A LUNATIC FEAR

BOOKS BY B.A. CHEPAITIS

A LUNATIC FEAR

B.A. CHEPAITIS

WILDSIDE PRESS

A LUNATIC FEAR
Copyright © 2004 by **B.A. Chepaitis**
Cover design copyright © 2004 by **JT Lindroos**

Published in the United States by **Wildside Press**
www.wildsidepress.com

ISBN: 0-8095-0063-9

It all started with the moon. If only the earth could have gone around the sun by itself, unperturbed by the complications . . . which the moon introduced.—N. Katherine Hayle. *Chaos Bound.*

PROLOGUE

Mary Lambert was walking along the footpath of the Ranalli River Bridge when she saw, in her peripheral vision, a man sitting on the railing. She passed him and kept walking, then slowed as it began to register that there was something odd about him.

Although it wasn't unusual to see someone standing on the footpath, leaning their elbows on the railing and staring down at the river below, it was unusual to see someone actually sitting on the railing, swinging his legs, tossing a stone up and down.

She slowed her steps. Twisted her neck to look over her shoulder at him.

He didn't seem upset. He tossed the stone up, caught it, tossed it again. Might as well be whistling, she thought. He had the look of an educated man. Wire-rimmed glasses. Tousled grisly sandy hair shot through with grey. Nice face. Friendly. He reminded her of her brother. But her brother had committed suicide, which was probably why she stopped instead of just continuing her after-work walk, the easiest part of her day and the time when she most did not want to talk to anyone. But he was sitting on a bridge, and he looked like her brother, and she was a psychologist.

It wouldn't hurt, she thought, to say hello.

She turned back and walked to him. She stood next to him, leaned against the railing.

"Hey," she said, pulling a cigarette from her jacket pocket. "Got a light?"

He caught his stone, held it for a moment, stroking the surface. Then he turned to her and squinted, pointed up at a sign over their heads. She craned her neck back to read.

No smoking, drinking, running, skating or dogs on the footpath.

Mary laughed, and shrugged. "Nobody's around. How about it?"

"Fine by me," he said. He pulled a lighter from his pocket, flicked it into flame and held it up.

She leaned over to him, let the flame touch the tip of her cigarette and pulled in smoke. "Thanks," she said, and made herself comfortable leaning on the railing, looking out over the river. Late afternoon sun kissed the surface of water and bounced up to them. The silver ribbon of river ran under them as smooth as liquid glass. Pretty river. Pretty afternoon.

"Nice view," she said.

"Yes," he agreed. "I thought this would be right."

"Right?"

"As the last thing I see," he said, smiling at her.

Mary nodded, feeling cold run through her. "You gonna kill yourself?" she asked.

He held up the stone, rubbed at it with his thumb. "Yes," he said. "I'd rather. It's a lousy world, isn't it?"

"Sometimes," she agreed.

She took a good look at his face. It was young and old at the same time. The smoothness of his skin placed him at thirty, tops. But the pouches of flesh under his brooding eyes and heaviness in his mouth made him look older. Like her brother. He had that same look of mingled calm and despair. The gnawing sorrow of his death suddenly relived itself here, in this man's face and eyes. Too much sorrow. Too much hopelessness. She looked away, out over the river.

He said nothing. Continued to toss the stone up and down. Up and down.

"Why is it a lousy world for you?" she asked.

He shrugged. "The usual reasons. An absence of love. An absence of hope for anything but stupidity. I mean, look at the third generation of pesticides—still poisoning the earth for a pretty lawn. Look at T-waves, and their results. Death and insanity in general. We survived the Killing Times, but what for? More of the same?"

She took a long drag off her cigarette while her mind busied itself with categories to place him in. He wasn't a mutoid because they all had some physical characteristics to tag them. A blue patch of skin on the face or neck, or a shortened arm or leg marked the genetic anomalies associated with having parents who were exposed to the biobombs of the vigilantes who roamed the cities during the Killing Times.

No. His problems were emotional, she thought. Like her brother. Intergenerational trauma was her first guess. That was what got her brother, too. He was a baby when serial killing rose to epidemic proportions and murder became the norm of the city streets. He couldn't remember any of it, but their parents did, and something of their trauma seeped into him.

"Maybe you should stick around and try to make things better," Mary suggested.

He turned the stone over and over in his hand and shook his head. "What for? All improvement becomes the next point of disaster."

"What?"

"The Christians," he said. "Jesus wanted to make change, and we got Christianity. And the crusades, and genocide for the sake of conversion, and—well, that's just one example. There's lots more. Genetic engineering causes new anomalies as fast as it cures diseases. Pesticides, of course—meant to cure world hunger, right? But maybe none of that bothers you."

"It bothers me," she said. "But I don't despair."

He chuckled. "Yes you do," he said.

The words entered her softly, like seduction, like sex.

Yes you do. You despair of change. You just keep yourself so busy you don't feel it except in the odd Friday afternoon when the sun slants in a certain way and you know you're alone. Utterly and absolutely alone is how you'll live and die, and you will die. You'll die and rot in the ground after a lifetime of kidding yourself that you matter. That anybody matters. That anything does.

A spiral of darkness began to unwind in her belly, creating a sucking motion that pulled her in and down toward this hollow center. Mary knew what he meant. She felt it on late Friday afternoons when she was done with her last client, looking forward to going home, and suddenly the emptiness of home seemed an appalling wasteland that represented not only the whole of her life, but the whole of life itself. There was no real pleasure in the world. All happiness was illusion. Not love or money or a friend or a cause to fight for made a dent in knowing how pointless it all was. There was an abyss waiting for her. She would fall into it and disappear, as if she had never been. The hole in the middle of the universe randomly spit out life for no apparent reason, sucking it back into nothingness for reasons that were equally random.

Now, standing on this bridge with a man who looked too much like her brother, Mary knew that saving him was a futile attempt to keep her own sorrow at bay. She couldn't help. There was no help for the sorrow of existence. There was only compassion, and companionship among those who shared the tragedy.

"Nothing gets better," he said. "It looks like it might for a while, then you see it never will."

"Yes," she whispered. He was right. The news this week was about too many suicides, a Pesticide bombing in the mall, and the Death Sisters, as the tabloids called them—three women who were arrested for gruesome homicides in a part of Connecticut that prided itself on low crime. Suicide, murders, and someone releasing pesticides in a mall to prove a point. So many dead, and it was so horrible, but they were all destined to die, anyway, so did it matter at all? Did this clinging to life matter?

He reached over and squeezed her hand, pressing the stone into her palm, then pulling away.

"I'd like you to have this," he said. "To remember me by."

She stared down at it. It was very plain. Smooth and oval, a greyish white. But it felt good in her hand. The weight of it, pulling her into a centered place where this despair didn't matter.

"You're going to jump," she said, no longer trying to talk him out of it.

"Yes," he said. "Will you sit with me before I do?"

She swung her leg over the rail and joined him. Sat next to him, stroking his arm. The dying and the newly born both needed touch. No words meant anything to them, really.

They sat together like this, while the sun blazed into red, and sank below the horizon. Then, placing a hand gently on her arm, he said, "We could go together, you know."

She blinked at him. Yes, she thought. Of course. That's what she longed for on those Friday afternoons. Someone to go with. Compassion and companionship. She felt relief.

"Yes," she said. "Yes. Let's do that."

He nodded at her. "It's better that way, isn't it?"

He held her hand and helped her to stand on the railing next to him, each of them clutching a girder as they got their balance and looked out one last time at the dying of the day, the silver of the river, the recession of light into darkness.

"Take a good look," he suggested. "Let it all be in your eyes."

She laughed. "Yes. All of it, in my eyes."

He squeezed her hand. "Ready?"

"Ready," she said.

They stood, just touching fingers and spread their arms wide. She swallowed the last rays of the sun into her retinas, and dove toward the rushing water, the cement parapets, the rocks, the currents, the end of her life. The ecstatic freedom and horror were so great that she didn't even notice that the young man still stood on the railing, clutching the girder of the bridge.

He watched her swan dive into the cement parapet, saw her skull crack like an egg on the side before the water took her. He could imagine the rest. Her body floating down to the bottom of the river, her hand loosening its grip on the stone which would float beside her, down and down into that slowness, into that silence. It would be a while before she came back up.

He lowered himself slowly to sitting, then swung himself over the side of the railing and onto the footpath. He walked on, looking for the next bridge.

CHAPTER ONE

The black foam rubber padding of the narrow corridors was only dimly lit by the red lights that blinked at the line between ceiling and wall. Jaguar Addams kept her back pressed to the wall as she made her way silently toward the opening into the next part of the maze. She could see motion at the periphery. Her opponent was waiting for her. Her weapon was ready, but she'd have to come up with a better move than open attack to win this round.

Jaguar liked to win, even if it was just a training game. That, she knew, was why the directors wanted her for training exercises. She'd do her best to win, and she wouldn't play by the rules, something the new Teachers and team members on Prison Planetoid Three had to learn to deal with. On the Planetoid, expecting the prisoners to follow the rules would get you dead fast.

Jaguar looked at her weapon and considered her options.

Very limited. The best one was to turn off her shield. The small blinking lights along the top gave her opponent something to shoot at with their laser fire simulators. If they were gone, she'd be invisible in her black jumpsuit. Of course, that wasn't allowed, which made it even more fun.

She turned off her shield. Standing in the darkness, she sensed rather than saw movement. The slightest click told her that her opponent had followed her example.

"Son of a bitch," she muttered, and thought some more.

Jaguar caressed her weapon. The simulators carried digital memory that communicated with the shields they wore to keep score. When someone made a direct hit, it was recorded in the computer banks. When the hit was low or high, that was communicated, too. She was an empath. Could she add to that memory, change it, or communicate with it? Direct it?

She didn't know. But she was, in general, very good at blowing up technology.

She pressed a hand against her weapon, and had a small, subvocal conversation with it. She searched for the feel of human thought on the other side of the opening.

Then, she raised her weapon, rounded the corner, and rolled.

She closed her eyes and fired, thoughts directing energy in the dark. The shot ricocheted off a darkened vest, and a number of lights around them began to blink on and off, make noises like small firecrackers exploding. Her opponent fired back, but it was already too late.

"Game over," a voice said over the loudspeaker. "Get Stan. She fucked it up again."

Light flooded the corridor. Jaguar pulled herself to standing, went to her opponent, and helped him up. "Nice shot," she said to him. "You almost had me."

He brushed off his knees and glared at her.

"Jaguar," a new voice said over the loudspeaker above them. "What did you do?"

She pointed to herself, widened her eyes innocently. "Me? Do?"

"Yeah," the voice said. "You. Do. Did you—uh—"

"I think I won, Stan," she replied.

"Never mind," he said. "Just—come up here a minute, would you?"

She patted her opponent on the shoulder. "Better luck next time."

She went to the door that was inset discreetly into the black padding, opened it, and wound her way upstairs to where the technicians played. Stan Kowoski was sitting at the control panel, swinging his head back and forth morosely and pressing buttons.

She stood behind him, put a hand on his shoulder. "Hey Stan," she said. "How's it going?"

"It was better before you got here," he said.

"I keep telling you guys, if you don't want me in the training games, don't request me."

He turned large sad eyes up to her. In general, she thought, he had the aspect of a basset hound with doleful secrets to keep, but he was good at his job. He specialized in laser technology, and, like any man with a love of his art, would regale her with detailed explanations of how they worked and the potential they had which wasn't yet being utilized. Some of it she even listened to, but for the most part she had more fun making him nervous.

She made him nervous because she was an empath, and the empathic arts were not within his technological control. They made him twitch and lay his ears back flat. In fact, in all the time she'd worked with him, she'd never once heard him use the word empath, or empathic arts. He would discuss psi capacities, but only in technical terms, regarding how they impacted the implants used to keep prisoners from running, or how well the Planetoid testing technology was able to discern and define what exact capacities prisoners might have. Of course, he was of the old school, and had started working on the Planetoid when Board code was still against hiring anyone who tested high for psi capacities. That ruling had recently been rescinded, and empathic work was more accepted as a useful tool for Teachers trying to understand the fears and psyches of their prisoners. Still, the empaths themselves were regarded suspiciously, because the empathic arts were still a rare and frequently misunderstood skill.

"It's your supervisor who insists," he said, staying focused on his board, "He says it's important for the new people to work with—um—you. "

"Empaths," she whispered. "You can say it. There are no children in the room."

He tugged at his collar. "Did you?" he asked mournfully. "With the laser memory?"

"Maybe just a little," she said, holding up a thumb and forefinger spread about an inch apart. "I wanted to see what would happen."

"What happens," he said, "is that the system backfires. Too much memory, and it can't digitize it fast enough. So it backs up, and lets off steam at the loose end."

"Fascinating," Jaguar said. "I'm so glad we know that."

"Right," he said, "But if you don't—wait a minute."He reached for a button that was buzzing madly, and pressed it.

A disembodied voice spoke into the room, from a source Jaguar couldn't fathom. "Call for Dr. Addams. Supervisor Alex Dzarny wants her in his office. She's on assignment. As of now."

"Got it," Stan said, and swiveled his sad eyes back to Jaguar. "You hear?"

"I heard. That's okay, Stan. It's probably for the best."

Jaguar walked the few blocks between the training center and Alex's office, enjoying the warm sun on her back, and the scent of growth in the air. Springtime on the Planetoid. Lovely.

Although winters were not as crisp as they were on the home planet, and summers weren't always as hot as she liked, the people who had done the creator's job of setting up an earthlike Planetoid instead of a bubble dome had done a good job with spring. She wondered if it was easier to create moderation than extreme, or if the planners just preferred moderation.

The Planetoid, which had been constructed from an asteroid base, a mass generator to create atmosphere, and shuttleloads of material from the home planet, was enough like earth that they could temporarily make a prisoner believe they hadn't left home. Unlike the early bubble dome Planetoids, here there were cities such as the Toronto replica she worked in, ecosites, and the great lakes they'd created in the holes of this small world. Thousands of tons of dirt and compost had been shipped up from the home planet, along with hundreds of species of trees, insects, animals and birds, over the course of the years it took to build. Carefully placed buildings and mountainous structures, created the illusion of horizon, and wave shields put the right stars and a moon of the right size in the night sky.

They hadn't created enough of the arid plains and mesas that Jaguar loved, but shuttles ran frequently enough for her to get home when her blood and bones cried for the baking heat and limitless views. And in spite of the sky island sense of boundaries she sometimes felt here, she knew she would stay.

She'd been working in the prison system as a Teacher for more than seven years, her job to create and run programs that led criminals to face and overcome their deepest fears, going on the post-Killing Times theory that all evil, and all crime grew out of fear. It was a theory she agreed with, and work she believed to be important. She'd survived the Killing Times in Manhattan. She knew what fear could do, and what happened when crime was badly dealt with.

She also knew that in spite of suspicions and misunderstandings like Stan's and the Board governors', it was easier to be an empath on the Planetoid. Only in places like 13 Streams, the New Mexico village where she'd lived after the Killing Times, were the empathic arts seen as normal. In tribal terms, they were just medicine, used badly or well depending on the skill and integrity of the empaths, who were normal people, doing normal things. But that was not so elsewhere on the Home Planet, where the general public tended to see empaths either as freaks, or potentially dangerous lunatics who used mind control on innocent people. Some religious fundamentalists thought they were responsible for the Killing Times

On the Planetoid, the work was dangerous enough that boundaries of proper behavior were broader, and empaths were tolerated because their skills had proved useful. There were also other empaths here for Jaguar to work with. Alex, for one, whose skills she was compelled to appreciate. He had the arts of the Adept, which allowed him to see through the days in ways she couldn't. Time unfolded for him differently than it did for other people, which might explain his supreme patience, and the way his eyes sometimes shifted focus to see beyond the walls she tried to build against him. Spider magus, she'd call him at those times, weaving multilayered webs of finely interconnected lines, then waiting within the structure to see who would fall in.

Her skills in the arts covered a lot of ground, but she was not an adept. They thought and worked in complex strategies, where she liked direct action, moving through obstacles rather than strategizing to clear the road. But Alex was trustworthy. She'd had to trust him with her life, and he'd come through. She was pretty sure that was a mark of his general integrity, rather an attempt at seduction.

Alex didn't seduce. He just told her outright that he wanted her. He wouldn't push—he had far too much courtesy and pride for that, and he valued their working relationship too much—but the offer was there. The desire was there. He wouldn't lie about that, either.

In a way his attitude made it more difficult for her. He'd made his choice. She had just refused to decide one way or the other. And while he wouldn't push her, she knew she could fall just as hard by tripping over her own feet. Lately, she'd found herself looking at his hands, wondering what they'd feel like, wondering what it would be like to be with another empath. She'd never made love in empathic contact. She could do that with Alex, if she wanted to. But she didn't want to. Or even if she did, it was just too risky. Lovers could be found anywhere, but good supervisors were irreplaceable, and what if something went wrong?

She kept this thought firmly in her mind when she entered Alex's office, without knocking, and waited the time it took him to realize someone was in the room. He looked up from his files and saw her standing there in her black jumpsuit, sleek and shining as the cat whose name she bore.

"What?" she asked him.

He waved a hand at the chair across the desk. She coiled herself into it, leaned back and raised her legs, resting the heels of her boots on the corner of his desk.

He tossed her a file folder. "Your next case. Let me know what you think."

She opened it, and read.

He sat and watched her read, swiveling his chair back and forth, taking in the sheen of honey in her walnut hair as it slipped like silk over her shoulders, enjoying the motion of her hand as it made the small gesture of curling it behind her ear. She paid no attention to his stare when she focused on her work. He could be kissing the back of her neck and she wouldn't notice. He enjoyed the notion, and turned it this way and that in his mind as she continued to read.

When she was done, she flipped the folder closed and slid it back across the desk to him. She let her head drop back over the high back of the chair and rubbed at her temples.

"What do you see, Dr. Addams?" he asked.

"We've got three women from the home planet," Jaguar said. "From the same Connecticut town. Three homicides. All bizarre."

"What else?" Alex asked.

"The testing routine reveals none of the core complex of fears we usually see with these kinds of crimes. And the cortical scans show a slewing of beta weights in the neural flow charts."

He nodded. "What's that tell you?"

She let a long breath out toward the ceiling, then lifted herself upright and looked at him hard. He felt the pull as she drew him into subvocal conversation, where it would be more difficult for him to evade or hide.

You plan on handing me the ticking bomb?

There was sharp suspicion in her thoughts. She already knew what this was.

No, Jaguar. Just seeking some confirmation.

A moment of silence while she made a deeper empathic contact and probed him for hidden agendas, for anything that smelled of danger.

Empathic contact was different than simple telepathic communication. The empath shared experience directly with the person they were in contact with. It was vaguely uncomfortable. Like running through a rainstorm skinless, or like a dream where you're not sure if you're falling or flying.

During the empathic moment, your only control was your capacity to exit, or consent to an absence of control. Your emotions and thoughts, your soul, were not your own during the interaction. Alex believed that's why more people didn't practice the arts, though they could be learned with varying measures of skill by anyone who made the effort. But the necessary trust, the fearless relinquishment of control, and the quiet discipline it took to come back to yourself afterward, took too much time, patience and moral courage for most people to bother with.

Jaguar was the most skilled empath he'd ever met, and this made contact with her easier, but sometimes she stalked him the way a cat stalked new territory, sniffing at his thoughts to measure them against the blade edge of her suspicions. He was willing to let her, though the feel of her investigation was difficult. As if an angel stroked his face with sharp and delicate fingers, asking if the exquisite pleasure of that touch hurt. Can pleasure hurt? Is desire painful? Fortunately, he was skilled enough himself to move into telepathic communication when it got to be too much. He spoke through her investigation of his psyche.

Jaguar, licking my soul isn't necessary, is it?

The motion of contact ceased. The feel of brief laughter in a soft wind moved through him and exited smoothly. She sat across from him, looking all business, except for the shadow of a grin that disappeared before it could be called into remark.

"The women have phase psychosis," she said. "Exogenous. When the beta weight anomaly is that large, there must be some exposure to Artemis Compounds."

He rubbed at his chin. Okay, he thought. She was reading it the same way he was. Now he'd take her out for a little test run. "The existence of exogenously induced Phase Psychosis is unproven," he said judiciously. "Besides, manufacture or possession of Artemis compounds is illegal, excepted in very restricted research settings."

"Yeah," she replied. "And I know a lot of pigs with little pink wings, too. These women claimed PMS as a defense, didn't they?"

Alex nodded. "Two. The third went for post-partum depression."

"Works out to about the same thing. Nice way of saying female trouble. Hysterical women." She tapped the files with her finger. "But we've seen this before, and it's not hysteria."

"We've seen similar incidents," he corrected. "Don't assume prior to gathering your facts."

"Alex," she said, "why'd you call me in if you don't think it's Artemis?"

She was right. He called her in because she would spot it. But, unlike him, she would be blind to the political ramifications. Or, seeing them, she just wouldn't give a shit. And that was the other reason he called her in. She would pursue the truth regardless of political consequences, and if his suspicions were correct, the consequences could get nasty.

Artemis compounds came from moon mining, and the Hague had instituted a moratorium on moon mining two years ago. It was up for either repeal or extension in six months. Corporations were lobbying hard for the repeal, and lining up to stake claims on the particular Lunar resources they wanted to exploit.

That was the word they used. Exploit. Alex heard it on the news, saw it on the web, had been in rooms where people had actually said it with no sense of folly. Every time he heard it, he winced for the speaker who didn't seem to understand that exploitation of natural resources had brought the planet to the brink of disaster more than once, and exploitation of extra-planetary resources would probably do the same. Exploitation in general was just not a good idea.

But there was big money to be made, and that's what the corporations saw. More than two hundred years ago Black Elk said of the gold miners who came through Lakota land that they sought the yellow metal they worshipped, which made them mad. Similarly, the lust for moon mining was literally a form of lunacy.

Lunar dust contained minerals readily available on the home planet, but the refining process had unexpectedly created a new grouping of synthetic chemicals that had the high molecular charge useful in shuttle fuels, and the unique electrochemical qualities associated with laser memory bank systems. There was speculation about its uses in regenerative medicine, too. Artemis compounds, the byproducts were called, and they were hailed as the next techno-savior of the world. Research and production plants were up and running with the speed of light.

But female workers in the plants and women who lived around the plants began miscarrying, or hemorrhaging to death. A few went on mad killing sprees. One woman burned her home with her family in it. Another set fire to the plant she worked in. Unions lodged complaints and insisted on protection for female workers. Neighborhood coalitions formed to keep plants out.

Corporations, backed by their own researchers, claimed there was absolutely no connection between the women's problems and Artemis.

The number of women affected didn't make up a statistical significance, and other variables could have led to their problems. Many were Killing Time survivors, and suspect for post-traumatic stress anyway. Those who miscarried were questioned about their exercise routines, diet and sexual habits. And as the scientists pointed out repeatedly, none of the men had any problems.

Still, the complaints continued, and moon mining protestors were joined by the Pagan and Indigenous People's Coalition, who appealed for preservation of the moon as a sacred site. A Coalition spokesperson was murdered, and the publicity led politicians into the fray. Finally, the Hague declared a moratorium on moon mining while conducting investigations into the long-term consequences of exposure to lunar by-products.

While corporations hustled to develop plans for safe plants using everything from isolation shields to space station facilities, the first year of study bogged down in inconclusive evidence. By the second year, watchdogging on dive and carry pirating of lunar surface material grew lax. Everyone suspected that without stronger evidence, the moratorium would simply be lifted, and everyone wanted to be first in understanding and using the new mineral possibilities. And it would happen in a few months, unless something conclusive prevented it.

Alex knew that if they made a definitive connection between Artemis and their prisoners, there would be more than a few people who wanted that connection buried, perhaps along with the people who made it.

"If it's phase psychosis, we need proof," he said. "Something the Hague can't ignore."

"Okay," she said. "I'll work the women. See what I can see."

"You have ideas for a program?"

She turned her eyes up and tapped a finger thoughtfully against her lips. "I'll work them together, and I'll want a site on the home planet."

"Why the home planet?"

"The closer we are to the site of their crimes, the sooner I'll be able to determine if there's a local cause. Besides, they're out of phase, Alex. They have to kiss the earth."

Alex considered. Planetoid prison colonies were created to keep the prisoners away from the home planet. In a case like this, they didn't need protest happening at the start. "We brought a few tons of the mother here when we established the ecosites. It'll have to act *in loco parentis*. If it doesn't work out, we can move you. What'll you do with them?"

"I'll sweat them."

He raised his eyebrows at her. Sweating with women in Phase psychosis. She'd be literally breathing in what they released. If he knew her, she'd be trying empathic contact with it.

"The sweat lodge, Jaguar?" he asked. "Isn't that—"

"—Necessary," she said. "They have to detox and they need the ceremony." She tilted her head at him."I know what I'm doing, Alex."

"How will you avoid eating the toxins?" he asked.

She waved a hand at him. " The same way you avoid eating any shadow. Contain it, block it off, let it go. You know the routine."

Yes. He knew the routine, and so did she. In fact, her boundaries were probably stronger than anyone else's he knew, in all ways. That was how she'd avoided shadow sickness all these years, in spite of the criminals whose psyches she'd touched. She allowed just what she wanted to come in, and nothing or no one else. It was, he thought, a blessing and a curse.

"What're you looking at for core fears?"

She shook her head. "I won't start with fears. I'll start with desire."

He frowned at her. The Planetoid system was based on the premise that crime grew out of fear, and prisoners needed to face the fears that generated their crimes. Desires weren't usually a part of the program. "Desire, Jaguar?"

"Desire, Alex. I'll find their fears in the same place."

"Explain, please," he invited her.

She pulled in breath and let it out. "It's complex. A three body problem, like the orbital relationship between moon, sun and earth. Or Planetoid, moon and earth, in this case."

"What's the triangle?"

"Fear, desire and power," she said. "You know this quote—From Davidson, *The Etiquette of Empaths*—'True power gives birth to generous desire, and false power generates only fear.' "

He nodded. "Fear chokes desire into greed, and greed is a washing of blood over power," he finished the quote for her.

"That's right. These women ate too much power, with nothing to ground it in. It made their true desires visible, and it's scaring the hell out of them. That's my working premise. The program'll work, if I'm right."

He swiveled back and forth in his chair. "If you're right, Jaguar," he said.

She turned her sea-green eyes to him. Pieces of gold light swam endlessly there. Crescents of moon-gold, caught forever in her eyes. As she established empathic contact with him, he felt the tidal pull, listened to the whispered hush of knowledge she was giving him.

And what will you do if I am?

She felt him considering this, weighing it. And his response.

What will you do, Dr. Addams?

She let the tip of her finger rest against her lips, then drew it down to her chin. She spoke, this time out loud.

"The real question is what they'll do," she noted. "We'll know more after that."

He swiveled his chair away from her and stared out the window. "Okay," he said. "Get it rolling. I'll call in the ecosite people and set up a spot for you. In the old forest site?" he asked.

"That's good," she said. "I'll start tomorrow if you're ready."

"I will be."

He paused and went through his mental list, checking to see if he'd left anything out. There was nothing, except to remind her that working with Phase Psychosis was tricky. Working with minds that battled illusions created confusions, no matter how strong your boundaries. He needed to remind her to be cautious. He swiveled back around to face her, and looked blankly at an empty room.

Silently, without even the sound of breath, she'd already gone.

He cursed softly under his breath. Then, a knock on the door told him more company had arrived.

"Enter," he said, and the door opened. Team member Rachel Shofet came in.

"You wanted something?" she asked.

He handed her the file folder he'd recently given Jaguar.

"Jaguar's on assignment, with these three," Alex said. "You're backup team."

She looked down at the file. "These are the Death Sisters, right?"

"That's what they're called. Read up as soon as you can."

She nodded and turned toward the door, but he stopped her.

"Wait. There's something else. I want you to do some research."

She turned back to him, grinning. Rachel, once a prisoner on the Plane-toids, and before that a closet Talmudic scholar in a community that didn't allow women that right, was relentless in tracking down information. Nothing got by her.

"I want a list of all the existing Hague research facilities for Moon

Mining and who's running them," he said. "And any connection, however remote, between those facilities and these women. Someone who knows them, a tree hugger who ran protests or someone whose mother did. Any connection."

She chewed on her upper lip and regarded him thoughtfully. "The Death Sisters have something to do with moon mining?"

"It's a possibility we're considering."

"That'd be bad," she noted mildly, as she typed these instructions in. "Anything else?"

"I'd also like Governor's Board agenda memos."

Rachel lifted her head from the notes she was making. "Board agenda memos? You mean minutes of meetings?"

"I mean memos. The kind they shoot back and forth over their computers and on laser files."

"I don't have access to Governor's memos," Rachel said. "Not officially. Not to their private lines."

"But you can get it."

She cleared her throat. "Technically, that's a violation. In the code books."

Alex swiveled in his chair and said nothing.

She sighed. "How far back?"

"Six months'll be fine."

She nodded. "What in particular are you looking for?"

"Discussions about moon mining. Artemis byproducts. Hague Repeal discussion."

Rachel blinked and shook her head. "What's that got to do with the Planetoids?"

Alex swiveled in his chair and made a temple of his hands. "There's rumors that the Planetoids are being considered as sites for a processing plant when the moratorium is lifted. I want to know who's for it, and who's against."

"I guess. Is—um—Jaguar aware of this?"

He shook his head. "I haven't discussed it with her yet. I don't want to get her motor running until I have more than local gossip to fuel it with. But if you come up with anything, I'll let her know right away."

Rachel nodded, satisfied with this.

"There's one more thing," Alex said. "I'd like a listing of recent crimes in the home planet town of Watertown, Connecticut for the same time as the Death Sister's crime. Any kind of crime, but only those committed by men."

Rachel groaned and rolled her eyes.

"It's a small town, Rachel."

"Then there'll be plenty of small crimes, you can be sure. When do you want all this?" she asked.

"No rush," Alex said, grinning. "Tomorrow'll be fine."

Rachel shot him a look, but Alex knew her. First thing in the morning anything she could find would be downloaded into his computer.

CHAPTER TWO

The deep green coating of the night surrounded them, a liquid blanket of breathing leaves and moss, the scent of rotting and growing and growing and rotting smooth in their nostrils.

Jaguar surveyed the women crouched at her feet. Their eyes were big and their naked skin shone in the soft moonlight. They stared up at her, not moving, not speaking, the rate of their breathing the only indication of their fear. They were her prisoners, and she'd brought them to the old forest ecosite between day and dusk to begin what looked like a challenging program.

"You're murderers," she said. "All of you. What punishment do you deserve?"

Terez Alfonse lowered her head, silky blonde hair covering her face. Karena Halsey poked a finger into the dirt, her painted nail carving small holes through dead leaves. Fiore Cruz bared her teeth in a grin. Nobody spoke, but she could hear the hiss and spark of their answer.

Death, they did not say.

Jaguar chuckled. "Death would be too easy."

Karena rocked back on her haunches and moaned. Jaguar's hand shot out and slapped her in the face. The moaning ceased. She cast her gaze around the ecosite, with its high pines, birch saplings that stretched toward light, and floor padded with soft, wet leaves. "We're going to make a sweat lodge," she said. "Start gathering wood."

The women stared at her blankly, and Jaguar shook her head. They were all some flavor of Christian, used to the polite smiles and good clothes of

Sunday church services. Spiritual ceremonies conducted naked on the damp earth were foreign to them. "Just do what I tell you," Jaguar said, and set them to their tasks.

She took on the job of cutting saplings and bending them to the curves that would be the dome frame of a sweat lodge, which they would cover in the canvas and skins they'd carried into the woods from her vehicle. Fiore chopped wood into kindling for the fire they'd build. Terez gathered stones that would be heated in the fire. Karena dug a pit for the center of the lodge, where the heated stones would go once the ceremony began.

Their three bodies moved like patches of moonlight through the trees. They worked without speaking, only occasionally asking for her attention nonverbally, to make sure they were doing their jobs correctly. Jaguar worked and listened to the language of their gestures as they performed their tasks.

She saw how Terez, young and blonde and lovely, carried stones tentatively, one at a time, stumbling frequently over tree roots. She would place a stone near the circle where the fire was to be built, then stop and stare at Jaguar. When Jaguar smiled at her, she jerked her head away and went back to work.

Terez was a mathematics professor who had the perfect marriage until she killed her husband with a meat cleaver while preparing a stir fry. Her crime was discovered when a colleague of her husband came to the house to see why he missed an important meeting, and found a blood-spattered Terez sitting at the table, staring at a plate full of cold human parts mixed in artful arrangement with miniature corn and straw mushrooms. All she would say at the trial was that she was tired of being a vegetarian.

Since her sentencing to Planetoid Prison Colony number three, she'd said nothing else, and it was Jaguar's job to find out what lay under her continued silence.

Karena worked awkwardly, shoveling dirt slowly, stopping to hold her hands up to the moonlight and sigh, brush the dirt off her rings, clean out a nail. She would pat at her head, as if to keep the curly dark hair that was cropped close and groomed hard in its place. She didn't seem aware of Jaguar's watchful eye. All her concern focused on somehow staying clean as she worked the earth. In contrast, Fiore's muscled back bent to her task with ease, and she didn't stop to wipe the sweat off her face and chest as she swung the ax against wood, then hauled it to the fire circle. Periodically, she would straighten her spine and lift her eyes to the moon, breathing deeply as if light and air were both equally necessary for her lungs.

Jaguar listened to the spark and hiss of their unspoken fears. They wanted her to kill them, she knew. It would be easier than facing the tangle of desire and fear they were caught in.

The women worked together to pile the stones and cover them with wood and brush. The air, heavy and humid, defied the fire at first, and the three women struggled with matches as kindling caught and spit and refused to burn. Fiore watched impatiently, her dark skin shiny with sweat, and the silver streak in her black hair accenting the high color of her face and eyes.

She was forty-four when she discovered she was pregnant for the first time, after being told she'd never bear children. The pregnancy proceeded without trouble until she began having labor pains in her sixth month. She was home by herself, but she didn't call a midwife. Instead she gave birth alone and easily, and her husband came home to find her licking at the remains of the tiny head.

Fiore pushed the other two women aside and grabbed the matches from them. She knelt in front of the fire and struck three against the box. In her hand the blaze caught, her breath spreading the flames around the circle and toward the wood at the center, casting sharp points of shadow and light across the faces of the women. Interesting, Jaguar thought, as she began to chant the song she'd been taught to start the ceremony for women.

Two hours passed as the rocks heated and Jaguar chanted and the moon ran in her course through the sky. The women began chanting with her, waiting for what they supposed was their punishment. They showed no signs of fatigue. The energy that coursed through them from the Artemis compound wouldn't let them rest. Jaguar could feel the pull of it as the ritual space unfolded around them.

When the fire died down, Jaguar let Fiore kick the logs out of the way to reveal the glowing stones, showed her how to pick them up with the pitchfork, welcome them into the lodge with sage and water, slide them into the pit at the center. Then, she led the women inside the lodge.

As she knelt and pulled back the canvass that covered the opening to the dome, she looked down and saw that blood stained the inside of her thigh, a warm trickle of red sliding from her skin onto the earth. Fiore, looking at her from inside the dome, laughed as if she knew. The other women took up her laughter. They were all menstruating, sweat and blood mingling in a space much darker than any night.

27

The lodge gave them each enough room to stretch out fully if they wanted to, but the warmth and dark made it seem small as a womb. As soon as Jaguar pulled the canvas down over the entrance and poured water on the rocks, heat rose to a palpable mass around them. Jaguar heard the women suck in breath and she laughed.

"It'll get hotter than this," she muttered, and poured more water on as she began the opening chant.

Even in the first round, where they honored the spirits of the East, it was a hot sweat. By the second round the other women had lowered themselves to the baseline of the lodge where they sucked in cool earth and moaned while she chanted. She could feel the breathy openness of empathic space in them and around them. None had tested positive for psi capacities, but they were sweating, and sometimes that opened regions long closed. And there was no telling what effect the Artemis compound would have on any latent skills they might have. Nobody had ever studied that. She'd find out more in the third round, when she would make her first empathic contact with them.

She could almost hear Alex cautioning her against this, especially in the third round, the round of the West, referred to as The House of No Words in Jaguar's tradition. This was the place of death, the place of the ancestors and the black jaguar. Here you ceased being fully human, and fully among the living. You spoke only in the howls that came from the bottom of your belly and the scream that lived inside your throat. If she contacted them here, she would be touching primal energy, and that was risky. But it was also effective, and when the door was closed between the second and third round, she silently told Alex to mind his own business. She knew what she was doing.

The inescapable fury of heat blanketed their skin, and the absolute darkness was broken only by the glowing red eye of stone at the center of the pit. Jaguar tilted her head back and howled, and the other women followed suit, hissing and keening as she crawled around the pit, feeling her way toward them. She reached Karena first. Karena, silent except for a whispered groan.

Placing her hands around Karena's head, she intoned the ritual words that asked permission to enter this psyche. Terez and Fiore screeched, but the sound of their voices left her as she felt her way through Karena's interior world. Hollow silence. Infinitely sterile emptiness, clamoring silently to be filled. To be filled. To be filled.

Karena was the odd woman out. She was from Staten Island, not Connecticut. She was here because she'd walked into a department store and pointed a gun at a cashier. He frantically handed over the money in his drawer, but Karena shot him anyway, then turned her weapon on the other dozen people there. When the police arrived, she was struggling with a shopping bag, dragging it toward the door. The policeman who took it from her looked inside, and dropped it quick, spilling dismembered hands and feet and ears and breasts all over the marble floor.

"I was hungry," Karena told the police.

Jaguar drifted in the vast white emptiness Karena cradled at her core, touching it gently, letting it become part of her own knowledge. She would go no further with her. Tonight was just the first contact with each woman, a brief and gentle listening.

She released her hold and groped through the darkness to a screeching Terez, whose hands clawed desperately at the base of the lodge as if she would dig her way out. Her beauty was almost palpable even when vision was denied. Jaguar stopped her hands, then caught and held her face gently, spoke quietly into the squealing terror of her mind, and found herself slipping into a space as rich and fertile as the rainforest.

There was rapture here, fleshy and sinuous with desire. A pounding and pulsing life-force, wanting to feast not so much out of hunger, but out of a sense of abundance. And all around it, a wall, thick and oppressive. No. It said only no and no and no again.

"Yes," Jaguar whispered back, "and yes and yes again."

She let her go and crawled around her to Fiore, who barked and howled and called out all the noises of wild animals caught in the grip of commune with the night. Jaguar had to struggle to keep a firm grasp on her, as she thrashed and worried her noises like a dog with a bone.

There was great joy in the storm of her voice raised in wild freedom, profoundly serene in its own rage. A serene and free rage. A wild calm. Some improbable conjoining of all that. A complexity, powerful and rich and complete as fire. To Jaguar it felt almost like home. With reluctance, she released her and crawled back through the slippery wet earth to her place.

She took a ladle of water from the bucket and tossed it onto the stones. As the heat hissed into an even greater beast of living steam she breathed deeply, releasing any toxins she might have absorbed from the contact, letting it out through the air of her lungs and the water pouring from her skin.

Aaiiyah, the women called out to the night.

Aaiyah they sang into the darkness and into her and into their own souls.

Jaguar could feel the motion of sound against her skin. She held her hand up for silence, and though they couldn't see the gesture, they were suddenly still. Jaguar spoke through the stillness.

"I myself, spirit in flesh speak," she said softly, and slid into her own center to meet what swam there.

Saw a woman feral and balanced. Saw a forest of knowledge she crawled through in darkness.

Touched the edge of a wordless whisper. The sigh of movement. That swift blackness which led her with vision thirty times more accurate than human sight.

She breathed in the blessing of that presence, and let it pull her into the spinning darkness, felt herself curling like a leaf within a coil of wind, lifted toward a translucent moon, almost full, trying to burst into fullness. She reached for it, all of her pulled to that source.

Grandmother. Nissa.

She was lifted to a place where light poured down around her, bathing her in that same wild calm she felt from Fiore who must be a daughter of the moon, a huntress, a fire spirit acquainted with the instincts of night. Light as cool and sweet as a child's hand in yours poured through her. Light as cool and sweet as dreams.

She rested in it, let it rest in her. In this light, she saw herself facing a man. Someone young and old at the same time. Sad and quiet and full of rage. She saw herself walking to him and feeling the warmth of his desire mixing with her own as the great grandmother light of the moon poured cool over both of them. He raised a hand to her face, and it was covered in blood.

Aaaiyah. Aaaiyah Nissa nissa.

She saw his hand covered in blood and the moon hissing out a silken scarf of more blood to cover his arm and shoulders and face drowning her in blood and more blood. A woman bathed in blood, and then Alex was there, blood flowing over him and he disappeared under it.

Blood on the moon, and the scream of pain that followed.

She opened her eyes, gasped, and shook herself out of the vision.

Blood on the moon.

"Open the door," she said hoarsely to Terez, who sat nearest. Terez flung the canvas covering aside and the three women crowded to it, steam flowing out in front of them like a river.

Jaguar lay down and let them breathe. They had one more round to go,

30

but they'd get water and a little cool air before they started. She needed to regroup. Needed to climb back in to her own skin so she could conduct the last round.

Blood on the moon.

Phase psychosis. Artemis compounds. There was no more doubt about it. Women bleeding, going mad. Blood on her thigh, and on the thighs of all the women here, and on the moon.

She knew what to do next. In the morning, she would start with Terez.

The women slept late, and rose to move silently through the activities of breakfast preparation and cleanup. As they worked, Jaguar noticed that Terez followed her with large eyes, always aware of where she was, what she was doing.

They ate bread and fruit that Jaguar had brought, drank water from canteens. No one spoke, and each face carried in it the glow of last night's sweat. Jaguar could see a shift in pupil size, in skin tone, indicating that the detox was beginning.

After breakfast was cleared and the three women sat leaning into trees, listening as if some answer ran through the sap, Jaguar turned to Terez. "Come with me," she said. Terez rose silently and followed her through the thick trees.

Jaguar stopped at a stream that trickled through the woods. She squatted by the side of it, cupped her hands and lifted water to her face. The moon was still apparent in the south, white and ghostly in the clarity of morning sky.

The water felt good against her skin. She let her hands linger in it, brought them, slippery and cool, to her neck, sighed with pleasure as liquid slid down her breasts. She leaned over and took another handful of water, spreading it over her ribs and belly, then between her legs, opening her thighs and stroking the insides gently, noticing as she did so that she'd stopped bleeding. She'd noticed earlier that the other women had ceased bleeding, too.

As she washed, she could feel Terez staring at her, unspoken questions boring into the back of her neck. Jaguar stood and turned to her, and immediately Terez lowered her eyes. Her face flushed and she took a step back.

"Yes," Jaguar said, "and yes again." She reached over and ran a hand through Terez' hair, combing the silken tangle with her fingers. It felt like air pouring over her skin.

"Your hair is like moonlight," she said. "Weightless and piercing."

Terez made a small sound, almost a grunt of pleasure, almost a whimper of fear.

"Do you know about the moon?" Jaguar asked, running a finger over her cheek. "Her light is so soft, you'd never guess how much she can do just by being there."

She grasped a handful of Terez' hair and twisted it around her hand as she spoke. "Women used to bleed with the moon, when they slept outside and were exposed to the light. Did you know that?"

Terez shook her head, the movement as small as possible.

"The moon pulls the body toward desire and knowledge. That's why men fear it, and fear women who worship it. They know that real desire gives you a power that can't ever be stolen or controlled."

Terez raised large blue eyes to Jaguar and said nothing.

"You're afraid," Jaguar noted, "but not afraid that I'll hurt you."

She unwrapped Terez' hair and dropped her hand to her side. "You're afraid I can't hurt you enough. That you'll never be able to pay for what you did, or who you are. You'd like me to run razor blades in pretty little circles around your face, or whip you. But I'm not going to do that. Quite the opposite. I'm going to show you how to be what you are."

Jaguar took a step forward. Terez took a step back.

"What do you want?" Jaguar asked.

Terez hung her head down onto her chest and peered at her own flesh. She touched it tentatively, as if it was an animal that might bite. She pressed her thumb into her sternum, held it there, released it, stared at the imprint of flesh against flesh. She lifted her hands and held her own face as if it belonged to someone else, drew her palms across her mouth, licking at them, tasting them. Then she squeezed her eyes shut tight and pushed out one word.

"Dance," she said.

Jaguar laughed. She stretched her lithe body in a line toward the sky and felt the pleasure of her own muscles rippling in the heat of the sun. She swayed in the dappled green shadows of the forest, flesh ambient with light, her motion the motion of trees in the wind, birds that landed in their branches. She caressed the curves of her own body, caressed the curves of the air that held it. Then she reached over and grasped Terez by the hips, moving them in rhythm with hers.

Terez pulled back at first, then ceased struggling and moved into the cadence of her body's song as she pressed closer to Jaguar.

For too many years Terez lived somebody else's life, as if she was just visiting her own skin. But under the sweet act she'd put on for husband and neighbors and friends, Jaguar could feel the burden of her desire, the heaviness of longing and the bitterness of fear within it. It was the burden of the moon as its face moved across the face of the earth. An oceanic shifting of waters and the subtle pulsing of the heart's rhythm toward its own center. She was always trying to get back to herself, as fast as she tried to run away. She grasped Terez by the hair, lifted her face and ran a finger across the thirsty lips.

"This," Jaguar whispered into the weightless light of her hair. "You want this."

Terez groaned and moved more deeply into the dance, into the body that rocked hers toward knowing.

Then a slight motion in the shadows of the trees caught Jaguar's attention. She peered over Terez' shoulder and saw Fiore standing behind a tree, watching them. Her eyes did not approve or disapprove. They just absorbed. When she saw Jaguar see her, she held her gaze for a brief moment, then turned her attention to Terez. And when Terez bent her mouth to Jaguar's neck and ran a tongue across her skin, Fiore stepped out from behind the tree and moved closer.

"Yes," Jaguar whispered, "and yes again." She took Terez' hands and pulled them away. Terez grappled to retain her hold, but Jaguar jerked her wrists and then pushed her back. Jaguar moved Terez' hand toward her own belly and pressed it down on the soft flesh.

"This. You want this. The erotic source of power. But you won't find it in me. What you want is in you."

Terez peered down at her own belly, saw her hand pressed on top of it, Jaguar's hand holding her fingers against the flesh.

"See who you are," Jaguar said. "Be what you see."

Terez began to tremble lightly, ripples of energy moving through her skin.

"Dance," Jaguar whispered.

Terez swayed and moaned and held herself close. Fiore, watching, moved closer. Jaguar, watching Fiore, moved back toward the trees as Fiore came and put a hand on Terez' shoulder. Terez opened her eyes wide and stopped swaying. Fiore spread her hands and ran them down Terez' smooth white back, cupped her small hips, and danced. Jaguar nodded, and silently faded back into the trees.

Day swallowed the white eye of the moon that led them here, and they continued their dance.

When afternoon transformed into dusty evening, Jaguar returned to the clearing by the stream. She found Fiore and Terez laying on their backs, looking up toward the tops of the trees and to a sky that was quickly emptying itself of light.

"We'd better get back," she said. Fiore stood and brushed herself off, then walked off into the trees, but Terez remained still.

Jaguar squatted next to her and tapped her shoulder. "Terez," she said, "look at me."

Her wide sky eyes were clear and focused. Jaguar touched her forehead and felt the return of words, slowly, as if she was a child just learning language as a tool.

Good. That was good. That meant her plan was working, and she was on the right track.

Jaguar ran a hand down Terez' face. "Are you still afraid?" she asked.

Terez frowned. It seemed to take her some time to remember how to respond to a question. After a while she shook her head slowly back and forth.

Jaguar nodded. "That's the gift the moon had for you. An authentic self. Now, you own it."

CHAPTER THREE

Alex's workday often finished at odd hours, depending on the assignments under his supervision and his involvement with them. For the next few weeks, he knew that involvement would be deep, and the hours would be long. Now it was close to midnight as he sat in his rocking chair, re-reading the information Rachel's research had uncovered for him. None of what he read made him happy.

The data on other crimes in the area of the Death Sisters offered nothing he could pinpoint specifically as a case of male phase psychosis, and it had taken him some time to go through the months of petty crimes to glean a handful of men who were only possibly interesting to him. These were Joseph Blau, convicted on charges of aggravated assault; Harry Liffen, serving a sentence for assault with a deadly weapon; Brendan Farley, who just paid a fine and incurred a community service sentence for his third public nuisance and demonstrating without a permit charge; and Pete Iman, convicted of public lewdness.

It wasn't so much the crimes that interested Alex as the fact that each of the men worked for some subsidiary of Global Concerns. That might mean nothing—just a blind alley he was wandering down for a bit—or it may turn out to be important. He couldn't tell yet, but he was inclined to pursue it. In the morning, he'd call the Connecticut Cop shop and see if he could find out anything more about these men. In the meantime, the Board Memos Rachel turned up were of more immediate concern. These involved the Planetoids and Artemis directly.

A few months ago, certain corporations suggested that the Planetoids would be an ideal spot to locate Artemis plants after the Hague repeal, which they assumed would happen. On a Planetoid, they could keep Artemis away from the home planet populace, and utilize the already established shuttle service for shipping and distribution. The memos specifically mentioned the undeveloped portions of Planetoid Three as ideal, pointing out the available prisoner labor and the potentially enormous income the operation would bring to an expensive system.

Some of this was not news to Alex. Planetoid One had long since developed small industries where the prisoners worked, and both Jaguar and Alex had wasted a lot of breath objecting to it. They both knew that once the prisoners became part of a production operation, the system was open to abuse. It would be to easy to forget they were here to rehab, not to warehouse.

Planetoid Three had so far avoided the problem because it was a Planetoid of city replicas, not bubble domes. There wasn't any room for the kind of industry Planetoid One supported. Or so Alex thought.

The memos all came from the same corporate conglomerate and went to a variety of Board governors—including Paul Dinardo, who was governor for Alex's zone. But Rachel couldn't retrieve any outgoing responses from the governors. All had gone through the automatic delete and expunge classified route, which meant that nobody was willing to take a public stand for the plants. Or against. At least it wasn't official yet, which meant he could still make incursions through Paul, who surely owed him one after the last go round they'd had with the army.

All of this told Alex that the situation was even more complicated than he'd anticipated. He let the case folder rest on his lap and he stared out the window at the silver surface of the Lake Ontario replica. He was deep into reconsideration of his initial assessment when he felt warmth at his back, like breath applied by a mouth held close to the back of the neck.

He hadn't heard anyone enter his apartment, but that didn't surprise him. He never heard her when she chose to be silent, just as she didn't see him when he chose not to be seen. What surprised him was the warmth of her presence, and the way she was letting it fold through him. The smell of the moon was all around her, beautiful and distracting. It glowed and spread through him.

"When you make love," she asked, "do you keep your eyes open or closed?"

He didn't shift. Didn't lift his head or twitch. He just let the question settle in to someplace where it wouldn't cause too much trouble. "That depends, Jaguar," he answered.

"On what?"

"The woman. The context of the lovemaking." He paused, then asked, "Would you like some specific examples and illustrations?" He felt her shift behind him. He had disturbed her. That was probably good.

He twisted in his chair and faced her. She was looking at him with an expression he could not interpret because it was far too complex a mixture of elements. "Would you?" he asked again.

She tilted her head to one side and considered him. "Your point," she noted. "We'd better move on."

He grinned, and turned a hand palm up toward her, inviting her to continue.

"It's phase psychosis," she said. "Exogenously induced."

"All of them?" he asked.

"Yes," she said, walking around to stand in front of him. "They've been exposed to Artemis compounds. Heavy exposure over a fairly long period of time."

He held her gaze steady. "How can you tell?" he asked.

"I can smell it," she said.

"Pardon?"

"I smell it. In their sweat. Direct contact. Not airborne." She stared at him hard, daring him to tell her she was wrong. He didn't.

Instead, he held her gaze steady, reached up and took her hand in his. His thoughts moved into hers easily. They'd done this so many times, in so many ways, there was very little to block contact unless one of them chose to actively push the other away. Apparently, she didn't choose that tonight.

Show me, he requested.

She shrugged, and then opened to him, drawing him in to her experience, what she saw and felt from the women, what swirling of energy created the patterns she perceived within them. Wordlessly, she took him through their visions and her own, including her vision in the sweat lodge.

The feel of her vision was unlike the feel of the others in surprising ways, and the content jolted Alex almost out of the vision itself. Blood on the moon, and a man with blood on his hands. And the man—he startled at the brief yet intense glimpse of face, so soon covered in blood. His surprise was so sharp that Jaguar almost halted in her progress, feeling it coming from him.

Okay, Jaguar. Just—give me a second here.

She let him linger in the vision, and then at his signal moved on through the night and into the morning, where he observed her at work with Terez.

The sun on her bare back as she leaned over the stream and dipped her hand into the water. The curve of her hips as she swayed with Terez, dancing her into her own desire. He felt it directly, as if it had been injected into his veins. Fear and desire. Desire and fear. The most potent and potentially combustible combination he knew, and Jaguar danced with it as if it was the easiest thing in the world.

And under the experience of the moment she shared, he felt her gauging his response to it. Jaguar's programs were never traditional. More than once, he'd fought with her about them, though she'd always ended up doing as she thought best in the end. She waited to see if he'd argue with her now.

Your call, Jaguar, he said into her questions. *Always has been.*

When the moment faded to black, he pulled his hand back from hers. Stood and pressed his hands against his lower back.

"Terez is coming along already," she said. "I think the others'll clear just as quickly if I keep sweating them."

"We still need proof," he said. "Something we can bring to the Hague."

She put a hand on her hip. "Xipetotec flay them all. What kind of proof?"

"Not the kind you just showed me, I'm afraid." He rubbed at the back of his neck and considered. "Let's go in the kitchen. I want some coffee and we have to talk."

He made coffee in the warm darkness. She perched herself on his counter while he worked, watching him silently from this post, swinging her legs back and forth. He could feel her eyes, still full of the moon, resting on him, as he moved from stove to cupboard to counter, making coffee, being normal, trying not to let his hand slip and find itself suddenly on her thigh. She was not, he decided long ago, the easiest woman to have around.

When the brew was finished, he poured her a cup, set it down at his kitchen table and took a seat. She sat across from him, letting the steam from her cup rise to her face and breathing it in.

"We need to establish how the women were exposed to Artemis," he said. "Odds are they know. They might even know where the manufacturing's going on. If you clear them, maybe they'll tell. How long do you anticipate for the program?"

"Couple of weeks, if all goes well. Of course, there's no telling what snags I might run into."

"Okay. Rachel's digging up everything she can about the people in their lives. Husbands. Bosses. Family. You get what you can from them, too." He swirled his coffee in his cup, brooded over it a minute. "What do you know about phase psychosis in men?" he asked.

"How much does anybody know? The initial claim was that it didn't exist at all, so nobody's looked into it. My theory is that given what we call acceptable male behavior, we might not even notice. It's still a testosterone friendly world. Why do you ask?"

He stirred his coffee, brooded over it a moment. "Curious," he said.

"Shaking your web, spider magus?" she asked.

"No," he said. "But apparently I don't have to."

"What's that mean?"

"Your vision in the sweat. That's an adept vision."

She made a sound of impatience at him. "I'm not an adept," she said.

He grinned. She wouldn't like seeing herself in that light. "Possibly," he said, "exposure to Artemis ups the ante on latent psi capacities. Maybe you're a latent adept."

"Am not," she growled under her breath.

Alex laughed. "Don't worry. I'm sure it'll dissipate as soon as the assignment's over. Makes me wonder about your women, though. What they might come up with."

"That's been on my mind. None of them tested positive for any psi capacities, however . . . "

"However . . . you're not an adept, either, right?" Alex concluded for her. "But you had a vision, and it was in adept space."

"How do you know that?"

"I could smell it, Jaguar. The man in it. You didn't recognize him?"

"Did you?" she asked.

He called the memory of the vision back into his mind and considered it again. He was almost sure on first sight. Second and third views only confirmed that sense of surety.

"Brendan Farley. Lives in Watertown, Connecticut. Got arrested for demonstrating without a permit not too long ago. He's had previous arrests for similar incidents. And he works for La Femme."

She narrowed her eyes at him. One of the reasons she mistrusted adepts was because the information they worked with was metaphoric in nature, tricky to interpret. They might see a lot, but how they interpreted it made all the difference in the world to their actions, and most didn't have a clue how to interpret well. Alex, she had to admit, was damn good, which was the only reason she listened to him at all on the topic.

"That's the guy in my vision? You're sure?"

"Positive."

"La Femme—one of my women worked there. Karena."

"That's true."

"Well, what's a penny ante activist who can't keep his nose clean doing in my sweat lodge vision?"

"I'm not sure, Jaguar," Alex said. "But I think it means more trouble."

"What kind of trouble?" she asked.

"Many kinds," he said, and swirled his coffee in his cup, thoughtfully observing the motion he'd created.

"Could you be specific?" Jaguar requested. "If I have to swim with the sharks, I don't want to play hide and seek with an adept at the same time."

He put his coffee cup down. "Specifically, there's Corporate trouble. Big money and big politicking trouble. Specifically, when we drag all this out into the light, someone's bound to get pissed off, and we'll be standing right in line to be pissed on if we don't manage it right."

"You think you can manage moon madness?" she asked, "It's like gold fever. Greed and fear are in charge of this one."

"Actually, on the home planet, Global Concerns seems to be in charge of this one." In response to her raised eyebrows, he added, "They're leading the lobbying efforts for repeal of the moratorium. With a battering ram."

She whistled long and low. "Global Concerns—that's Lawrence Barone's outfit, isn't it?"

He was always prepared to be surprised at the bits of information she did and didn't carry around in her head, but this was very unexpected. Big business ranked as low on her continuum importance as bureaucratic angst. That she should know the name of a corporate executive was about as likely as him knowing what she was up to at any given moment.

"How do you know that?" he asked.

"I read," she said cryptically, then added, "And I'm very fond of the writing of Anna Burhasa."

"Oh," he said. "Burhasa. I should've guessed."

Of course Jaguar would know about that. Anna Burhasa was a novelist, playwright, screenwriter, poet from the earlier part of the century. She started out poor and obscure, but the Nobel prize for her play *Gods and Fishes* changed all that, and she was suddenly a very wealthy woman. Her money started the Burhasa foundation, which, among other things, had helped places like 13 Streams get solar technology and a larger plot of land.

Her personality was as colorful as her writing. She traced her roots back to the Etruscans and always wore her family crest—a leopard's face surrounded by grapevines—in her jewelry. She was a political activist, frequently arrested for civil disobedience, and threw the best parties in any town you cared to name. She traveled the world and wrote about it, took a variety of lovers, male and female, and wrote about that, too. She married three times, and the third marriage lasted until she was shot in the streets of LA, an old, old woman busy rescuing children during the Killing Times.

Unfortunately, neither fame nor wealth protected her from the vicissitudes of divorce. Her second husband, Martin Barone, who had accused her of witchcraft in the divorce proceedings, finagled rights to some of her early works, and even though she deliberately didn't allow those works to be published until after her death and his, his son by his second wife, Martin Junior, claimed the rights, and the courts said yes, he could have it. Martin was Larry Barone's father, and with his inheritance, Larry, who had a talent for business, financed the start of Global Concerns, Inc. If Anna was in a place where she knew her money was financing the Barone empire, Alex thought, she'd be royally pissed.

"Very good, Jaguar," Alex said. "I'm impressed."

"Don't be," she said. "What I like, I learn about. And I like her." Jaguar stood, stretched. Took a stroll around the room and then returned to her seat. "Which means I already have a prejudice against Barone and his outfit. Global concerns my ass."

"Global Concerns covers ten different corporations, and eight of them could make lots of money off Artemis," Alex commented.

"What're his connections to the Planetoid?"

"That's the other thing I wanted to talk to you about," he said. "It's worse than we thought. There's been memos going around about renting out portions of the Planetoid for crystallization plants."

He watched her face go through its changes. Chin lifted, eyes narrowed, mouth pressing into a thin line. Jaguar had a way of thinking with her body, processing information through her skin and hair. He let her, waiting to see what would emerge when she was finished.

"Who do we need to be careful of here?" she asked. "What governors want it?"

She tumbled to that quick enough, he thought. "I don't know yet. Rachel's looking into it. I should know more tomorrow, after I talk to Paul and see what he has to say for himself."

Jaguar moved back to the table and sat across from him, leaned on her elbow. "Will you tell him what's going on?"

"Enough. He doesn't like to know too much. You know how he is."

She snorted derisively. "You think you can trust him, Alex? If there's corporate monkey business going on, who's to say he's not involved? Governor's are like ungreased fists, ready to—" She made a gesture rich with clarity.

"I trust Paul to be Paul," Alex said quickly, "He likes things kept simple."

Jaguar chewed on this thought and her lower lip. "That's true. You think this Brendan Farley is involved?"

"More than likely," he said. "Maybe someone the women knew. I know I'd like to find him."

"Careful what you wish for. He'd be very dangerous, if he's messing with Artemis."

Alex laughed. Jaguar telling him to be careful was a new phenomena.

"I mean it," she continued. "Lunar material—you have to handle it with absolute respect. You know that, don't you?"

"I believe so," he said patiently. "After all, I'm old enough to vote, and drink, drive wings, choose my bed partners with care."

She made a noise like growling at the back of her throat, reached across the table and grasped his wrist. Squeezed hard. In her touch, he saw her vision again, this time feeling the blood that covered him, drowning him, soaking into him.

Do not fuck around with this stuff. It will eat you alive.

Through her hand he could feel the motion of pull, the motion of desire that flowed through the moon, through the tidal pull of blood in veins, through her. As she touched him he could feel the influence of the moon, a power she would let flow through and out of her. He knew the discipline it took her to resist using that power, and he honestly wasn't sure if he could do the same. Power was as seductive as love, or fear.

"You be careful, too, Jaguar," he said softly. "It's already in you."

She released him, and turned a slow smile toward him. "I know what's in me, and I know what to do with it. There's more danger here for you than there is for me. Don't forget that, and don't hold anything back. If you find this man, let me know."

He shifted in his seat, looking away from her. "I will. Barring death or gags, I will."

"All right," she said. "Okay. Back to work. The women are waiting." She stood and stretched her long arms toward the ceiling,.

And quietly as wind, she was gone, leaving Alex to brood further over his coffee, his job, and the imprint of her fingers on his wrist.

CHAPTER FOUR

In the morning, Alex's first move was to call the police department in Watertown where, after a series of forwards from desk to desk, he was put in touch with a Detective Jurgensen, who had the Farley file. His face, as it appeared on the telecom, was round, tired, and intelligent.

"Detective Jurgensen," Alex said. "Did anyone tell you why I'm calling?"

Jurgensen grinned, making his face even rounder. "Not a gott-damn clue," he said. "However, it's not often I get a call from the Planetoid, so I thought it might be interesting."

"It might," Alex agreed. "I'm hoping it is to me, at any rate. You have the file for Brendan Farley?"

Jurgensen rolled his eyes and grimaced. "Farley. Christ. Now there's a piece of work."

"Really? I understand he was just a misdemeanor. Didn't get a permit to demonstrate or something?"

"Didn't get a permit to stand in the middle of the street screaming about use of pesticides on lawns. Screaming," Jurgensen repeated. "In a nice neighborhood, too."

"Ah," Alex said. "You know him well?"

"Hell, yeah. This wasn't his first arrest. Believe it or not, he's got a helluva rap sheet. All civil disobedience crap. He's an environmentalist," Jurgensen concluded, saying this last word with as much scorn as he could manage to insert into every syllable.

Alex was a little disappointed at this news. He was looking for behav-

44

iors that were out of the norm for the person involved. It sounded like getting arrested was all in a day's work for Farley. No indication of phase psychosis there.

"So there was nothing unusual in his arrest. And you haven't seen any behaviors in him that were—maybe a little exaggerated, or suspicious to you?"

Jurgensen's blue eyes widened into great circles. "Funny you mention that," he said. He looked to his left and to his right, as if checking for listeners, lowered his voice and leaned close to the screen. "We got no proof, understand, but we like him for the mall bombing."

That, Alex thought, was more like it. "Mall bombing?"

"Pesticide bomb, set off in a mall just outside of town. Killed seven, injured thirty-two. Helluva mess. Farley's always going on about pesticides, and he's got a degree in chemistry, so he looks real good for it. Only, we got no physical evidence yet." Jurgensen waved a hand at the screen. "We'll get it, though. Then," he pointed at Alex, "we'll send him to you."

Alex grinned back. "Sure. We got room. When did the mall bombing happen?"

"Two—no, three weeks ago."

Perfect, Alex thought. Just about the same time the Death Sisters were in action. Jurgensen picked up on this as well.

"We thought maybe he made a pact with the Death Sisters, y'know? Then, we had all those jumpers, too."

"Jumpers?"

"Yeah. Bunch of people—I think five—all pick the same week to go off the bridge. We get maybe that many suicides in a year, not a week, so it was pretty back around here." He tilted his head and regarded Alex. "So now you gonna tell me how all that's connected, because I have a feeling you know."

Alex shook his head. "I'm looking for the connections, if there are any. Maybe you can help me with that, and send me what you have on Farley."

"Sure. I'll get it out today. And when you figure it out, you'll call me back and let me know what it was all about, right?"

"I'll do that," Alex said. "It'll be a pleasure."

Alex flicked off his telecom and stared ahead at his wall for a moment, letting all this information sink in. Okay, he thought. What next?

And that was easy. Next was Board governor Paul Dinardo, who was on the home planet, in Washington, just around the corner from the legislative bodies the Planetoid system received funding from.

Governors spent most of their time in liaison work with the home planet government. Except to write up protocol or approve protocol changes, they left the actual work of the Planetoid to the supervisors and Teachers, so long as nobody made any noise. A low profile was a valuable commodity in the Planetoid system. First, the invisibility of the system itself kept the home planet populace happy. They could gaze skyward and know there was somewhere for the dangerous criminals to go, away from a world they wanted kept clean and neat, especially after the violence of the Killing Times.

And second, the kind of work done with prisoners on the Planetoids was something the legislative bodies liked to keep invisible. They wanted the Planetoid people to do the job, but they didn't want photos of work in progress, unless it was presentable to their constituency.

It generally suited all concerned to keep things that way, unless they were like Jaguar, who ran with scissors, and pointed them up.

This trait in her aggravated the hell out of their Board governor. She would have been fired long ago if she wasn't the best they had, and if Paul didn't know that if he fired her, Alex would follow. Paul trusted Alex, who rarely made messes, and often kept other people from making them. If Alex ran with scissors, he would at least keep them pointed down. He punched in Paul's code, and found him in his office. When his face appeared on the telecom, it looked distracted, and Alex could see his computer on and scrolling in the background.

"Busy day, Paul?" he asked.

Paul rolled his eyes. "I got a few senators up my butt about a thing or two."

"Would it have anything to do with moon mining?"

Paul startled, put down his cup of coffee, reached behind him and closed down his computer screen. He pressed a few buttons on his telecom.

"Go secure," he told Alex.

Alex pressed similar buttons, and smoothed his own aspect into serenity.

Paul leaned forward and stared into the screen. "How do you know about that?" he asked, then held up a hand to stop him. "Never mind. Just tell me *what* you know."

Alex inclined his head in acknowledgment. Paul didn't like to talk about empathic work, though he knew Alex was an adept and often used those capacities in his job. "I know the moratorium on moon mining is six months from expiration, and the pressure's on to let it expire."

"Yeah," Paul said. "Everybody who watches the news knows that. There's about six different mega-corps all wanna be first in line. What else?"

"I've heard talk about putting Artemis plants on Planetoid three when the moratorium's repealed."

Paul narrowed his eyes. "Whose talk is that?" he asked.

Alex leaned back and folded his arms across his chest. "Talk among friends. Is it true?"

"It's true. The Senate likes it. Makes us profitable, and it's an election year, God help us. Senator Delaney says develop the unused sections outside the replica cities. I say she's nuts. I told them forget it. We're an open system, and it's too dangerous. Same problem here as they'd have on the home planet. We got some big boys against us, though, so I ain't calling it until it's over."

Alex let his shoulders relax. At least he didn't have to fight with Paul about it. "I'm surprised they want us and not One."

"It's prettier here," he said. "Besides, One already puts its prisoners to work, and we don't."

"Yet," Alex commented.

"Not yet, and not ever," Paul said decisively. "We work 'em, we start needing 'em. Then we're not rehab anymore, we're a labor pool."

"I'm proud of you, Paul," Alex said. "You're evolving."

"Too bad the Senate don't believe in Evolution."

"What Planetoid people support the idea?"

"A few governors," Paul shrugged. "Shafritz. You know him? He's zone 9."

"I know him. Tall thin guy with a lot of beard and a fake laugh."

"Yeah. That's him. Then there's John Kusick, who votes for anything I don't want because he's still sore that zone 12 does better than zone 9 in the football pool."

"Zone 12 does better than 9 in just about everything, Paul. It has better governance."

Paul shot him a look that asked if this was flattery. Alex said nothing. It wasn't flattery. It was just the truth. As governors went, Paul was better than most because he usually knew when not to interfere. He had his problems, but he beat the hell out of Kusick or Shafritz.

"Who's against it?" Alex asked.

"Miriam Whitehall. You know her?"

Alex nodded. She was an attractive woman, pleasantly curved, with soft brown eyes and soft curly brown hair. She tended toward the liberal in her politics, and flowing dresses in her wardrobe, and Alex remembered that her voice was nice to listen to. She had once expressed a personal interest in Alex, and he might have reciprocated, but he had a feeling that she wasn't as soft as she looked, and it didn't seem worth the possible consequences.

"Is that it? Just Miriam?"

"Far as I can tell. The rest are waiting to see which way the wind blows. Hell."

"What would it take," Alex asked, "to get a definite ruling against use of the Planetoid?"

"A hammer on the right heads?" he suggested. "A really big hammer?"

"How about solid causal evidence linking phase psychosis to Artemis byproduct exposure?"

Paul lifted his coffee cup and took a sip. "Yeah?" he said casually. "What kind of evidence?"

"I have some prisoners who exhibit the symptoms of phase psychosis. I'm in the process of linking them to Artemis exposure. We may get some very solid information there."

"The last time women made that claim, they got their asses wiped."

"What if it was a man?" Alex asked.

Paul put his coffee cup down. "What do you need?" he asked.

Alex sighed. He supposed it was true, what Jaguar said. That men still had that extra six to nine inches of legitimacy that seemed to expand infinitely in these kinds of situations. She called it a legal hard on. Crude, but accurate.

"I need extra research hours for my workers, and access to some private files—like Larry Barone's."

"That's a lot of toys, and it ain't even Christmas. If you get 'em, how do you play with 'em?"

"I play nicely, Paul. And I play with friends. Like you."

Paul drummed nervous fingers on his desk. "Okay," he said. "I'll clear the hours, and I'll see what I can get for Barone, but that'll be tougher. Alex—you really got something?"

"I think I do, Paul."

"Can you nail it?" he asked.

"Maybe."

Paul shook his head. "There's a lot at stake here. What's your plan?"

"In particular, I'm not sure. I have to let a few things unfold. Jaguar's working with the three women."

Paul's forehead creased and uncreased itself. Then he shrugged. "I suppose," he said, "that was inevitable. Keep tabs on her, will you?"

Alex grinned. "Always."

"Yeah. Right. Stay in touch. Let me know what I need to know, okay?"

Alex nodded, and signed off.

He spent a minute tapping a finger against the edge of his desk, and an image of Jaguar came into his mind—she was sitting in front of his desk, saying this was a three body problem. The moon, the earth, and the Planetoid. And his morning was the same—a three body problem, including Governors, Corporations, and Cops. He'd done Cops and Governors. It was time for Corporations. He asked his computer to give him the number for La Femme Personnel headquarters, and it made the connection for him.

A very smooth, fair face filled his telecom and showed him a perfect set of white teeth. "May I help you?" the face asked, looking as if it really wanted to help in any way at all.

"Maybe you can," he said. "I'm calling from Planetoid Three—I'm Supervisor Dzarny, in charge of a prisoner who once worked for La Femme, and I need her personnel records, and some time with her supervisor to ask a few questions."

The smile showed itself again, and the face nodded. "We like to cooperate with the legal system in any way we can, Supervisor. I'll put you through to the appropriate party."

Her smile disappeared, but was soon replaced by one almost exactly like it, also looking ready to help him climb mountains, if need be.

"Supervisor Dzarny," the smooth voice said, "I'm Janet Crowly, Personnel director."

"So nice to meet you," Alex said. "Have you been told why I called?"

"Yes, and we've confirmed your ID, so we can proceed, if you'll give me the prisoner's name."

Alex gave the name, and the smile disappeared.

"I sent a note to your researcher, didn't I?" she asked.

"I don't know. Did you?"

"Well, yes. Of course I did."

"Maybe she didn't get it yet. Tell me what it said."

"Well, her file's been expunged. I—I checked three times. It's not there."

Alex knit his eyebrows and made himself look imposing. "Ms. Crowly," he said, "this is a serious legal matter."

She blanched. "I know. I just—I can't explain it, either. I don't expunge personnel reports. I can't. Nobody can, really, except—"

"Except?" Alex asked.

"Except nobody," she said quickly. "Nobody."

"I think I'd like to confirm that," he said, "with your supervisor. Can you put me through?"

"Oh," she said, her hand flying to her mouth. "To my supervisor?"

"That's right. Now, if you don't mind."

The screen went blank, and soon another face appeared, slightly older, but no less well tended than the others. Only, he couldn't see the teeth because this face wasn't smiling. In fact, it looked grim.

"Supervisor," she said, "Margaret Riley. Janet tells me there's some kind of problem?" Her tone indicated that the very idea of a problem was in unspeakably bad taste.

"Regarding records for one of your past employees," he said. "Karena—"

"Halsey. Yes," she said. "She was expunged from our files."

"So I understand. But Ms. Crowly says files are not expunged."

"Only under certain conditions. After what she did, we didn't want her name associated with our products."

"Didn't it occur to you that her employee records would be useful in her rehab?"

"We assumed you could get any pertinent information from the trial transcript, the police interview and so on."

"Yes," Alex said. "Well, sometimes they don't cover the kind of information we're looking for. I'd like her former supervisor to talk with my researcher. Do I do that through you?"

"Yes. Just let me check on him. If you'll hold a minute."

Alex nodded. She disappeared from the screen briefly, and was replaced by a fractalling design, accompanied by a Bach fugue. The fractals spit out periodic logos or ad copy for various Global Concerns products.

Margaret returned before Alex was stricken with the urge to buy anything, and she looked as if she felt she'd need to defend herself.

"It will not be possible," she said firmly, "for your researcher to speak with Mr. Farley."

"Has he been expunged, too?" Alex asked.

"Of course not," Margaret said with some warmth. "He—well, he quit. About two weeks ago. Just walked out."

Alex frowned. "Do you still have his file?"

"I'm sure we do."

"Then forward that to me. Would it have a photo?"

"They all do."

"Good. Send it on, then. I'll give you the address."

He did so, and signed off. He should have a photo by the end of the day.

When Margaret Riley saw Alex's face disappear from the screen, she thought she'd better apprise her local manager of the situation, in case it did become a legal matter. She punched in a number, and was put through a number of secretaries until she him.

"I'm receiving inquiries about Karena Halsey," she said. She explained the situation briefly. "I thought you might want to know. And there's a Planetoid request for the file on her supervisor—a Brendan Farley."

The manager's face stayed neutral, as did his tone. "Who is inquiring?" he asked.

"Supervisor Dzarny from Planetoid Three. Do you want his number?"

He nodded, considered for a moment, then said, "Send him what he wants. And let me know if he wants more."

"Very good," Margaret said, and signed off.

When she was gone, the manager drummed his fingers on his desk. He'd been given some names that were specifically of interest in Corporate headquarters, and both of these were on the list. He called his district manager and passed the information on. The district manager thought it best to let the buck pass from her desk to the next one up, and so on, until at last, the private secretary for CEO Lawrence Barone got the call.

She was irritated at the interruption, which occurred when she was trying to proofread a rather tricky bit of lobbying verbiage, but she was trained to respond, and so she passed the message on immediately to his message box, where the buck stopped.

In his office, when Larry Barone listened to the terse message, he sat at his desk and lowered his face into his hands. He'd been working hard, lobbying for the Hague repeal, and establishing a site off the home planet was crucial to his efforts. He was told it would be simple. 'Leave it to me. I'll take care of everything,' were the words he remembered from his associate in this operation. But this could complicate things. His thoughts circled possibilities for danger or opportunity. He'd have to find out where the women were, who was working with them, what was already known. He'd have to find out what Dzarny was up to. He'd have to determine if he could place any trust at all in his current source of information, who told him it would be simple. And he'd have to start figuring back-up plans, just in case.

He rolled his shoulders around, trying to release the tension at the back of his neck. He was considering his next move, when there was a quick knock on his door.

"Come in," he said.

The door opened, and a woman in her late forties, with hair the color of wheat and a figure like the goddess who ruled that plant stepped onto the thick carpet of his office floor.

He held a hand out, gesturing her to him. "Darling. Come in. Come in."

She closed the door behind her. Observed that he pressed the button which set the lock mechanism. She walked toward him, leaving her shoes at the door, and unbuttoning her dress as she neared his desk.

He smiled as he unbuckled his belt and removed his jacket and tie.

"Miriam," he said, sweeping his arm across his desk to clear space, "Always such a treat."

At the start of the next sweat, Jaguar noticed that even though the women were still fundamentally nonverbal, they were beginning to show signs of change. Karena's hands were lined with dirt, her fingernails torn and paint peeling off. And she didn't seem to mind. Jaguar picked up a handful of mud and spit into it, rolling it around her hand. She took a finger-full and smeared it on Karena's face, painting her with jagged streaks of brown earth. Karena jerked back out of her reach.

"Be still," Jaguar commanded, and she stood, blinking and afraid. Jaguar described a circle of earth on her forehead, a spiral on her cheek. "This is what you want," she murmured more gently. "To be dirty."

Karena sighed and relaxed. That was good. Very good. There was still old material to clear, but her consent in this moment was a very good sign. They were all doing well.

"Go get more wood," Jaguar told Karena and she walked away silently.

Fiore tended the fire, which was blazing nicely. Jaguar went and stood by it, found it too hot even for her, and took a step back. She didn't know how Fiore was able to get so close without spontaneously combusting, but she seemed unbothered by the wall of heat. Her dark eyes caught and swallowed the sparks that flew up around her. When she leaned too close to the flames, a line of fire bit at her hair, sizzling the grey into a frizzled mass of black. Jaguar moved to her and smothered the fire with her hand, sucking in heat and smoke and choking it back out as she stepped back, coughing.

Fiore whirled on her swiftly.

"You were on fire," Jaguar coughed, turning away, seeking air.

FIore breathed out heavily through her nose and returned to her work.

The fire blazed itself down, and the rocks grew red and alive beneath it. Jaguar moved the women inside, starting with the chant for renewal used in the sweat following the onset of menses in girls. The women wouldn't understand, but their bodies would.

As she chanted, Fiore picked up the repetitive syllables and the tone, and began chanting with her. Jaguar was surprised at the strength of her voice and the fervor with which she used it. Her body knew. Her body wanted this. Needed this. A fiery woman.

I am fire.

Jaguar stopped chanting. Someone had spoken into her. Empathic contact. Fiore?

In the darkness of the sweat, with only the red glow of the rocks to see by, Jaguar reached across the pit, balancing precariously at the edge of it, and grasped Fiore's face in her hands, pulling her toward the center where stones burned and were not consumed. Fiore leaned forward and fell, her hands pressing against the red hot rocks.

She did not scream. No fire chewed at her hands.

Jaguar let her go, and she pushed herself back to her place without so much as a whimper.

"Chac Ma," Jaguar whispered reverently. "Look at that."

Fiore was an empath. And pyrokinetic. Her tests hadn't indicated any psi capacities, and Pyrokinesis always showed clear in the advanced neural workup. But Fiore could hold fire in her hands, create it with her thoughts. Jaguar would treat that most respectfully. She couldn't try to learn more here, in this closed space with the two other women present.

She'd have to think about this before going any further. An empath. Pyrokinetic. It could be very interesting.

For the remainder of the sweat, she watched Fiore's eyes watch her, two sparking stones that ate fire in the howling dark.

CHAPTER FIVE

Miriam, dressed once more, sat on the other side of the desk in the leather armchair, looking as innocent as a mother or a nun. She could do that. Play hardball, roll naked on the floor, and turn around to show the world a Madonna's face. It was a useful talent, Larry Barone thought. Now it was time to see her business face.

"What's happening with our prisoners, Miriam?" he asked.

"Not much," she said. "The women are assigned to a Dr. Addams." She wrinkled her nose in distaste.

"Someone you don't like very much?"

"Someone nobody likes very much. With one or two exceptions."

"I've heard her name before, haven't I?"

Miriam nodded. "You may have. She gets in trouble. No sense of discretion."

Miriam was being far too offhand about this. She was hiding something. Larry searched his mental files to see if he could remember where he knew the name from. The news? Yes. Something in the news.

"There was something about her crashing the VR system, wasn't there?"

"Ye-es," Miriam said hesitantly.

Then Larry remembered the rest. Jaguar Addams. He went through some files of Planetoid people a year ago, when he first started thinking about Planetoid Three as an Artemis site. Her file was thick and interesting. She was an empath, with a ninety-eight percent success rate and a history of taking on the big boys. She didn't play by the rules, and she almost always won. He'd read about Supervisor Dzarny, too, now that he thought about it. Another empath. Addams' supervisor. Shit.

"Jesus, Miriam. She's the one who took out Division for Intelligence Enterprises. She's with the women? Our women? They were our test subjects, for Chrissakes. If she gets to them, it's all over."

"Darling," Miriam said quickly. "Don't worry. I'm having it taken care of."

"How?"

"You'll see." She leaned over the desk and patted his arm. He jerked it back. He hated it when she did that. "It's okay. Really. I know the system. I know how to work it."

"Then why is her supervisor asking questions about Brendan? He's supposed to be an invisible presence, to quote you, and now Dzarny wants his records from La Femme."

"Alex Dzarny," Miriam mused, her forehead creasing slightly, then smoothing itself as she smiled. "He's part of the plan, darling. Though I'm surprised he got this far before—" Her words trailed off to silence.

"Finish your sentence, darling," Barone suggested.

Miriam turned her attention back to him. "You know I have it all set up," Miriam said. "Can't you just trust me?"

Larry narrowly avoided laughing. "Sure. Once I know the set up. And approve it."

Miriam's mouth turned itself into a small smile. "Remind me never to throw a surprise party for you. Listen, it's simple. When the Planetoid destabilizes, sweetheart, if there's a worker involved, insurance won't pay any claims. You know that. Assured wrote the policy." She held her smooth hand up, and turned it over, palm up.

"Dzarny's our worker?" Larry asked. He had to admit, he liked that. It was elegant, and very like Miriam.

"He'll save your company more than fifty million dollars." She waved her hand in the air, tossing away any thought of trouble. "Brendan will find him before the day's out. I'll see to that."

At this, Larry's skepticism returned. "He's unstable."

Miriam laughed. "He has to be, Larry. Don't worry. He's under my control. Besides, Alex won't get anywhere. He's a fool."

"Because he didn't respond to your charms?"

Miriam's voice grew cool. "His choice of women is questionable. *And* he's a fool. He's been against every development of the Planetoid from the start. Unprogressive, and loud about it."

"Better luck next time," Barone noted.

"Fuck you, Larry," she snapped. "We are to proceed, and if you back out now, I'll give you away like an old pair of shoes."

Larry laughed. He enjoyed pushing at her sweet woman persona, just to see what its limits were. Generally, if you messed with her opinion of herself, or with her grasping for money and power, she'd lose it. Ego, money and power were pretty much what she was about, underneath all the politicking. She once told him that what she liked best about him was that when she fucked him, she was fucking the world. "Fucking it, and coming out queen," she said, her eyes wild with delight.

Not that he minded the attitude. Half the fun of sex with Miriam was the challenge of who would be conquering whom in a series of physical inter-actions that were more like wrestling matches than lovemaking. Both of them, vying for the turf of each other's bodies. But that was pleasure, and this was business, which was looking dicey.

"I just want to make sure everything *goes* as planned," Larry said. "If the women talk—"

Miriam pushed herself to standing. "What'll they say? And who will listen to them say it once the Planetoid's destabilized."

"What about Brendan? If Dzarny gets to him—"

"Not a chance. The women might rehab, but men can't come back from Artemis. Not at that level of exposure. They're too weak."

Though her arrogance never ceased to amaze him, he had to admit that she knew what she was talking about. Men's reactions to Artemis were off the chart, compared to women's. They just needed more of it to get there.

When Artemis was legal, the men who worked in their research plants showed no trouble, but Miriam pointed out that nobody had spoken with the men's wives, because as a rule when men had trouble, it was their wives who experienced it. She also reminded him that their exposure was minimal, and to only a few of the compounds. Women probably just had a different level of tolerance. And there was bound to be individual variations, too. She had no negative reaction. In fact, she'd had some real benefits from Artemis, though she wouldn't elaborate on what they were.

Larry finally agreed that it would be good to establish reactivity parame-ters They'd tried out another man before Farley, and it wasn't pretty. He'd had to call in a few big favors to get rid of the body.

They hadn't planned to test any more men after the last disaster, but when Brendan worked for La Femme, where they were testing various properties of Artemis for their effects on skin regeneration and sexual energy, he had been too curious by half about their "secret formula." With his background in chemistry, he was able to distill one of their lotions to its basis, and then showed up outside Larry's office with a handful of moonstones he made from it.

Miriam suggested they might as well make use of him. "He wants Artemis, let's give him Artemis," she said. "And we can do some more tests on exposure in men. Besides, I have an idea for how to use him."

But he had to admit, once she got the exposure level right, she had complete control over Brendan.

Miriam took him to her apartment and disappeared for three days. She said she'd made an important discovery. Artemis made men more passive and more aggressive at the same time. More passively aggressive. And much more useful. That was when it was becoming clear that getting Planetoid space for an Artemis plant would be tricky at best. The Governors were balking, in spite of the money. Senators were wavering, too. Sure, they wanted the moratorium lifted, but they wanted a litigation-free space to work in. In light of that, Miriam's idea was a good one, but from where Larry sat it wasn't anywhere near airtight. Too many variables. Too much left unplanned.

That was one difference between them. She liked to improvise. He liked to plan. She said planning gave him the illusion of control. He said she was too lazy to formulate strategy. They'd already decided that they had to take steps to destabilize Planetoid operations. Brendan became a means to do that.

It was a good idea, but he wasn't a man to trust blindly, especially with a woman like Miriam. Granted, he needed her now, but soon she would become redundant. He already had some options for what to do when that happened. In the meantime, he had his own ways of monitoring the situation.

He smiled at Miriam. "Back to work," he said.

"I know. Me too. I'll be on the Planetoid for the week."

"Taking care of all the glitches, I trust."

"Of course."

"Let me know if there's anything you need me for."

"I will," she promised.

As soon as the door closed behind her, he opened his desk drawer, and sought a small piece of paper which he kept unrelated to any other. It had a number on it for someone who would be particularly useful in the near future. That someone might be difficult to get, however, and it would be best if he started trying now.

CHAPTER SIX

Alex liked to walk, and did so whenever he had the chance. Thus, the next afternoon found him walking through downtown, and toward the zoo, which fronted a number of Planetoid prison facilities, such as the VR site, the House of Mirrors, and the Normal Houses, which were called that because they looked like a normal suburban neighborhood. Some prisoners were housed here during their rehab, and Alex was going to check on one, at the request of a Teacher who wasn't quite sure if he was making the progress he ought to.

He didn't mind this part of the job. It got him out of the office and away from paperwork for a while, allowed him to stretch his legs and relax. But right now his mind was more on Artemis. He was anxious to hear from Jaguar, learn about her progress, but he didn't want to interrupt her with contact. She'd get to him as soon as she had anything to offer.

Of course, there was no point in speculating about that ahead of the facts, but that didn't stop Alex from speculating. He had a twitch about this case, and he was deep into the twitch when he crossed the bridge that spanned the Lake outlet between downtown and the outskirts where the facilities were placed.

He was so deeply into it that he walked right past the man leaning on the rail of the bridge, nodded at him and went on, before it registered that the man's face was familiar. He stopped walked, and turned around to look again.

He looked harmless enough. Bland face. Sandy graying hair. Nondescript face. Eyes the color of nothing much behind wire-rimmed glasses.

His own frame was wiry rather than muscular, and Alex noted that his wrists seemed weak, arms flaccid as they hung loosely over the railing. He was holding something small in one of them, turning it over and over thoughtfully.

But he was familiar. He was a face Alex knew.

"Ye gods and little fishes," he murmured to himself. "Can it be?"

It certainly looked like it was. Brendan Farley. Just standing there, as if he'd been waiting for Alex to come along.

Alex walked back toward him, intending to ask directions as a means to starting conversation, but when he got there and said hello, his program changed.

The man turned to face him, then turned away again.

"I suppose," he said, continuing to stare straight ahead, "you know who I am."

Alex jerked his head back, then tried to cover the gesture unsuccessfully. Okay, he thought. We'll play it that way.

"Sure, Brendan," he said amicably. "I do." He went to the railing and leaned against it next to the man. "I'm Alex Dzarny, by the way, but maybe you know that already."

"I do," he said.

Alex said nothing while he let this news settle in. Careful what you wish for, Jaguar had said. Careful when you get it.

"I'm glad to meet you," Alex said, honestly. He held out a hand for shaking. Brendan didn't take it. Instead, he closed his nondescript eyes, opened them again, and turned them on Alex.

They were filled with cold. Filled with empty spaces like the dark at the back of the closet. The swirling eddies of sorrow, creeping despair, afternoons alone and nights without comfort for body or soul. Alex found himself swimming in the death of animals, the death of plants, the death of all bodies with no hope of regeneration. Cells drying and lifeless. Toxins creeping in where life once resided. Despair as thick as night.

Jesus, he thought. That's no good.

He hadn't made empathic contact. Why should he be feeling so much? It was out of hand already. Too much. Too big and too close.

Don't fuck around with this stuff. It will eat you alive.

Through a fog of despair, he closed his eyes and found the still, quiet space at the center of his chest and rested in it a moment. He breathed out, and extended the stillness in and around him. He opened his eyes. It still felt a little thick outside, but his own emotional space was clear for now. Better. That was better.

Farley looked him up and down, and pocketed the small white stone he'd been turning over in his hand. "We should go," he said.

"Go where?" Alex asked.

"To the shuttle station."

"Oh. Are we taking a shuttle somewhere?"

"Come on," Brendan said. He pushed himself away from the railing and began to walk across the bridge.

"It's a ways from here. You know that, don't you?"

"We'll grab a taxi once we're off the bridge."

They did so, riding in silence, and were let off at the shuttle station. They went inside, and Brendan peered up at the signs that told departure and arrival times.

"What are you looking for?" Alex asked.

"New England corridor. At least, I think—" He frowned, and dug into his pocket, took out a piece of paper and chewed at his lip while he read. "Yes. Connecticut. New England corridor."

"Why Connecticut?" Alex asked.

Brenda pocketed the paper and smiled wanly at Alex. "It's what The Mother told me to do. Get two tickets for Connecticut."

"Two tickets?"

"Yes. Of course. One for me, and one for you. For tomorrow. Could you do the honors?" He indicated a ticket stand to his left. "I don't have any money."

Okay, Alex thought. Okay.

He got into the line, and Brendan stayed close behind. When the tickets were purchased, he handed them to Brendan, who took them and stared down at them, as if trying to remember what they were, and why he had them.

"Is everything okay?" he asked Brendan, who continued to stare at the tickets.

"I think—there's something. I—can't quite remember."

He raised his eyes to Alex, and a profound, unguarded sorrow showed in his face. It was the sorrow of a child who doesn't understand why he's being beaten, what he's done to deserve the beating. Alex wanted to comfort him in some way, but he didn't have a clue what to comfort him about, and didn't dare make empathic contact to try and find out. Instead, he decided to try and distract him, and maybe get some information at the same time.

"What brings you to the Planetoid? Did you come here just to find me?"

"No. Not just. It's a delivery job. I deliver things sometimes. I'm a messenger boy."

"For anyone in particular?"

Brendan nodded his head up and down, up and down, as if keeping time to an internal music Alex couldn't hear. After due consideration, he said simply, "I work for The Mother."

Alex waited for more. It didn't come. Brendan stared back down at the tickets, and began talking to himself, muttering under his breath. Then he shivered, squared his shoulders, and started walking fast, making his way toward the exit. Alex stared for a moment, then trotted to catch up.

"Hey," he said, when he caught up, "what's the idea? I thought we were in this together?"

Brendan blinked at him as if he'd forgotten about him entirely, and Alex imagined that he had. "Sorry," he said. "I—didn't think."

"What's up?" Alex asked.

"I hear The Mother."

Now that was interesting, Alex thought. Psychotic? Or telepathic? Perhaps, Alex thought, both. Phase psychosis, and increased psi capacities from Artemis.

"What does she want?" Alex asked.

"We have a schedule to keep. I—forgot. Sometimes, I forget." His face expressed torment, and he balled his hands into fists and punched them into his leg. "Stupid," he said, hitting himself again. "Stupid stupid stupid."

Alex reached down and grabbed his wrist, stopping his hand. "Listen," he said, "tell me what you have to do, and I'll make sure you don't forget."

Brendan regarded him suspiciously. "What?" he asked.

"I'll help you remember," Alex repeated.

Brendan was still for a moment, but he did unbunch his hands and relax his arms. He pulled back from Alex, took the paper out of his pocket, and read. Then he put it back in his pocket, and smiled at Alex. "We should go," he said at last.

"Go?"

Brendan nodded. "It's time to go."

"Go—where?"

"To the ecosite. The rainforest ecosite." He made a clucking sound of disapproval. "Though why you make them here when we can't take care of them on the home planet is anybody's guess."

"I think we have a different attitude about that sort of thing on the Planetoid," Alex noted. "I thought we were going to Connecticut."

"Not yet. That's for later, I think. We're to go to the rainforest ecosite. It's near the works."

"The—works?"

"You know. Energy, water supply, so on."

"That's important?"

"Of course."

"Why?"

Brendan put his head back and peered up at the ceiling. His hand went to his pocket for his list, then stopped. "I'll tell you later," he said.

He reached into his pocket and pulled out the smooth white stone he'd been playing with on the bridge, turning it over in his hand.

"What's that?" Alex asked.

Brendan smiled up at him. "Something you'll need." He held it out, and Alex took it.

It was smooth and white, felt cool and good in his hand, just the right weight for holding, just the right texture for smoothing between palm and thumb. He smoothed it.

As he did, a feeling of deep calm enveloped him. Clarity and coolness all around him. The stone seemed to pull him into himself, into his own hand, as if he could invert, slowly and softly, and become part of that compressed matter. As if that inversion would give him all the answers he needed.

He was going with Brendan, to find out what this was all about, to save the Moon, the Planetoid, Jaguar, whoever else needed saving. He felt his own strength, capable of saving so much. Wasn't that his life? Saving the unsaveable. Saving those who didn't even know they needed it. Hadn't he saved Jaguar years ago, when she first came to his office as a 19 year old, looking for work on the Planetoid? Hadn't he made sure she got the college degree she needed, and when she returned to work on Planetoid One, hadn't he saved her from getting fired? Hadn't he saved her from getting fired or killed again and again?

Of course she wasn't grateful for that, but he, of course, didn't expect gratitude. It was just what he did, saving people. And he could save Brendan, too.

He smiled and looked up, saw that Brendan was smiling back.

"Let's go," Brendan said, and they did.

CHAPTER SEVEN

In the morning Jaguar was woken by the sound of someone whispering in her ear. She rolled over in her sleeping bag and mumbled something rude. The voice continued to whisper in tones that were slightly disapproving, "Message for Dr. Addams. Immediate retrieval requested. Message for Dr. Addams. Immediate retrieval requested."

"Fuck me," Jaguar groaned, and felt around on the ground for her belt sensor. Why she promised Alex she'd take it, why she kept her promise, and why she didn't remember to turn it off were all questions she couldn't answer.

Her hand touched plastic and she dragged it through the dirt to her face, pressed the retrieval button and listened with her eyes closed.

"Jaguar," Rachel's voice said. "Can you come to Alex's office? I need to talk to you. I mean, I *really* need to talk to you."

Jaguar sat up and rubbed at her face. Rachel, calling her in? She wouldn't do that unless it was important, so Jaguar knew she'd have to go. Around her, the three women slept, breathing lightly. They'd be okay. If they tried to run, their implants would stop them before they reached the edge of the ecosite. And if she hurried, she could be downtown in an hour, back in another. Depending on what Rachel wanted, of course.

She pulled herself out of her bag and padded on bare feet over to Fiore and touched her shoulder. Her eyes opened immediately, as if she'd been waiting for Jaguar to wake her.

"I have to leave you alone for a few hours. I'm putting you in charge."

Fiore's head jerked up and down. Jaguar took this as a sign of understanding. "Don't do anything stupid," she said. "If you try to leave the site, you'll be stopped."

Another quick jerk of her head. Fiore understood.

Jaguar started to walk, and got to the treeline before she remembered she was naked. That probably wouldn't be a good thing, once she got on the road. She turned around and went to the pile of clothes that belonged to the women. Hanging in a tree above them was her ceremonial dress. She took it down, slipped into it, and made her way through the woods to her car.

In her car, she caught sight of her face in the rearview mirror. High color in her cheeks and some twigs in her hair were the only signs of where she'd been. She shook her head out and drove.

She was entering the Supervisor's building when she realized that she still wasn't wearing shoes. Nothing to be done about that now. Besides, her dress almost covered it. She took the elevator up to Alex's floor, made her way to his office with only one pair of raised eyebrows to greet her. She opened the door to his office and closed it behind her. Then, she stood and stared at the seat he usually occupied.

"You called me?" she asked the person who was staring at his computer.

Rachel lifted her head from the screen she'd been peering at and ran her gaze up and down Jaguar's form. "Where's your shoes?" she asked.

"A bear ate them," she replied. "That's my story and I'm sticking to it. Where's Alex?" she asked, looking around.

"He's not in," she said. "That's why I called."

"What do you mean he's not in? He's always in."

"Today must not be always," Rachel said grimly, and she stood up, walked around the desk to where Jaguar stood.

"Well, where is he?" Jaguar asked, hand on her hip, foot tapping lightly, her equivalent of a twitching tail.

"I don't know." Rachel said patiently.

"Don't know?"

"Alex," she said, "is missing."

"Missing? What do you mean missing?"

"Will you stop repeating everything I say? Missing. M-I-S-S-"

"Rachel, what the hell is going on?"

"I wish I knew," Rachel said. "Stan Kowaski was all over me because Alex was supposed to be at a training orientation. Then Miriam Whitehall called, furious because he missed a teleconference. Very important, she said." Rachel wrinkled her nose. "I don't like that woman."

"Neither does Alex, but apparently she's on our side. When'd you see him last?"

"Yesterday afternoon. He took off early to go to the Normal houses and check on a prisoner. He was supposed to come back. Here," she handed Jaguar a file folder that was on the desk. "I got some information on him—not from La Femme—but he never came back to get it."

Jaguar opened the file, and saw a picture of Brendan Farley. She stared at the picture, waiting for her mind to wrap itself around the news it bore. She knew the face. Had just seen it in a sweat lodge vision, where blood poured out over Alex.

"Hecate," she whispered softly. "Rachel, who is this?"

"It says right there," Rachel pointed to the name.

"I mean, what's he got to do with Artemis?"

"I'm not entirely sure. He worked at La Femme. Supervisor. Actually, for Karena Halsey—one of your prisoners."

Jaguar blinked up at her and was silent. She knew that whatever made Alex go AWOL, it had to do with Brendan Farley. An adept vision, Alex said. She had no problem admitting she didn't like it much.

Still, it was useful to know, she supposed. And she did know. Alex was chasing this man. And if he caught him, he might have hold of more than he imagined. He'd be careful. As careful as he could, though he had no experience dealing with this kind of energy. If he thought he could do it alone, he could get himself trapped fast.

She took a stroll to the window and stared out of it. Pressed a hand against the glass. She ought to be able to find him. It would be easier if she could place him in space, but she still ought to be able to find him. She could still hold the image of his face, her knowledge of his spirit, and call to him on that basis.

Alex. Where are you?

A moment of silence passed, and she let it. Rachel was far away, outside this space where she would find him. If she spoke, Jaguar wouldn't hear what she said.

Then, the motion of opening. A shift in energy, subtle as the smell of rain about to fall.

Jaguar?

Relief flooded her. It was Alex. But something was wrong. He said her name as a question. Sounded not quite right. He sounded—surprised. Confused.

That's right. Where are you?

I'm with Brendan.

I know. You need help?

No answer, though she still felt his presence. But he was distracted. Something else pulling at him. She wished she could get a sense of his location. There seemed to be a thick fog all around.

Alex?

I'm okay. Tell Paul I'm getting him a man.

What?

He'll understand. Just tell him that.

Alex—

—I can't. Not now. I'll explain when I—

Then, a searing across her forehead. The empathic contact cut, quickly and painfully. She pulled her hand from the window and pressed it to her temple.

"I thought he had better technique than that," she muttered.

She shuddered, and turned back to Rachel, who stood holding herself very tense and still, arms straight at her side, eyes wide.

"It's okay," Jaguar said hesitantly. "At least, I think it is."

Rachel muttered some words in Hebrew, pressed her hands together in an attitude of rather Christian prayer, and then shook her head. "Are we supposed to do anything?"

Jaguar shrugged.

"Well, where is he?"

"I don't know, exactly."

"Is he on the Planetoid?"

She ruffled her hair, let her hand rest at the back of her neck, and thought. She didn't couldn't tell. "Maybe?" she suggested.

"Maybe?"

"Maybe not?"

"Jaguar," Rachel said.

"Rachel," she replied, then looked around the room. She pointed to Alex's computer, "You can run this thing, can't you?"

Rachel suppressed her laughter. "Of course. It's just an XRE 17 with a tri-sort web module."

"Right," Jaguar said. "As you say. So could you pull up some information for me?"

"Well, don't you know how—never mind," she amended quickly, when she saw the look on Jaguar's face. "What's your pleasure?"

"I want—anyone on the Planetoid who's even remotely connected to any of the companies Farley worked for. That'd be—" she opened Brenda's file and flipped to his work history. "Assured, Biomed Inc, and La Femme."

"Anyone?"

Jaguar thought. "Governors, Supervisors, Technocrats."

"Middle and Upper Administration," Rachel said. "Levels 7 through 12."

She went to the computer, and Jaguar flipped back to the beginning of Brendan's file and read. There was a listing of his activities with environmental groups, with more news stories, and some information about his place in various groups. He protested pesticides in Seattle. Had a civil disobedience request in California for chaining himself to a genetic engineering plant that dealt with modified growth hormones in cows. He was on the board for the Clean Rivers Coalition, and a few other places as well. Apparently he liked to keep busy.

She scanned his work history, and saw that, with a degree in biochemical engineering, he'd started out working for places like Assured, where he was an investigator, probably responsible for blocking many of the cleanup monies that company should have paid out. He went from there to working for BioMed, Inc, another Larry Barone outfit, but only stayed a year, after which he worked as a retail personnel supervisor at LaFemme.

Jaguar lifted her eyes from the file and thought about this. An odd career move, she thought, unless his track wasn't leading him to top-notch work in biochemistry.

"Rachel," Jaguar asked, "what exactly is La Femme?"

Rachel turned away from the computer and giggled. "You really should get out more, Jaguar. It's the biggest cosmetic company going, one of Barone's, and the place where your prisoner worked."

"I knew that. About Karena. And Barone. I just wasn't sure what they did there. It seems odd, doesn't it, that Farley would go there from working at Assured and Biomed. Assured does a lot of environmental disaster coverage, right?"

"Right. They cover the Planetoid, in fact. In case we get hit by a passing asteroid, or the atmosphere blows. That sort of thing."

"How cheering. Anything going on the computer?"

"Nothing pops up from the collate protocol."

"Then—how about the same Planetoid group, and connections with the Barone companies listed here."

"I'll give it a shot." Rachel hit some buttons, waited while the machine made noises, and then peered at it when the screen shifted.

"What is it?" Jaguar asked, peering over her shoulder.

"Not much. Just people you'd expect to have had contact with Assured. The administration that handles insurance policies, signs off on them. All the Governors come under that heading."

"Shit," Jaguar said. "How about stockholders in any of Global's stuff?"

Rachel shrugged and went at it, but when information appeared, it was unhelpful because most were listed under DBAs or company names rather than individual names, and none of those Jaguar recognized. "See?" Rachel said. "Companies hide in other companies and people hide in them. It's pretty tough to get through that kind of stuff. They want to keep the tax man away."

"Can't you get anything else for me on Barone?" she asked.

"Tricky," Rachel said. "He's private, so I don't have access to his codes through the Planetoid system. I don't know if I'd need a warrant of some kind to go for more."

"What if he has any affiliation with the Planetoid?" Jaguar asked. "Besides Assured, I mean."

"Why would he?"

"He seems to own everything else. Maybe he's got a piece of one of the stores or—or technical operations here." She pulled herself up straight. "Just check, okay?"

Rachel requested the collate drawer. The computer hummed, and made clicking noises while she typed in commands. Then it made more noises for what seemed like a long time.

"What's it doing?" Jaguar asked suspiciously.

"It's thinking," Rachel replied.

Jaguar frowned. "Shouldn't you do something?"

"Let it think, Jaguar. We've posed it a problem and it's solving it."

Jaguar went and looked out the window, stared at the people walking on the street below and thought deliberately of nothing in particular. It was a trick she used sometimes to coax the questions she needed to ask to the top of her brain.

"Here we go," Rachel said, and Jaguar moved back to the computer.

"What is it?" she asked as she stared at the screen.

"More code, but I can get the decrypt file. Basically it says there's a collate between Barone and us, but it's not saying what. Could be some communication he had that put him in the log. Could be—anything. It'll take a few hours to find out."

"Fine," Jaguar said. "I should get back to my prisoners anyway. I'll call in later. In the meantime, give me Brendan's file. I'll take hard copy."

Rachel slapped a hand against the desk and swore.

"Rachel," Jaguar said, shocked.

She swiveled the chair and presented an equally shocked face to Jaguar. "It's gone."

"What?"

"Gone. G-O-"

"I heard you. I just don't understand you."

"The file. Look at that." She motioned toward the screen and Jaguar read:

A fatal exception has occurred. Resolve lower read/execute right in line 5267727/W-O. It may be possible to continue normal functions.

Jaguar stared at the screen. "What's that mean?"

"Either the program's burned—unlikely—or somebody's tagged it. I mean, changed the protocol to make it unreadable."

"Would Alex do that?"

"Maybe," Rachel said. "But he'd have to be here to do it, and he's not."

Jaguar took a step back and ran a hand through her hair. "Can you track it?" she asked.

Rachel shook her head. "I can't even get near it without blowing a whole bunch of other protocols, and Alex wouldn't be too happy if I did that. Mess up his files."

"Well, who could have done it?"

"Supervisors. Governors. A really good hacker."

"Okay," she said. "At least that gives us a place to start looking."

"Us?"

Jaguar shrugged.

"Right," Rachel said. "If you have a teaspoon, when I'm done with this I'll start clearing some of that water out of the ocean, too."

Jaguar left her to her work.

CHAPTER EIGHT

"Put him through," Larry said, and waited while the broad face and head of blonde hair appeared, smiling, on screen. Pasquale, he called himself. No last names. Or sometimes, he called himself the Golden Retriever. He was an arrogant, eccentric, and sometimes very helpful man, and though Larry's trust in him was limited, he was glad to talk to him now. He'd called back fairly quickly, too. Larry wasn't sure that was a good sign. Probably it meant he already knew more than Larry wanted him to, but that would be par for the course with Pasquale.

He had appeared in Larry's office when Miriam first started messing with Brendan, and he suggested that Larry might need his services.

"What services?" Larry had asked.

"Tracking and delivery," Pasquale had said.

"Delivery?"

"Of information. Of people. Things. You need to have some of each. Especially information."

"How do you know that?" Larry had asked.

Pasquale's broad shoulders moved up and down. "It's your job to know some things, and my job to know others. That's how I make a living. Look," he added, "You want references, talk to your friend Joe Derry. I've worked for him."

The reference checked. In fact, Joe told Larry he was a lucky man. Pasquale picked his clientele very carefully, and couldn't be had for love or money unless he chose you. Larry tested Pasquale first, hiring him to investigate the specifics of a stock trade he had his eye on, but couldn't get enough information on to make a decision about. The next day Pasquale called and told him to stay away. The man running the trade was about to be arrested for fraud.

"Ridiculous," Larry said, "I had him checked through every legal circuit I know. He may be a loser, but if he was a fraud, I'd know it."

"Then buy," was all Pasquale had said before he hung up.

Larry didn't buy, and the man was arrested two days later. At that point he wanted to get Pasquale back, but had no idea how to contact him. It didn't matter. Pasquale showed up at his apartment. Larry hired him for the duration, to keep an eye on Miriam.

"How will I find you if I need you?" Larry had asked.

Pasquale chuckled. "Don't worry about that. If you need me, I'll find you."

And he always did. Like today, when Larry had been thinking he wanted a talk with Pasquale, and he called. Larry had almost come to expect it.

"Things are heating up," Larry said to him now. "Miriam's going to the Planetoid."

"Yeah," Pasquale said. "I know. You want me on her there?"

Larry thought a minute. "Just keep tabs and let me know what she's up to. I want to anticipate and prevent any possible hazards on this assignment."

"What about Dzarny?" Pasquale asked. "You want me to track him, too?"

Larry subdued a moment of irritation. He had never mentioned Dzarny. He hated it when Pasquale showed off that way. "Not yet, but it may become necessary. I'll let you know."

"Maybe," Pasquale said, "I'll let you know first. What about the Addams woman?"

Larry sighed. He hated it, but it was so very useful. "Anything you can get would be appreciated," he said.

"So long as you show your appreciation with dollars and cents," Pasquale said, and hung up.

When he was gone, Larry found that he felt lighter, less anxious. Irritating as he was, Pasquale was even more reassuring than a gun in his pocket.

When Jaguar returned to the site, she found Karena already gathering rocks, and Fiore collecting wood with Terez. They were making progress, climbing back into relationship with each other and the world. Terez had no hesitation about reaching over to touch Fiore on the cheek, smiling at her shyly, and Fiore returned the smile. She let them set up for the sweat they'd do later that evening, then set about giving them lunch. They ate more slowly, tasting their food now, and they shared their food nicely.

"Listen," Jaguar said when they were done. "Why don't you all take some time to rest before tonight? You can work on your tans."

At this, Karena actually giggled, and Fiore and Terez turned to each other. Fiore, breaking away from Terez' gaze, looked to Jaguar. "Can we walk?" she whispered.

Jaguar nodded. "Not too far. Be back by dusk."

Slowly, they rose and wandered in different directions, Terez following Fiore into the woods, Karena raising her face to the sun and heading due south toward a small clearing. Jaguar knew this kind of time was a necessary part of their healing, but she was glad she had the file to go through to keep her impatience from rising up and throttling her. Waiting was not her strong point.

The women returned at dusk, and Jaguar lit the fire for the sweat. When she chanted the pre-sweat cleansing song, Terez joined in, making the sounds with her—barely audibly, but making them nonetheless.

Inside the lodge, Jaguar made light empathic contact with all three women, and felt the shift in their energy, as if a listing ship began to pull itself right. In Karena, along with this shift, she felt the dark rumblings of a creature long denied voice, and she knew she'd have to take her next. They could start in the morning, and Jaguar had an idea of the best way to work with her.

As they honored the west and Jaguar opened herself into a howl that would release any toxins she might have absorbed she felt Alex's thoughts moving inside her.

Jaguar. You sweat well.

She paused and adjusted to his presence. Felt him enjoying this moment.

Where are you? she asked.

On the move. A pause in thought. Then, his voice, with an odd, far-away feel to it.

To where?

Not sure. Possibly Connecticut.

Are you okay, Alex?

There was a long pause, and she could feel him considering the question. Then, the answer came, unexpected and inexplicable.

I can see everything, Jaguar. Everything.

She felt the brush of a hand against her face as he exited. It was so present that she brought her own hand up to her cheek. That was odd, she thought. But she couldn't attend to it right now. She had three women staring at her in the dark, and she returned her focus to them. When the sweat was finished, she led the women out of the lodge and had them raise their arms to the rounding face of the moon.

Nissa, Nissa, she sang the Seneca words with them. *Nissa, Nissa, Gaiwayo.*

Our grandmother. All is well.

All is well.

CHAPTER NINE

Alex had little specific memory of what happened between night and morning. He remembered the feeling of being on top of the world, a knowledge of how great his own power to save was, and he remembered Brendan watching him, smiling, agreeing with what he said, though he didn't remember his own words. He didn't realize they'd slept on the beach of Lake Ontario until the morning, when he woke with his face in the sand, Brendan staring down at him, holding out a small white stone.

"You dropped this," Brendan said. "You shouldn't lose it."

Alex stared at it. That stone. It had something to do with losing himself, with not knowing how to control his own behavior. Artemis material. It had to be. He scrambled to his feet and took a few steps back, drew in to himself briefly and re-arranged his own energy. Then he shrugged at Brendan. "You hang onto it," he said. "I might lose it again."

Brendan nodded solemnly, pocketed the stone, and stood up. "Are you okay? It can hurt, just at first."

Alex frowned. "What can hurt?"

"Contact. With the Mother. She's so strong."

"Oh. I'm—okay. Did we sleep here?"

"Of course. We stopped and ate, you made a call, then we came this far before you were tired."

Alex tried to retrieve memory, and was vaguely successful. He remembered the feeling of power. Remembered—who did he call? He heard a brief blip of male voice. Paul Dinardo. What did he tell him? That they were going, and he had to look after Jaguar. He was afraid—did he say that? That he was

77

afraid he'd kill her? Why would he say that? He turned his frown to Brendan, who replied to his unspoken thoughts.

"Because you know you will," Brendan said. He looked around, looked up at the sun, which stood at midmorning. "It's getting late. We need to go."

Alex thought briefly about taking him down, bringing him in, then decided against it. He'd get more information by sticking with him on his own journey. He was okay as long as he stayed away from the stones, he thought. Time enough to bring him in when he knew a little more.

"I'm ready," he said, hoping that was true.

They left the beach and walked on the outskirts of the city, heading toward the Rainforest site. Brendan was talkative, asking intelligent questions about environmental issues on Planetoid, listening intently while Alex explained how they managed things like waste, and erosion and atmosphere. Brendan was interested in every aspect, it seemed, and asked questions about the use of laser-bounce technology for communications, about the VR site, about the mass generator that made their atmosphere possible.

"Wait," Alex said at one point, "Couldn't we catch a cab? It's still a few miles." He felt drained, as if he'd been taking powerful drugs, and was experiencing the consequent crash.

Brendan smiled at him sadly, as if he understood. "You'll get used to it," he said. "It's better if you just keeping holding them, though." He reached into his pocket, presumably for a stone.

"No," Alex said quickly. "I'd—rather wait until we get there."

Brendan looked disappointed, but removed his hand, empty. He waved a hand ahead of them, to the bridge that separated city from outlying areas, crossing the silver surface of a lake outlet. "Let's stop on the bridge for a bit and rest."

They started across the footpath built for pedestrian enjoyment, and at about the halfway point Brendan stopped, looked up and down the bridge, and went to the railing. He leaned his elbows on it. "This is a good spot, isn't it?"

"All right," Alex said, and leaned his elbows next to Brendan's.

The lake at their feet was a mirror for the blue sky over their heads. It was a pretty day. Not too hot or too cold and lots of sun. He looked forward to getting to the rainforest site, and wandering under the canopy of trees, listening to the birdsong. It was a place so full of life, Alex thought it must surely have a good effect on Brendan, who seemed to be lost in Thanatos drive, the urge toward death.

Brendan was silent, giving Alex some time to sort out his thoughts, try to understand what Artemis was doing to Brendan, and to him. Jaguar had called it the three-body problem—desire, fear, and power intermingling in the psyche. For him, obviously power meant the power to save. For Brendan, it meant the power to die. But since that power intermingled with fear, Alex also had a fear of not being able to save, and Brendan a fear of living. And their desire—was it also the opposite, or was it more complicated than that? Did he want to save to fulfill another desire altogether? Did Brendan fear living because of some desire that Alex couldn't yet perceive?

And in any case, how would he manage himself, and Brendan while he figured this out?

Alex was on this when a woman walked by, nodded at them.

Brendan observed her approach and Alex noticed how the presence of other people barely skimmed the surface of his molecules, while at the same time he was in intense contact with everything around him. He wondered how that worked.

Brendan stared at—past? through?—the woman, reached into his pocket and pulled out a small white stone. Turned it over again and again in his hand. Alex gasped, as the world around and inside him began to shift. Shit, he thought. Can't I control this at all?

The woman slowed as she approached them, then stopped and smiled. "Nice day," she said.

"Nice place to see it," Brendan agreed.

She stopped and leaned on the railing next to him. "Good place to find answers, if you got questions."

Alex, working on his breathing, on finding a safe place inside himself, heard her as if she was very far away, or as if he was viewing the scene from within a bubble filled with some liquid that rendered him incapable of action. He was not there. He couldn't move to be anywhere else. He struggled against the feeling, and got nowhere very slowly.

Smiling broadly, Brendan held out the stone to her. "Pretty, isn't it?"

She took the stone, cupped it in her hands. Alex watched as she leaned further and further over the railing. No, he thought. She shouldn't do that. He had to stop her, save her. He was responsible for that. But what if he couldn't? What if he failed? Folded in on himself and didn't act in time, acted in the wrong way? Maybe it was better to do nothing, try for nothing because anything he did might be the wrong thing. Fear washed through him and held him still.

He saw the woman leaning further and further over the railing.

"No," he gasped, and willed himself into motion, his hands grabbing at her, holding her, while her body twisted over the railing and dangled high above the water. "No," he said again, feeling her slip from his hands which were sweaty and felt the heaviness of her as if she were a two-ton weight. He'd had dreams like this. Bad dreams where he was trying to hold on to someone and they kept slipping away or he grew clumsy and his hand wouldn't properly work, the thumb and finger forgetting how to grasp and hold.

"Grab hold of me," he said desperately, "Grab hold."

She smiled up at him. Clutched at his belt. Something ripped. Alex turned and saw Brendan, his hands held out in blessing as she let go and fell down and down.

Her body missed the water, landing on a footing and staying there. It all happened so softly, Alex could hardly believe it was real.

"We have to get help. I have to call this in," he said, reaching for his cellcom, but it was gone. She'd torn it off in her struggle to release herself from him. He looked up and down the span of the bridge. He'd have to walk back, get help. Do something.

He turned on Brendan, who smiled at him beatifically. From his pocket he pulled another stone, and pushed it into Alex's empty hand. It happened so fast, Alex didn't have a second to—

You see how easy it is. How much they want to go. How good they feel when they do it. It's all good, and you did save her after all because if she didn't go, what would she have here? Waste and death and pain. Just waste and death and pain. You saved her.

Alex felt a sensation of relief, of release. What it meant to save someone—maybe he'd been wrong about that. Maybe Brendan had something to teach him, rather than something to learn from him, and in any case, he couldn't leave him now. Had to stay and help him, too. Save him. So many people who needed to be saved.

Brendan put a hand on his shoulder. "Let's go," he said.

He walked across the bridge toward the rainforest, and Alex followed.

"Larry, darling. I need you to do something for me. Are you secure?"

"Always. Are you?"

She sighed, mildly offended at his lack of trust. "Larry, how long have we known each other?"

Too long, he thought. Since they met at one of those idiotic dinners where business people pretend to be philanthropists and give each other awards for taking tax deductions through charity. She'd asked his advice about stocks, and he'd recommended some. He had no idea she'd be so good at playing the market, end up with so much stock under the cover of a company he'd helped her invent. In fact, she was now a major stockholder in La Femme. She'd been playing him, vying for control of his turf since they met, and now she was still vying for the turf they'd share on the Planetoid.

"We've known each other for some time," Larry said neutrally.

"Then don't worry so much. I only need one thing from you. Remember that conversation we taped, talking about Artemis and me telling you how it would be unthinkable?"

He remembered. They had made a few tapes like that, supposed telecom conversations, which might be needed to help maintain the appearance of Miriam being against the plants.

"I remember," he said.

"Put a date on one. For tonight, between nine and ten. Okay, love?"

When he opened his mouth to ask why, she held up a finger and wiggled it back and forth.

"Now, now. Let it be a pleasant surprise," she said, emphasizing the word pleasant. She flashed him a smile, the one that said she was a warm and loving woman who took care of her man. Sometimes he thought she actually believe her own bullshit.

"We'll be in touch," she said, and signed off.

When Larry's face disappeared from the screen, Miriam sat at her desk, smiling. She enjoyed her interactions with Larry. He was good in bed, and he had the kind of wealth that creates power as well as material comfort. He lacked vision, but she had enough for both of them.

She reached into her desk for one of the stones she kept there.

There were many Artemis compounds, each with its own properties, uses, and hazards, but she liked the moonstones best. They were the heart of the moon, she thought, and had all the same qualities as that body of cool light. They cleared the mind, made night vision possible, and increased the strength of women who knew how to bear big power without collapsing.

She smoothed the stone in her hand and relaxed her mind, relaxed her breathing. She had learned early on that to go into this tensely was painful, and gave her headaches. But if she simply breathed in the Artemis, let the energy of it flow into her, then she could see things she never thought possible, know more than she ever knew before.

It made her laugh when Larry questioned her capacity to handle Alex. Of course she could handle him, just as she could handle Brendan, or any man. Men were such silly creatures, relying on foolish structures like logic and administrative flow charts because they lacked the capacity for complex thinking. She could dance rings around them, with or without the moonstones, though they certainly helped, making it oh so easy to be in the minds of those she needed to control. They would serve her well in her goals, which were as clear as her vision.

She would own her very own world. She would exploit it and run it. The clarity of that vision was the gift of Artemis, available for her use but not for Larry, or Alex, or any man.

Of course, the gift wasn't for every woman, either. That Addams woman didn't want anyone to use it, but her fear would not stop progress. Miriam knew what her plans were with Karena, and how to use them to suit better ends. Jaguar, she thought, was as foolish as any man.

But Miriam was not. As she caressed the smooth piece of the moon in her hand, it amused her to think that she would almost literally be killing two birds with one stone.

The next day, Jaguar left Fiore and Terez in the forest, with instructions to go nowhere beyond their camp circle. She knew that the implants in their legs would stop them, but she also wanted them to understand their limits and accept them. It would help them heal. They settled into themselves like two more trees in the forest, and were silent.

Jaguar dressed herself and Karena, and they walked the two miles of woods between the camp and her vehicle. As they drove, Jaguar noted that Karena's face closed into a pinched ball of tension. She would be the hardest of the women to work with, Jaguar thought. Both Terez and Fiore seemed to have some depth of character preceding their crimes, but Karena had very little in the way of internal resources to guide her through the process of self-knowledge. Jaguar was prepared for her to fall apart at a moment's notice, and if she did, Jaguar would give her over to the medics and continue to work with the other women.

"Nervous?" she asked.

Karena bit at her lip, hands working hard in her lap.

"What're you afraid of?"

She took a deep breath. "That it will hurt," she gasped out, then lapsed into silence.

"Don't worry," Jaguar said. "I never heard of shopping being that painful."

When Jaguar pulled into the parking lot of a mall Karena sat there, staring dumbly ahead.

"Come on," Jaguar said. "You love to shop. I'm just giving you what you want. It's not my fault that you despise yourself for wanting it."

Karena made a small noise inside her throat. Jaguar laughed.

"You're always just a little hungry, aren't you?" she said, "Or maybe not so much hungry as ready to consume, regardless. Get out of the car, and let's go."

She pulled her up by the arm and Karena allowed herself to be led across the lot, through the mall entrance, and into the first department store. They were in the lingerie department, and Karena turned to a red silk nightgown, burying her face in it and moaning. Jaguar rifled through a belt pack and pulled out a card.

"Work the plastic, girl," she said, tapping her on the shoulder with it. "I'm right behind you."

Karena released the nightgown, touched the card with the tip of her finger, then giggled. She covered the giggle with her hand, but it bubbled out from between her fingers.

"Go on," Jaguar said, pushing the card at her, "knock yourself out."

With a swift tug, Karena grabbed the card and turned focused eyes to the racks of clothes.

Jaguar trailed after her from rack to dressing room, dressing room to checkout, as she piled up clothes. Karena paid, Jaguar glad that this was a reimbursable expense, then they went into the mall, where they combed the shelves and racks of stores, Karena's eyes focused as a hawk sighting prey. Shoes and scarves, nail polish and pantyhose, face creams and underwear and strange little hairpieces. What she wanted seemed as endless as what was available for purchase.

While they walked from one store to the next, Jaguar saw, in her peripheral vision, a newscom rolling the days events across the screen. A headline caught her attention, and she moved closer to read it. Someone had gone off the bridge between city and ecosites. That was bad, she thought. Connected? She hoped not. This didn't need more complication than it had.

She looked back to the store she'd just exited—an accessory store, where Karena fondled cheap jewelry. She moved back toward the store, then stopped abruptly and stood very still.

One of the Board governors was in the store with Karena. Miriam Whitehall, casually trying on a pair of sunglasses Jaguar knew she'd never buy. Miriam liked everything natural. She never wore sunglasses. She put them back, and turned to Karena, put a hand on her shoulder. Karena startled, turned around, and took a step back. Miriam placed a hand on hers. She was saying something. Jaguar couldn't tell what.

She walked quickly back to the store and got there just in time to block Miriam's exit. "Hello, governor. What brings you here?"

Miriam smiled. "Shopping," she said. "Of course. And you?"

"Shopping," Jaguar said. "Of course."

Miriam nodded at Karena. "With a friend?"

"Of course again," Jaguar said.

"You have interesting friends," Miriam noted.

"So I'm told."

They stood facing each other. Jaguar would be damned if she'd move first. "Well," Miriam said a split second before the silence grew unbearable, "I'd better go. Reports to file and so on."

Miriam took a step to one side, and Jaguar got out of her way. As she stepped around Jaguar, Miriam turned back and smiled one more time. "Give Alex my love, will you?" And she made her way down the mall.

"Bitch," Jaguar said mildly to her retreating back. She grabbed Karena's elbow and led her out. "C'mon," she said. "Time to go."

She led her toward a telecom, placing her on one side and commanding her, doglike, to stay.

She punched in Rachel's number. She didn't waste time with amenities. "Anything from Alex?" she asked, as soon as Rachel appeared.

"Nothing."

"How about our various research projects?"

"Not too much. If you can hang on a minute, I'll punch it up."

Jaguar looked at her prisoner, who stood blissfully clutching her bags, oblivious to Jaguar.

Rachel swiveled away from the screen, and then back to it. "So far, who could delete files—governors can whenever they like. No notice. No permission. Supervisors under special circumstances, but they need

Board clearance on it. So it's likely a governor, since there's no record of clearance. That help any?"

Jaguar tapped a finger against the telecom. "Is there any way of telling which governor did it?"

"I'm trying to, but I think if they want it hidden, they can hide it. They just put a wormhole in and—do you want the details?"

"I think not. Anything on connections with Barone?"

"He owns no Planetoid businesses, and has no investments here, except for Assured, of course, which insures the Planetoid. There's the usual politicking, especially recently. He's met all the governors at one point or another, and keeps up conversations with some of them."

"Like?"

"Shafritz. Malor. Those are the highest counts of calls I can track. Less with Miriam Whitehall and Paul Dinardo."

"Check on Miriam," Jaguar suggested, "for any connection, however remote."

"Any particular reason?" Rachel asked.

"Yeah," Jaguar said. "I don't like her taste in sunglasses."

"Whatever you say," Rachel said, and signed off.

Jaguar turned back to her prisoner. "Ready or not," she said, "it's time to go."

As they left the mall, Karena was still lost in the ecstasy of purchase. She crossed the parking lot clutching her bags as if they might escape before she got to the car.

Jaguar, clipping along beside her, grabbed her elbow. "Wait," she said.

Karena stopped and twisted her head around to face Jaguar.

"Look," she said, pointing skyward. "It's the moon."

Karena tilted her head back. The whites of her eyes showed, seeming to absorb the light they looked toward. She opened her lips and a hiss of breath escaped them like steam forced out of a tightly closed pot and she pulled back, lowered her head as if burned.

"She changes everything she touches," Jaguar said, "and she touches everything."Jaguar smiled. "She calls us back to ourselves, and makes us face our desire."

Karena whimpered and clutched at her bags.

"That's not your desire," Jaguar said. "It's not those things you buy and buy and buy. They're just a substitute, to keep you from knowing what you really want. Who you really are."

Karena's whimpering turned to a rumbling sound at the back of her throat, and she first clutched the bags closer, then held them out, away from herself and began to scream.

Good, Jaguar thought. Very good. She took a step back as Karena's fury reached the zenith of a piercing shriek and became motion as she flailed her arms, bags waving like clumsy wings. She ripped at them with her nails and her teeth as she tried to shed them, her strangled voice going from scream to a series of yips coughed up like old hiccups. People leaving the mall stopped to stare, and Jaguar saw a few workers in the prison system who had their hands on belt sensors, ready to call in trouble. She ignored them, and let Karena whirl her way through her rage. When all of her packages lay like dismembered bodies in the lot, Jaguar put a hand on her heaving shoulder, and pressed her other hand against her forehead.

See who you are, she whispered into her. *Be what you see.*

Jaguar felt her rage. She used getting as a substitute for doing and being. Like eating when you're lonely. Fucking when you're afraid. It was the wrong material, and so it was never enough. She gorged herself, then was enraged because she was still hungry. It moved through her, and under it was the something else she wanted, wild and without encumbrances, empty and light enough to fly. She didn't want things. She wanted freedom.

Yes, Jaguar said into her. *Don't be afraid. It's what you want. Who you are. It will hold you.*

That was the end of the three body problem, Jaguar knew. Under the misclaimed power, under the fear that supported it, was the real desire for which all other action was a substitute, a chimera. Karena whimpered and crumpled to her knees. Jaguar stepped back and gave her space, watching as she crouched on the ground, holding her hands in a cup in front of her, crooning into them as if they contained something precious.

Jaguar frowned. Was Karena holding something real? One last precious purchase she wouldn't relinquish? Jaguar saw moonlight glint off the surface of it.

She took a step toward her, then stopped.

"Karena," she asked, "what's in your hand?"

Karena didn't lift her head. Jaguar took another step forward, and when she was close enough to spit on her, squatted down in front of her, reached over, felt her hand close on something smooth and cool, and took it from her prisoner.

She held it up to the moonlight and watched it glow. A stone. Smooth and grey and glowing in the moonlight. Crystal in the tightness of its molecules, but ordinary in its color and shape.

Unexpectedly, the coiled wind of empathic space engulfed her.

Kill her before she kills you.

Jaguar gasped, looked at Karena, but it was too late. Karena's face had become a mask of rage as she pulled her hand back and slammed it into the side of Jaguar's head.

Jaguar went down and caught the cement with the side of her jaw. That was going to hurt like hell, she thought, and hoped she didn't break anything. The stone flew from her hand and skittered toward a sewer grate, falling down into it. Karena screamed in rage and lunged for her. Voices spoke to Jaguar.

She's got a gun. Kill her. She's got a gun.

Jaguar blinked and saw it in Karena's hand, pointed at her, safety released. Jaguar pressed the button that released the glass knife at her wrist. Karena reached her, fell on her, and then Jaguar saw blood everywhere. Blood sprayed across her face, the face of the moon, her prisoner. Blood, everywhere.

Saw Karena falling. Falling again and again. Heard voices. Heard someone in the parking lot screaming. Saw Karena fall and fall then land with a sickening thud, like the sound of punching into a pillow, like the sound of a blade hitting home into flesh.

Saw that she was on the ground, Karena under her, pinioned by her blade. Her eyes stared death into the full of the moon.

Jaguar lifted her face and looked around. A crowd had gathered. Cellcoms were being used.

"Shit," she muttered. "Now what?"

Those who patrolled the city streets of Planetoid Three's replica cities had a fairly easy job. Their most demanding task was making sure they didn't inadvertently interrupt a Teacher's program, mistaking it for a real crime. Usually, they were kept well enough informed of the running programs to avoid this, but once in awhile, a Teacher would take on an action that couldn't be predicted far enough in advance to warn the police.

For that reason, Officer Bailah took his time observing the body that lay broken and bloody at the bottom of the bridge. Instead of investigating, he called it in and waited for confirmation that this was indeed a real body, really dead.

When the coordinating offices confirmed that this woman was real, and really dead, he picked his way carefully down to the footings, and knelt next to the body of a young woman who lay on her back, staring into eternity. Clutching something in her hand.

The officer wrapped his hand in a handkerchief and carefully pulled the something away from her. Held it up and looked at it. It was a cellcom, with a Planetoid Prison system ID. And it belonged to someone he happened to know. Someone he'd worked with before. Someone he couldn't believe would have anything to do with anything like this.

It belonged to Supervisor Alex Dzarny.

CHAPTER NINE

Color flitted from tree to tree, accompanied by the sound of song. Explosions of yellow. Blue flying sapphires amid the deep emerald canopy above them, and now and then a shot of blood red flung through the air, singing about beauty because that's what they understood best.

Brendan and Alex were in the tropical rainforest, and there were birds everywhere.

Alex breathed in deeply of the smell of heat and humidity, leaf and rot and growth. It was a good place. He liked it here.

Brendan wrinkled his nose. "What's that smell?"

"Life," Alex said. "There's a lot of it going around here."

"I don't like it," Brendan said. "It's too active."

Right, Alex thought. Thanatos drive. Brendan was allergic to life.

Alex sat down next to him on the side of a small hill and listened to the edge of his energy field. It sucked inward forcefully, into that spiral of suicide that made you understand the relief of death, how it solved all problems and made all pain cease in an instant. It was a compelling force, seductive as sex, which was basically its opposite. He'd been around suicidal prisoners before, and knew that their presence shifted the way the world looked, but he'd never felt anything as powerful as he did with Brendan, as if despair had been boiled down into its elemental form, a vapor that permeated his whole system. Alex knew it wasn't his own despair, but he felt it all the same and it turned him to stone like the stones Brendan carried.

"We could go elsewhere," Alex said. "There's an arid ecosite. Pretty sparse landscape."

"Where is it?"

"About an hour south of here."

Brendan shook his head. "I don't think it's close enough. This is—well, it's better, I suppose. Those birds make a lot of noise, though."

Alex laughed. "I thought you were an environmentalist."

"People called me that. I didn't call myself that. It's not what I am."

"I see," Alex said. "What are you, then?"

"Nothing." Brendan said. "Like everyone else. Like you."

Alex turned away from that bait. "If you were interested in environmental causes, why did you work for Assured, or La Femme? They're not very good about the environment."

Brendan peered out somewhere far away from Alex. "I worked to make it stop. It all has to stop. You know, of course, they're destroying the world."

"La Femme, or Assured?" Alex asked.

"Women," Brendan replied.

Alex frowned. "Pardon?"

"Women," Brendan repeated. "You know. Men get blamed for raping the earth, but women want us to have babies and homes and all those things that damage the planet. Not that they can help it. It's their nature. Virulent, as opposed to virile. Or, you might say virulent, so that we'll be virile and they can have their babies and their sex and love and—you know."

He turned his pale eyes to Alex. "It's about life. They insist on it. And it has to stop."

Alex held his gaze. There was slowness gathered here like dreams when your legs won't move though you have to move. A thick hopeless absence of motion because what was the point of motion anyway.

"Women," he repeated, staying neutral.

"Women," Brendan echoed. "I wanted them. All the time. I've had a lot of them, too," he continued. "In college I had twins—Maria and Dolores. They were so succulent, it made my mouth water. They thought I was a stud because I was in geology. Outdoors a lot and so on. I thought I was a stud, too. Then I found out there's really only two things you could do with my degree—manufacturing and mining, or insurance. Unless you get a research grant, which I didn't have a chance in hell of getting. You had to know the right people for that, and I didn't know anybody except Maria and Dolores. I went for insurance because they were supposed to be doing something valuable, but—well, you know what they were after." He waved a hand toward the sky.

"Actually," Alex said, "I don't know."

Brendan regarded him with suspicion. "You don't?"

Alex shook his head. "I've been busy here."

"Oh," Brendan said. "Of course. Well, they made it easier to poison the earth. Provided a cushion for the industrialists, so they didn't have to be responsible for their stupidity. Just pay someone else to do a half-ass clean-up job, and make it all look good for the press. You remember the Holton disaster?"

Alex did. The Holton company dealt with nuclear waste disposal left over from the closed nuclear power plants. They had repainted the waste barrels, then left them in the basement of a school abandoned during the Serials. They remained hidden for a year after the children returned to the school, and nobody could figure out why they were getting sick and dying until a janitor was tracking rats in a back room of the basement and discovered the leaky barrels. The parents and the town got about $56 million for the cleanup, but insurance paid Holton more than that to cover their extra legal costs. After costs, they made a $5 million profit on the whole mess. And the kids were still dead.

"Assured was Holton's company. They lobbied for the new pesticides, too," Brendan said.

"I read the memos in their files. That's when I left and I went into cosmetics research. Mineral sources for women's beauty products. I thought it'd be more pure somehow, because I still thought women were pure." He shivered, whether from revulsion or fear, Alex couldn't tell. He noticed that Brendan had pulled another stone from his pocket and was turning it over and over.

"Scare you?"

"Yes," Brendan said. "Because then I began to understand. It's the women that make us what we are. We wouldn't need nuclear energy if the women didn't have to be beautiful with their blowdryers and their hair dyes and their nail polish. Their hair was always like silk. And the smell of them. Everything they did. It was all meant to keep us breeding, keep us making things, keep the machine producing, the vermin multiplying. I loathed myself for wanting them."

Desire, and fear. Fear of desire. That was all he had, but it was a lot.

"Y'know," Alex pointed out, "not all sex leads to procreation. In fact, most of it doesn't, and the population is at zero growth right now, so I'm not sure if your concerns are justified." He knew that reason wouldn't touch Brendan's fear, but he wanted to see what kind of response it drew. That would tell him more about how Brendan's system of terror worked, maybe show him the way in to begin changing it.

"Sex," Brendan replied pointedly, "leads to all manner of hell, whether we're procreating or not. Possessiveness, the urge to dominate and own and—and consume. We consume what we desire, and we're consumed by it. And if we're going to keep selling cosmetics and blowdryers and big houses and fancy wings, we need sex to be uppermost in our minds. Sex sells, so sell sex. It's the new opiate of the people, since religion went west."

Alex listened hard, trying to understand what Brendan said, and what he didn't say. His age placed him as second generation after the Killing Times, which meant he was a child of the storm, subject to the told memories of an event that his parents had lived through, but he had not. He could never deal with the trauma directly since he hadn't directly experienced it. He'd only known the fears of those who had experienced it and they never named it for him properly. It seeped into his psyche without context, and he had to build one for it. Whether he'd done so before or after exposure to Artemis, that exposure had multiplied his burden of unspecified despair. But it also gave him the power to achieve a cessation of pain through death, and made him believe he had to share the gift.

It made its own sense. It was no more difficult to deal with than other problems they found in their prisoners. Alex knew how to proceed.

"So you left cosmetics," Alex said. "And started poisoning people in malls instead."

Brendan stopped playing with the stone. Turned a hard stare on Alex. "What's it to you?"

"Nothing much," Alex said. "Just seems like you might have tried some other moves first. Celibacy, maybe, if sex bothered you that much."

Brendan shook his head. "I couldn't. I was too weak. No matter what I did, I wanted them. You know how that is, don't you?"

"I suppose," Alex said.

Brendan tossed the stone up and down, rubbed it thoughtfully. Alex could feel the temper and measure of his need to consume, and his terror of consuming. He could feel how he turned desire inside out and saw death as the only way to stop it, projecting the solution of suicide onto others. Yes, this was simple. This could be cleared. How strange of Jaguar to be so afraid for him.

"Sometimes I wanted a woman so bad, I was afraid of what I'd do to her if I had her," he said. "You know that, too, don't you?"

Brendan stared at him, and Alex felt it moving in himself. His desire for Jaguar, so strong he wasn't sure if it would consume her, or consume him. But no, that was different. That wasn't his. Wasn't hers. That was—Brendan's.

"No," Alex said. "No."

He watched Brendan turn the stone over and over in his hand, saw the way it seemed to absorb and then give off light, as if it swallowed pieces of the sun and then returned them, soft and glowing, to the world. He leaned toward Brendan and touched his hand lightly.

"What is it?" he asked, His words were thick and slow. He wasn't sure what they were attached to or what he meant. No, something said in him. No.

"A gift," Brendan said, "from The Mother."

He held it out toward Alex, who saw his own hand reach for it. His hand, slow and thoughtful, reaching for what he wanted. What he wanted.

Haven't you ever wanted a woman so bad you were afraid of yourself?

"No," he said. "No."

That you would hold her so tight she'd be crushed. Hold her so tight because you're angry at her for making you want her enough to crush her, angry at her for making you want her, for tormenting you with desire. You want to save her from herself, and you can't. And you begin to hate her for it, hate her and wish that you could crush her, and it would be over.

No, Alex thought. No.

He wanted to say this out loud, but his mouth wouldn't move fast enough to make the words. Brendan tossed the stone up and down, and the motion made soft trails of light around his hand. Alex watched, saying no to something. To what? Something.

The stone slipped from Brendan's hand, onto his lap, and from there to the ground near his feet. He took his glasses off, rubbed at them with his sleeve. Alex watched from a slow place.

"There's no capacity in humans for anything except greed. We're greedy, and won't even protect our self-interest in our greed."

Yes, Alex thought. He's right. That's why we say we'll exploit the resources of the moon. It was greed. But the moon was so beautiful, so full of richness, how could they be blamed for wanting it? He could feel her pull even now, mistress moon riding the sky, though she hadn't risen yet, in all her richness and resources.

"The women taught me that. We're greedy for them. So we have to make them do the right thing. Some will, but others won't. They want us to want them, so they can laugh at us and torment us. But The Mother will take care of them."

The Mother. Yes. She would take care of it. Alex seemed to know about her suddenly, as if he'd learned it from Brendan's mind though he hadn't made empathic contact with him. Had he? Or were they in constant contact, as if they were the same man, maybe all men represented by just the two of them sitting here in the rainforest trying to save The Mother from destruction. The last two good men willing to die and kill for The Mother. The last two to save her.

"The Mother," Alex heard himself say as if some part of his brain was working without him, "The Mother is a woman." His voice sounded sluggish and distant. Confused. "The Mother is a woman," he said again, this time with more certainty, as if he'd said something very important.

Brendan's face grew tight. "Listen to yourself," he said angrily, "That's all you can think of. She's a woman, and that's just someone else to fuck. Fuck your own mother. You would, wouldn't you? I know you would. Any man would, because they make us want to. They make us fuck them and fuck them and fuck them until we die from it. And they blame us for it, accuse us of rape and abuse and—and they twist it all around so it's our fault, not theirs. But it's their fault, with their soft skin and their silky hair and their big big eyes."

Alex shook his head. No, he thought. No. Something wasn't making any sense. Or maybe it was. Something was making sense. Ultimate sense. If only he could get unstuck from this slow place, this place where sound and thought were so thick and heavy.

"If she's a woman, doesn't she do that?" he asked, careful to make sure words emerged when he moved his lips which had gone thick and numb.

Brendan turned on him and put his face very close to Alex's so that Alex could see into his eyes, like looking through fog into an abyss. "Stupid man. Of course it takes a woman to know what to do about other women. But she's here to help us. Make it so we'll never want them again. She can bring us peace."

Never want them again, Alex thought because he couldn't really speak any longer.

Brendan grabbed his shoulders and shook them hard. "You know how it has to be. We have to save her, so she'll come and make it right and we won't have to *feel* this way anymore."

Save her? Alex thought. Yes. That was right. He knew about saving people. But how?

Brendan nodded at him, then waved a hand across the plane of the earth in front of them as if sweeping it clean. "Get rid of it. Make it all go away. Make it clean, for The Mother."

Alex saw what Brendan saw. The planet was cleared of human activity, of human presence, of human life. It was clean and bright and ran efficiently, following its own rhythms. The planet was clean and a new group of beings walked its surface, caring for the ecosites, living where Toronto Replica once was and—

No. Wait. That wasn't the home planet. That was the Planetoid. Planetoid Three. Alex tried to figure out what was going on, but Brendan kept talking, interrupting his confusion with more confusion.

"How?" he heard himself asking. "How?"

"Kill them," he said. "The only way is to kill them all. They're the only link."

Link to what, Alex wondered. He looked at Brendan, asking without words, and Brendan answered.

"To life. The link to life," he said, and nodded at Alex as if he was a teacher giving a lesson that was finally understood. "And they torment us with it."

He held the stone out to Alex, invited him to touch.

The appeal of death was what it wiped out the pain of desire. Pain. Desire, all washed away. And Brendan was right. Desire was painful. He knew that. What did he have to look forward to except his continuing desire with no satisfaction, and didn't she encourage that? She wouldn't change herself, so he had to bear the burden of desire. Painful, and constant. They give it to us, and use it against us, Alex heard a voice say, then realized it was his own thoughts, his own voice reverberating inside his head.

"Wouldn't you like to see an end to it?" Brendan asked and his words fell from his mouth glowing like the stone in his hand.

No, Alex thought. But he wasn't sure. Brendan held the stone out to him, and Alex almost touched it. Kept a finger moving toward it, but slowly, very slowly like the rhythms of the turning moon.

There's a way to stop it.

Yes. There was. He could see that. A way out. A way that worked.

If she was dead.

If she was dead?

If she was dead.

If she was dead.

Alex felt searing pain course up his arm, run toward his heart as if someone had stuck a hot needle into a nerve. He jerked away from Brendan, stumbled and fell back, his hands finding cool damp earth, his lungs seeking air, pulling it in hard.

The fog inside him lifted, and he sat in a clear space, feeling his feelings.

"Shit," he said through clenched teeth. "Dammit, that hurt."

Brendan put the stone back in his pocket and smiled knowingly. "I was like that at first, too," he said, "Afraid. But you'll see. There are answers. You didn't think there were, but there are."

And Alex thought he was beginning to understand some of them already.

Jaguar sat at the gleaming black conference table with her hands folded in her lap, wearing her best grey silk pantsuit, hair neatly braided, only one silver and obsidian earring in her left ear, the tip of her glass knife tucked well up her sleeve. She'd had to replace the one the cops took from her last night. They let her go home after she made her statement and answered hours worth of questions. Then, this morning, she was called to this meeting with the Board governors. That didn't look good.

Sometimes prisoners died in the course of their program, and usually after the Teacher made a statement they heard no more about it until they received formal notice that further investigation had proven them innocent of any wrongdoing. To be called to a meeting about a prisoner death could only mean trouble. This suspicion was confirmed when she noticed that none of the Board governors who sat around the table with her were willing to make eye contact.

George Shafritz whispered in low tones to Hira Shilo. Miriam Whitehall read her files. Frank Goodall leaned back in his chair and hummed tunelessly at the ceiling, drank from his glass of water. They regarded her not at all, as if she was the body at a funeral, just an object to talk about before they got on with the more important business they had with each other, the still living.

The door to the room opened and Paul Dinardo, Board governor for her zone, entered. He cast a quick look her way, then averted his eyes as he found his seat and mumbled an apology for his lateness. Once he was seated, he pulled her file from his briefcase, tugged at his tie, and gathered in the others with his eyes.

"Review meeting come to order," he said. Silence made its way around the table.

She noticed he continued to look at his file rather than at her. She noticed the small muscles in his jaw were working hard.

"Dr. Addams," he said, "We have your account of the prisoner death dated 5/19, and all present have had the opportunity to review the incident. Is there anything you'd like to add to the report at this time?"

"No," she said. "It's all there."

Miriam leaned across the table toward her and said in silky tones, "We understand how difficult this sort of moment is, Dr. Addams, and I'm sure you understand that our verification process must be complete and accurate. Since your report contained the briefest of paragraphs, Paul thought it might be as well to hear a fuller account."

She blinked in surprise, then turned full face to Miriam. For one split end of time, she allowed herself to dip into Miriam's eyes, feel the triumph that rested behind them. Before Miriam could respond in anger or fear, she pulled back.

"There's no fuller account than the one I gave in my report," she said.

"Then could you repeat it for us, please?" Paul Dinardo asked. He was being polite. Jaguar didn't like the sounds of that.

"All of it?"

He consulted his files, then looked to the other governors. "Just from the parking lot," Miriam suggested.

Jaguar sighed. She'd told it about five times last night, then wrote it down, so she supposed she had it memorized by now. "I was engaged in part of the prisoner's program in a parking lot outside Scarborough Mall, when she produced a laser weapon and threatened me with it. I told her to put it down, and she didn't comply. I approached more closely and drew my own weapon—a glass knife—and she moved in. In the ensuing fight , she fell on my weapon and was fatally wounded."

She waited. Saw Paul's face. Miriam's face. The glances they exchanged.

"Dr. Addams, what happened to the prisoner's weapon?"

"Happened?"

"Where did it go?"

She tilted her head at him inquisitively. "I suppose one of the guys from the cop shop picked it up after I went to the hospital with Karena."

"After a careful search, no weapon was found. And where did your prisoner get a laser gun?" George Shafritz asked.

Jaguar kept her face toward him. "Perhaps someone gave it to her in the mall."

Miriam nodded as if she was satisfied. Jaguar had put the meeting with Miriam in her report, so she must be aware of it.

Hira shook her head and tapped her long thin hand against the table. "Are you suggesting anyone in particular?" she asked.

"No," Jaguar said. The governors waited for elaboration. None came.

Hira raised her eyebrows at Miriam, who let a smile twitch across her lips. She transferred the smile to Shafritz, who passed it on to Frank Goodall, who tried unsuccessfully to relay it to Paul Dinardo. He sat with his head turned down toward his file, looking grim.

"Dr. Addams," Goodall said, "your statement includes report of a meeting with Governor Whitehall at the mall. Are you in any way suggesting that she might have given your prisoner a gun?"

"No," Jaguar said again. Again they waited for elaboration. Again she didn't oblige.

Hira Shilo laughed nervously. "Then, what are we doing here?" she asked the others. "I mean, really. Our decision's been rendered, and I do have a lunch appointment." The others murmured, consulted expensive watches.

Paul Dinardo's head jerked up. Hira stopped laughing. He lifted his chin in Miriam's direction. "Why don't you just tell her what you told me, Miriam?" he said.

Miriam turned her hand over. "If you really think it's important, Paul."

"I do."

She turned to Jaguar. "You claim to have seen me at the mall, but at the hour in question, I was in a telecom conference with a business associate. The conference lasted an hour, and took place at the Governor's Inn. There's a record of it."

Of course, Jaguar thought. No gun was found. Miriam was not at the scene. Alex had disappeared.

"Records are very easy to falsify," she said, a statement rather than a challenge.

"But CEOs are not bought cheaply, and though I'm not a poor woman, I'm not yet rich enough to buy off the perjured testimony of Lawrence Barone."

Murmurs went around the table. Jaguar felt her skin grow cold. Barone. Jesus. She was in trouble, and so was Alex.

"Do you mind telling me what you were talking about?" Jaguar asked.

"Not at all. We were discussing his recent request to have Planetoid Three used as a base for a Lunar material processing plant. I was explaining why we would have to refuse his request."

Jaguar looked around the table and noted the reactions of the other governors. Shafritz was shaking his head while Malor whispered something into his ear. Jaguar heard him mumble the words, 'talk about it later, Talek.' Paul looked blank. Hira's face was creased with concentration, as if she was trying to untangle a fine chain necklace and not succeeding. Miriam smiled at Jaguar.

Jaguar did something she'd never done before. She made empathic contact without permission, in a public setting.

She turned her sea-eyes toward Miriam and let her thoughts enter without permission, without care, without the courtesy she should take in these matters,. The entry was so easy, she thought for a moment that she'd found another empath in the room, but realized quickly she was wrong.

Miriam was no empath. But she'd been absorbing Artemis. Jaguar was getting familiar with the difference in feel between the two. She stayed just long enough to say her piece.

You won't get away with this.

And she heard Miriam's laughter. Miriam's response.

I already have.

Jaguar pulled away and lifted her eyes to meet Paul's. "What the hell is this?" she hissed.

"That's what we'd like to know," Shafritz declared, standing and pointing an angry finger at her. "You—you're—doing something, and you have no right here. No right at all."

Miriam, at his left, put a hand on his arm. "Hush, Talek. It's all right. Sit down."

"Yes. Please, Talek. We don't need to make this into a circus," Paul said, and then turned to Jaguar. "Do we, Dr. Addams?"

"I'd rather have a circus than an execution," she said.

"Don't be ridiculous," he said. "There's no execution committee here. It's an incident review committee, which I called to give you an opportunity to provide information that might forestall your suspension pursuant to further investigation. Unfortunately, you haven't told us a thing we didn't already know and under the circumstances," he looked around the room, and everyone present nodded as if saying yes to a question they'd asked before they arrived.

"Very well," he said. "Then the decision for suspension pursuant to further investigation stands, and if there's no further questions, this meeting is closed. Reconvene in four weeks."

Paul slapped his file folder shut. The others followed suit, and began to rise. Apparently it was all over.

"Wait a minute," Jaguar said. "I have questions."

Paul looked from Jaguar to Miriam.

"Don't worry," Miriam said, " Your pay will continue for the duration of the investigation."

"That wasn't my question," she said, and turned to Paul. "What's my Supervisor got to say about this?"

The small muscles in Paul's jaw twitched harder. Before he could answer, Miriam intervened, saying, "Your supervisor is unavailable for comment, Dr. Addams."

Paul jerked his face around to look at Miriam. In a barely perceptible movement, she turned her head left and right to indicate a negative. Don't say anything.

"No, Miriam," Paul protested. "She has a right to know."

"Know what?" Jaguar asked.

Miriam lifted a shoulder and let it fall. "It's your call," she said.

Paul looked at Jaguar hard. "Supervisor Dzarny has disappeared. And a body's been discovered. A woman who went over a bridge. There's evidence to suggest he had something to do with the death."

"But," Jaguar protested. "That can't be. He's—he said—"

"He said nothing," Paul cut in. His face looked desperate for her silence. Shut the hell up for once, he was almost screaming. Don't go there. Say nothing.

"Paul, that's ridiculous and you know it," she said anyway.

Miriam broke in. "There's a warrant out for Supervisor Dzarny's arrest. For murder. He's considered armed and dangerous, and orders are to take no chances in bringing him in."

Jaguar licked her lips. Miriam was so good at mediating difficult issues, so liberal in her politics, so clear in her progressive stance. Everybody liked her. Everybody trusted her. She was the governor people went to when there was any kind of conflict because they were so sure of her ability to resolve it without creating hard feelings.

Jaguar had a sudden memory of seeing Miriam at a Planetoid dinner—some official function Alex made her attend—and the whole time she kept flipping her honeyed hair in Alex's direction, and Alex kept turning her away like a curtain that was blowing in his face. She'd looked daggers at Jaguar when Alex led her onto the dance floor after dinner.

As if there was no one else present in the room, Jaguar focused on Miriam. She lifted a hand up and let it fall, nonchalant. "Just because he wouldn't fuck you, that's no reason to have him gunned down. I mean, I hear he's good, but no man is that good."

There was bluster from the others that ended with Paul waxing coherent, saying, "For Chrissake, Addams—that's out of line."

Miriam's voice carried the tone of a righteous martyr when she silenced him, saying, "No, Paul. Let her talk. It's meaningless prattle."

"Then let me clarify," Jaguar said. She directed her gaze at Miriam's watching eyes and spoke into her, touching that part of her where this truth lived.

You grew up poor, and then you lost what little you had during the Serials. Your home, your family, your sense of security. You were poor and powerless and alone, and now you want money and power, to keep you safe from your past. You think you'll feel safe if you have that. But you won't because what you really want is to know that you're loved. And love can't be bought with money, or coerced with power. You may want Alex, but no matter how rich or powerful you get, you'll never have him. Never.

Jaguar waited in the silence that followed, feeling the turmoil in Miriam as she tried to push this truth away and failed. She made a sound like growling, which Jaguar wasn't sure was audible to anyone but her, and pulled her gaze from Jaguar, breaking the contact.

"How dare you!" Miriam hissed. Jaguar leaned back in her seat and grinned.

"What is going on here?" Talek asked.

Jaguar laughed coarsely, and one of the governors in the room emitted a gasp. Miriam looked around at everyone in the room, stood and began to gather her files together. But Jaguar wouldn't let it go.

I dare a lot more than you ever would, Miriam. That's why Alex likes to dance with me.

Miriam lifted her file folder and then paused for a long moment. A slow anger burned in her eyes. With renewed confidence, she turned back to Jaguar and renewed the empathic contact.

How dare you say anything about love. You have it in your hands and you throw it away.

Miriam lingered just long enough to see that the shot hit home, then released Jaguar and left the room.

Jaguar's jaw worked hard. That was the only charge she'd been hit with today that she didn't know how to answer. In every other matter she knew her innocence, but not in this. She leaned back and closed her eyes.

"Dr. Addams," Governor Goodall said. "I don't know what you did, but I hope it wasn't—wasn't—anything against protocol. You'll receive a reprimand in your permanent file if you—"

"Stuff it," she said.

"What? What did you say to me?"

"I said stuff it," she repeated, and decided she would say no more.

She sat with her eyes closed, head tilted back, and listened to the scraping of chairs and movement of feet which indicated that everyone was leaving. She continued to sit until she felt a presence at her back.

"Leave me the hell alone," she suggested.

"Look," Paul Dinardo said, "if I could do anything, I would."

She opened her eyes and twisted around to face him.

"How about suicide? That might cheer me up."

He grimaced at her, pointed a finger, and pulled it back. "Then you'd just be stuck with the others. And if you think I'm bad—what the hell did you do to him, Addams?"

This made her blink hard. Feel a searing anger course through her jaw. Not another one. Accusing her as if she'd ever done anything except be who she was, anything except try to stay out of his way so they wouldn't hurt each other, wouldn't do the harm she knew they potentially could do.

"I haven't done anything to him," she said.

"Yeah? Then why is it one minute everything's going along. He's doing his job—okay it's a complicated job, but he's doing it. Next thing, all we know is there's a dead woman holding his stuff, and he's bought two tickets for the shuttle, headed to the New England corridor."

She frowned at Paul. "Did he go?"

"I don't know. We're asking around to see if he went, but you know how that goes. Most of the security is pre-boarding, and if someone else took the tickets, we might not track it for a while. He could be there, he could be here. He could be somewhere else. What I really want to know is why he gets so crazy about you. Why is it that every case he's on with you is trouble? I mean, I understand a little fun now and then between consenting adults, but I'll be damned if I'll lose a good supervisor just because he's lost his head over a—" he blustered, controlled himself.

"Over a what, Paul? An empath? A piece of ass? An injun? Which derogatory appellation are you groping for with your feeble little mind? And why do you assume I know anything more than you do?"

"Because," Paul said, "he told me you were involved."

"Told you? You spoke with him?"

"Yeah. He called in."

Jaguar stood and grabbed his arm. "What kind of shit is this?" she demanded. "You just sit there and don't tell me while these rat fuck pencil pushers take my job away?"

He regarded her smugly, apparently feeling all Alpha, Jaguar thought, because he knew something she didn't. He removed her hand from his arm, and took a step back. "Just shut up and listen a minute, can't you?"

She bit back on all the questions that wanted to fall out of her mouth and settled back in her chair.

"Okay good," Paul said, and huffed out a breath. "Before all this happened, he told me about the—situation. Or, at least, what he thinks of it. The moon mining and the women and so on."

"The women I'm working with have Phase Psychosis," she said. "Maxxed out from exposure to Artemis. And someone is trying to push through crystallization plants on the Planetoids. Is that the situation you mean?"

"Yeah—not so loud, okay?" He cast glances around, peered out the door quickly. "And what the hell is wrong with you, gunning for Miriam? Using that stuff here—Jesus, Addams. I stick up for you, you know that—and Miriam is the only Governor on your side."

"No she's not, Paul."

"Yeah? Well, I saw the tape of the conversation she had with Barone and you didn't."

"Miriam was at the mall last night," Jaguar said, then sat back hard in her chair. Either he believed her, or he didn't. "Skip it," she said. "What else did Alex say?"

"He said you could prove it. About the Artemis thing. Can you?"

"Not now," Jaguar said. "I was getting there. When did you last hear from Alex?"

"Two days ago. Right after he left his office, I guess. Jesus, this is a mess, Addams. You're aware of that, aren't you? "

"Probably," she noted, "a little more directly than you are. Can we get to the part where you tell me what he said?"

"It was just crap. A message on my telecom. Didn't make sense. Didn't even sound like him."

He threw his arms out, a gesture of helplessness. "He said he was leaving, because he didn't want to kill you."

Jaguar let these words find a place to settle in her psyche. "Didn't want to kill me?" she asked.

"Yeah. Just like that. Tell her I don't want to kill her. Tell her that's why I'm leaving."

"Are you sure he meant me? Not some other her?"

Paul struggled with himself a moment. "Beautiful. He used the word beautiful. 'She's so beautiful, I won't kill her. Even if the Mother wants it.' That's what he said. And that's why I ask what you did to him."

Jaguar sat very still and listened to her own heart beating out its recurring theme. Alive. I'm alive. Alive. I'm alive.

"Do you still have the message?" she asked.

"Are you kidding? I got rid of it fast."

"But you're sure you're remembering what it said?"

"Yeah. I'm sure. I wouldn't forget something like that."

"And you erased it," she said gruffly. If she could have listened to the message itself, she might have picked up residual information from his voice. She knew how to read physical evidence in ways Paul couldn't. Now she knew little more than she'd known before. He was with Brendan. He was being exposed to Artemis. He was in trouble.

"Paul, can you get me back with the women?" she asked.

Paul shook his head. "Can't do it. Got a second choice?"

"Find Alex."

"Right. If he ain't telling, well, you know how he is when he doesn't want to be found."

Jaguar chewed on her lower lip and thought. Alex had a remarkable capacity for invisibility. He didn't so much block her contact, as disappear from view altogether. Pulled in all his signals and made them shut down until he was nowhere to be found. It was very disconcerting. And if he thought he'd harm her, then he'd hide from her.

Hell, she thought. Hell and shit and rat fuck. It was a bloody mess. She pushed her chair back and stood. "If I need your help to find Alex, can I count on it?" she asked.

"Yeah," he said. "Sure."

She gave him a long, steady glare, saw that he probably meant it inasmuch as he meant anything, and nodded. She moved toward the door.

"Where're you going?" Paul called after her.

"Somewhere else," she said. "Any objections?"

"Just don't leave the Planetoid. You aren't going to, are you?"

She stared at him hard. "Do you really want to know what I'm going to do next?" she asked.

Paul pulled a handkerchief from his suit pocket and wiped it across his face. "No," he said, his voice muffled by the cloth. "I don't want to know a damn thing at all."

Jaguar left the building and she walked.

She walked down Yonge, past all the sporty shops and little bakeries and cafes. The smell of fresh brewed coffee trailed after her from the tables of people who chatted amiably in the sun, not one of them knowing how close they were to having their little world altered wildly or perhaps destroyed. She walked and continued to walk until she found herself at the Toronto Sanctuary, where she let herself in to the breeding complex and went to the cages where the two jaguars, Hecate and Chaos, spent their days.

She stood in front of their cage, hands on the bars that stood between them. Chaos, the male, stood and prowled to her, sat and stared at her as she stared at him.

"Where is he?" she asked, but he didn't answer.

Jaguars weren't trackers. They were opportunistic hunters, as she was, ready to change direction at a moment's notice. Alex was like that, too, which would make him more difficult to find. What she needed was a bloodhound. And she needed it sooner rather than later because they were being ambushed.

Miriam had as much as told her so. She knew what they knew, and was seeing to it that they were removed, for reasons Jaguar couldn't yet determine. It must have something to do with Artemis, but she knew of no connection between Miriam and moon mining except for this falsified conversation with Barone. A conversation she had on record, and had played back for the governors. A conversation where she came down adamantly against using Planetoid Three as a Lunar processing base. Jaguar had to give her some grudging respect for that move. With her soft clothes and consensus building ways, Miriam played a good game. Jaguar would have to play a better one, because there was even more at stake than Alex right now, though that was bad enough. If she couldn't figure this one out, the Planetoid was about to get sold down the river. Miriam had something in mind for that, Jaguar was sure. She just didn't know what. She wondered if Alex knew.

She sighed, and brought her thoughts into focus. She'd found Alex before, and she'd find him now. She didn't have a bloodhound, but she had Chaos. She had Hecate. She had her arts. She rubbed at the mint she carried with her in her pocket, breathed in the sharp, clean scent of it, and spoke to her namesake.

I myself, spirit in flesh, speak.

Chaos' gold eyes took her in and floated her in to that place where she saw most clearly. She gathered her energy, her intent, and sent it out toward Alex, toward his spirit which she'd drawn closer to than any other spirit in all her travels within the particular piece of flesh she occupied.

Alex, where are you?

Spirit traveling, moving through nowhere and standing still but going, and she found herself against a soft wall of light. Glowing and impermeable. It spiralled, thickened, spun itself into a great sphere that hung in darkness above her, splashed with a trail of blood. Her intent and her desire pounded against the barrier, but got nowhere.

Alex. Where are you?

The thickening mist consumed her thoughts, muffled them, dispersed them. They would not reach their destination. Not through this viscous obscurity.

The impermeable bank of compression surrounded her, and she couldn't breathe through it, couldn't stay afloat in it. It kept sucking her down. Down into a place where there was no air at all, and no reason for any.

Here? Are you here?

Fear wrapped around her. Was he here, in this place of obscurity and hopelessness where she couldn't reach him, couldn't grab his hand as he'd grabbed hers to drag her back from the place of death. Is that why he left that message for Paul? *Tell her I don't want to kill her.*

And if she couldn't find him? If he died or if he fell into that shadowed place where he would kill her and she had to face that again, the same way she had to face it with Nick? What would she do? Her days would be emptied out by his absence, and she'd never looked at that before. Never seen what she met here, in this place.

Fear. And desire.

Alex, where are you?

This fear would swallow her. She could find no emotional footing to get away from it. Nothing to hang onto here. No positive energy. Nothing. No positive energy.

She was a positive, being drawn into a negative. Physically and magnetically pulled. Desire pulled into fear.

Desire.

"No," she gasped. "Let me go."

And the fog lifted. The sense of suffocation dispersed. She stood alone, in front of the cages where Chaos paced and Hecate made noises at him. Alone with the winged creature named desire, beginning to stir.

She clenched and unclenched her hands, feeling the tingling that signalled a return to the present, outside of any empathic space. Her desire was pulled into fear, just as it had been for the three women she was working with. Both were a part of her, but one was eating the other. The part of her that remained interested and aloof was glad to know this, but the rest of her understood that it was only the beginning of the journey.

If her desire was pulled into fear, the only way to overcome that was to free the desire to increase its energy, so that the fear couldn't suck it away.

But what was her desire? The years she'd worked with him, found a friend in him, found someone she could trust—she wanted that to continue. There was a solid reality to his presence. He was always himself, even when it irritated the hell out of her. He had integrity, compassion, and the patience of the turning earth. She wanted to continue walking near that presence.

Was that desire?

Or was it the fire she felt when he kissed her? The growing warmth she tried not to acknowledge, even now after he'd admitted to his desire for her? Silly of her, she thought. There wasn't any reason why she shouldn't sleep with him, except that it could complicate her work life. But they were adults. Once the ardor cooled, they'd go back to working together and be fine. It might take time, but they'd do it because they both loved their work. But was that what she wanted? Was that her desire? To sleep with him, and then let him go?

Did she want to have him in her bed, in spite of the complications because desire knew no complications beyond its own needs? In her bed. Her arms and skin and flesh and mouth—did they want him? Her legs and belly and breasts—did they want him?

She didn't know because she'd never let herself know. Whenever it came up, she pushed it down, away, out. Told it no. But if she felt confident about maintaining a working relationship with him no matter what happened between them sexually, what did she have to lose?

That, she thought, was what she didn't want to know. What she had to lose. Standing here, putting her finger on it, the potential loss seemed way out of control. If she let herself want him, the beast would be loose, and she'd never get it back in its cage again.

Chaos rolled over on his back and made a noise of contentment. Hecate turned her golden head toward him and yawned. Marie told her recently that Hecate was pregnant. She'd managed to get them to mate after all, with her program of allowing them to relearn how to hunt.

Maybe, she thought, that's what she needed to do. Hunt. Like Fiore, who had the look of a huntress, watching the forest, watching Terez, watching Jaguar. If she hunted, maybe then she'd know if she wanted to mate.

CHAPTER TEN

The following day, Miriam Whitehall had a long conversation with governor Shafritz about the meeting they'd attended, and the trouble in Zone 12. She was concerned, she said, because she didn't know if the trouble indicated a deeper problem.

"I don't think so," Governor Shafritz said, speaking tentatively. He smelled a political move in the works, but wasn't sure what it would be. "Twelve's got a rep for the best."

Miriam rolled her eyes. "I know. Best technicians. The VR site. And the best success rate. But that was mostly from Dzarny and Addams."

"They were good. Did some spectacular jobs."

"And look where it's gotten them," Miriam said, clucking her tongue.

"A shame, isn't it? Not that Addams' behavior is a shock to anyone, but Dzarny. I never would've thought it. He seemed reliable as rain."

"Maybe," Miriam said, " But he's also—well, you know. And in so deep with that Addams woman there was bound to be trouble."

Shafritz did know. Everyone knew how Alex was about Dr. Addams, and hardly anyone understood why.

"They have a word for that, don't they?" Miriam asked. "When people like them go bad."

"Shadowed," Shafritz said. "I think they call it shadowed."

"Yes. That's the word. Shadowed." She brooded over it for a moment, then asked cautiously, "It's not catching, is it?"

"Catching?" Shafritz repeated.

"Can other people become—shadowed? I mean, if they're not—like Alex."

"No," Shafritz said uncertainly. "I don't think so. Why?"

"I'm concerned. We really don't know what happens to people under those circumstances, do we? And it does seem there's some sort of emotional breakdown going on in 12, doesn't there?"

Shafritz frowned over his shrimp cocktail and said nothing.

"What I'm really surprised at," Miriam continued, "is Paul Dinardo."

"Oh?"

"Yes. He must've seen this coming. Must've known there were problems. So why didn't he do something about it before it got this far out of hand? He's always supported the two of them. And he didn't look well at the meeting, did he?"

"Not particularly," Shafritz said, "But he usually doesn't."

"Well, I suppose he's under a lot of pressure, with the push to get a Lunar plant here once the moratorium is lifted."

"Do you think it will be?" Shafritz asked, trying not to sound too hopeful. He and Miriam were on opposite sides of this issue, and he felt strongly that it would be good to bring innovative industry to the Planetoid system. Especially with someone as powerful as Lawrence Barone backing it up.

"Unless we can find a better to way to fight it, your side will win the day," Miriam said.

Shafritz had to admit she was a good sport about her losses, even when she fought like hell to win. "I appreciate your equanimity in the matter," he said. "I really do."

Miriam laughed. "Well, if I have to lose, I like losing to the best. Mr. Barone really is quite a nice man. Very down to earth. And his ideas on management are quite effective. Aside from the Lunar processing, I think he'd be quite a valuable friend to the Planetoid, and I'm afraid we might be needing a few friends, if this kind of disturbance keeps up."

"Surely it won't, Miriam. With Dzarny and Addams out of the way, things should quiet down."

"I don't know," Miriam said. "I have a bad feeling about it all. I really do. I think we should keep our eyes open for more trouble. Mark my words, and if I'm right, you'll have to buy me a bottle of champagne."

"That would be no loss," Shafritz said. "No loss at all. "

Jaguar sat in the dimly lit bar, a glass of beer in front of her. Occasionally, she picked the glass up and sucked at it hard. Then, she put it down and stared at the remaining contents.

"Wow," Gerry said, "I mean, do you think he really killed someone? I can't imagine Alex doing that. Unless he's cracked up. Gone over the moon. Bonked out. I mean, he's always been like rock steady. Whaddya think happened to him?"

She growled softly, and her hand closed harder on the glass.

"And you must feel like shit, too," he continued. "I mean, you're suspended. And you don't even know if he's dead or alive, right?"

Her growl deepened, and grew louder.

"You wanna talk about it?" Gerry asked politely.

"Fuck off," she snarled back, and returned to silence.

He leaned back, his chair balancing on two legs, his hands crossed on his abdomen. She was supposed to sing with his band tonight, and he had a feeling he was out a vocalist unless he could bring her around. Somewhere in the recesses of his thoughts, which were as dimly lit as the bar, he understood that this wasn't the most important item on the agenda this evening. She was suspended. One of her prisoners dead, and she didn't even know what happened. And Alex was gone. Warrant out for his arrest. Gerry knew this was serious stuff, but the neural connections that would make it serious for him had yet to be completed.

He rocked back and forth on the two legs of his chair and hummed loudly.

Jaguar growled at his noise.

He tugged at his shirt collar, and kept humming.

Jaguar lifted a hand and slammed it down on the table, making the beer dance and causing the legs of Gerry's chair to slip out from under him.

He came down directly on his ass, and sat on the floor. Jaguar lowered her head and continued to brood.

Gerry swore softly, rubbed his tailbone and stood. "You want something stronger than beer?" he asked. "I'm heading toward the bar."

Jaguar raised her face and stared at him, as if taking notice of his presence for the first time that evening. "I have to find him," she said. "I have to find him."

"Yeah," Gerry agreed. He paused. Scratched at his balding head. "How'll you do that?"

"I don't know," she said. She wished she could at least determine if he wanted to be found. Alex could keep the lowest profile of any man she knew, and in fact had the capacity to create a temporary shield of invisibility around himself. It was an empathic trick he'd tried to teach her, but she just couldn't learn. He said it was a matter of ego. Hers was too big to hide easily.

But no. He promised he'd stay in touch unless he was physically prevented. She had to assume he was being prevented. But why, and more importantly, where? Here, or on the home planet? How could she decide which place to look first?

"Know anyone who keeps bloodhounds?" she asked.

Gerry snorted—his version of laughter. "I know a golden retriever."

"I need bloodhounds," she repeated.

"No," he said. "You need a golden retriever."

She peered up at him. "What?"

Gerry righted his chair, and sat down, this time with all four legs firmly on the floor. "Not what. Who."

"Then who?"

"The golden retriever," Gerry answered amicably, and when he saw the look on her face, hurried to say, "Pasquale. He's a sort of a friend, I guess. From when—you know."

Jaguar nodded. She knew. Gerry was a drug runner before he was a musician. That brought him to the Planetoids many years ago. He said his decision to stay here had a lot to do with the people he'd left behind, and wanting to continue to leave them behind.

"What's Pasquale got to do with this?" she asked.

"He's a sniffer. They call him the golden retriever."

Jaguar finally felt as if something interesting was happening. She knew the term sniffer. A sniffer was someone who found people, found information. Sometimes they worked for the home planet police. Sometimes they worked against them. It was not officially considered a psi capacity, the ability to find people and things, but Jaguar knew that was just a way of refusing to acknowledge the usefulness of the arts. People who could track used a combination of clear seeing and empathy that was very specific, very focused, and often very effective.

And Gerry knew such a person. Pasquale. If he was from Gerry's past, he probably worked against the law. But right now, she supposed she sat on the wrong side of the law as well, so what did it matter.

"Where is he?" she asked.

Gerry shrugged. " I suppose he's still alive somewhere. If I know him right, somewhere warm and sunny."

"Well, can you find him?"

Gerry scratched at his head more, and sneezed. For him, that was a sign of deep thought. "You mean it?" he asked.

"Yes," she said.

"Because," Gerry continued, "he's—well, he's a mercenary. Not someone you'd—I mean, Pasquale, he's a mercenary," he concluded lamely.

Jaguar stared coldly at Gerry. "Is he any good?" she asked.

"The best," Gerry said decisively.

"Then can you get him for me?"

Gerry twisted his nose around a little, as if tuning the dials of a radio, seeking the news. He clucked a few times. Then whatever egg he was hatching emerged.

"He gave me a coin. I did a favor for him, and he's the kind of guy who likes to repay favors. Said if I ever needed him, I should cash in my chip. Gave me an address to ship it to."

Jaguar lifted her beer to her mouth and emptied it. She put the glass down on the table hard, and ran a finger around the rim. Something like a plan began to formulate itself. She had people she could use, and was figuring out how to use them.

"Get him," she said. "Now."

Gerry shifted nervously in his seat. He didn't know anything much more unsettling than Jaguar, unless it was Jaguar with an idea. "What're you gonna do?"

Good question, she thought. She had just set one possibility in motion, but she certainly wouldn't wait around for a mercenary sniffer to show. She would see about tracking the stone Karena dropped. There was something about it. Sometime important. And she thought she'd like to catch up with Fiore, who had the eyes of a hunter. Fiore knew something, too. Maybe knew what where the Artemis compounds came from, but certainly knew enough to get Jaguar started in that direction. If she could track the source, she might be able to get the proof she needed. Or she might get the information she needed to help Alex. Or both. She needed Fiore.

"What I'll do first," she said to Gerry, "is find me a good woman."

"Huh," Gerry said, "I never guessed that about you."

Jaguar rolled her eyes. She pressed her hands against the table and stood.

"Hey," Gerry said, "Where're you going?"

She paused and looked down at him, as if he was already very far away. "I've got work to do, Gerry."

"That mean you're not singing tonight?"

"You can safely assume that," Jaguar said.

"Damn," Gerry said. "That's what I was afraid of."

CHAPTER ELEVEN

The earth was very brown and the sun was very bright. Somewhere between the two, the color green invaded him. It was in him and all around him. Above and below him. As they walked, Alex reached up for it. He held his hand up to try and touch it, wanting to know if it was something alive. An animal. A spirit. Matter trapped in color. Energy trapped in matter, waiting to burst free in its purest form.

Or perhaps eyes. Green eyes that pierced him with desire and called to him. Called to him. Eyes he knew, watching him.

But when he lifted his hand between the brown of earth and fire of sun, his foot caught on a root and he fell, his body slamming into ground with a thud. He lay there, breathing earth, with his eyes closed.

Ahead of him, the crunch of footsteps stopped, then started, growing closer to him. He opened his eyes and saw Brendan's brown sandals, noticed that his toenails were long and curled down over the end of his toes.

"I thought perhaps we should continue walking," Brendan observed.

Alex lay still, aware of his own breathing, aware of his body as an entity that contained, him, aware that his thoughts and emotions were moving in circles he couldn't contain. Time seemed to pass, but he wasn't sure how much.

"What?" he asked.

"The wind," Brendan said. "It's rather peculiar here."

Alex pushed himself to a sitting position and stared up at Brendan, who stood squinting toward the top of the tree canopy, his face pursed in disapproval. "I like the wind," he continued. "It moves around objects intimately, in its own way. But it's peculiar here."

Alex looked around. The world seemed to be returning. He saw trees and heard birds and the rustlings of animal motion. Colors had recombined themselves with the life forms they were attached to, and Brendan's voice was emanating from his mouth again, instead of occurring in the air around them.

He didn't know how long they'd been wandering the ecosite, except that it couldn't be too many days if he judged by the growth of his beard and his hunger level, both of which were still minimal. He supposed he was somehow tending to all his bodily needs, though he wasn't sure how or when. There were fruits in the trees. Space enough to pee. Streams to drink from.

Brendan rattled something in his hands. "Here," he said, handing Alex a bottle of pills. "Take one of these."

Alex rose stiffly and unsteadily and took the bottle from Brendan. He looked it over. It was a standard nutritional prescription used with prisoners who stopped eating during their programs.

"Who gave these to you?" he asked, surprised to hear that his voice still worked normally.

"The Mother," Brendan said. "She was concerned that I wasn't eating. I told her eating was a sensual pleasure, and an abuse. To eat off the body of the mother in that way is so, well, incestuous."

Alex opened the bottle and took one, swallowed it dry. "I see," he said. "Brendan, where do those stones come from? Did you bring them with you?"

Brendan's hand went to the pocket of his jeans and he pulled out one of the smooth gray stones, rubbed it lovingly. "They're gifts. From The Mother."

He turned full face to Alex and smiled. His eyes glowed softly behind his glasses. They seemed to swell and grow, increase in luminescence.

Alex felt the obliquity of earth inside them, the tilt of the axis and the swift motion. He felt himself coursing an orbit through space at 900 miles an hour. He put his hand out to steady himself, but it did no good. He was falling. Falling, like Alice into the rabbit hole, slow enough to watch the moon pass by, to see Jaguar's face as he rolled past her, to know something was happening to him and he'd better make it stop.

Something is happening to me, he told himself, and it has to do with those stones. He was falling, and there was nothing to grab hold of except Brendan, who held the stones.

He looked up and saw him smiling, nodding at him. Not good. That nod. He saw it on the bridge. He was nodding and holding out his hand for Alex to grab hold of but Alex didn't. He knew better. Instead he pressed a hand against Brendan's forehead. Was it his forehead, or was it the surface of the moon?

He pressed his hand against it and whispered into him.

Brendan Farley—See who you are. Be what you see.

Motion ceased.

He stood still.

He stood still inside a very white room where Brendan lay still on a metal cot, and a woman bent over him, singing to him, smoothing his forehead, smoothing his hair. He closed his eyes and slept, and she stood back, viewed Brendan, sleeping.

The woman dropped stones into his pockets like gifts, and left him alone.

Then, Brendan sat up and pushed Alex away. Pushed Alex away and Alex felt himself falling again, faster this time as if he fell out of a shuttle and through the absence of matter.

The way down was long, and his resting place unsure, but all the way he knew he was riding somehow secure on the backbone of the moon.

Jaguar strolled through the door of the Planetoid Personnel Building, pressed her thumb against the elevator button to give her imprint read, and got on when the doors opened. But when the doors opened to the basement, where the main computer banks were housed, a guard blocked her from further progress.

"Excuse me," she said politely.

"No, ma'am," the guard replied, and continued to stand in front of her.

"Yes, sir," she responded, and took a step up to his chest.

He walked forward, pushing her back into the elevator with his bulk and holding her there while he pressed the button that would close the doors and send them back up to the lobby.

When the doors opened again, Jaguar was staring over his shoulder at Rachel's wild eyes, with her hand reaching for the guard's lower extremities. The guard, who was intent on watching her right hand, which she was slowly raising toward his face in a fist, had no idea how close he was to having his heirs cut off at the pass.

"Jaguar," Rachel said frantically. "Here for your things? They're in my office."

"It's not *my* things that were chiefly on my mind," she growled.

"Ha," Rachel said. "Ha ha. Well, yes." She turned her bright smile on the guard.

"She's not allowed in here," he said gruffly. "I was told if her imprint came through, stop her."

"She can get her things," Rachel said, "as long as she's not alone. And she's not." She took Jaguar by the arm, led her around the guard and down the hall.

"Xipe totec flay them all," Jaguar said, "can't even get in the front door."

"You're suspended," Rachel hissed back at her. "What did you expect? They'd just let you waltz in and take whatever information you want? They *know* you, Jaguar."

She pulled her arm from Rachel's grasp, and walked at a rapid pace next to her, head held high.

"What did you want, anyway?" Rachel asked.

"I want a location for Fiore," she said.

Rachel stopped walking, stared at Jaguar's back as it moved down the hall, and then stopped. "What?" she asked.

Jaguar continued walking. "You heard me," she said over her shoulder, and Rachel scooted to catch up.

"What for?"

"I have an important fashion question for her. Like what do you wear to break into a Lunar crystallization plant."

Rachel blinked. "You're serious, aren't you?"

"Very. I also want to find out if anyone mentioned a small stone found in Karena's vicinity. Or maybe one in her pocket."

"A stone?"

"Stone. Small. Smooth. White. "

Rachel cast a glance up and down the hall. "We shouldn't talk here," she said.

At this, Jaguar came to a halt.

"Dammit, Rachel, why not? Haven't I done my work well here? Hasn't Alex been—" she stopped talking, clenched her jaw shut. Breathed hard with her eyes closed.

"Tell me what to do," Rachel said.

Jaguar took in breath and let it out. "I need help, but if you help me, you should know it could be big trouble. I won't be playing tiddly-winks, and I won't be playing by the rules."

"I know that. Tell me what you want me to do," Rachel said patiently.

Jaguar let go of tension. "Can you get the files on Fiore, and also anything at all about Miriam Whitehall's life off the Planetoid?"

"Whatever I can," she said.

"Good. And find out what happened to Karena's property. If there's a stone in the pile, get it, but put it in a sealed box. Don't touch it too much, okay?"

Rachel frowned. "How come?"

"I think it's what all the fuss is about. Meet me at Marie's as soon as you can, okay?"

"The sooner you clear out of here," Rachel said. "The sooner I'll get there."

Jaguar opened her mouth to say words that might begin to express how grateful she was, and found nothing to cover it. "Okay," she said instead. "See you there."

It took Rachel less than two hours to get what Jaguar requested. When she arrived at Marie's, Jaguar and Gerry and Pinkie Horton were already there, sitting at the kitchen table, drinking coffee and eating bread warm from the oven.

Rachel stopped and surveyed the scene. "A party?" she asked.

"Sort of," Jaguar said. "A rescue party. What'd you get?"

Rachel held out two discs, and Jaguar took them. "Where's Fiore?"

"Normal house 7 with Peter."

"Peter," Jaguar said. "Couldn't they find anyone less suitable?"

"He works with child killers," Rachel noted.

"Fiore's not a child killer. She's a hunter." Jaguar turned to the table, and waved an arm, inviting Rachel to sit. She found a place, and Marie moved from the stove, where she was cooking something that smelled good, and handed a basket of bread and a cup of coffee to Rachel.

"Thanks," Rachel said. "You joining us?"

Marie shook her head. "Just peripherally."

Jaguar took a seat. "Marie thinks we're nuts. Maybe she's right."

"I am," Marie noted laconically.

Jaguar surveyed the others. Gerry, looking vaguely interested in the proceedings when he wasn't focused on buttering his bread. Pinkie, whose blue Mohawk highlighted the green paint she circled her eyes with to ward off evil spirits. Rachel, looking far too normal to be sitting among them. And, of course, herself. Hair braided with feathers. Obsidian earring that marked her as an empath. The sage green shirt and loose khaki pants she wore when she helped Marie with the animals at the Sanctuary.

And Marie, in her usual coveralls, grey hair cropped close to her head, hands rough with the years of tending gardens to grow the plants she wanted for the animals she loved more than she cared for any human. Jaguar ran a hand across her mouth. She was about to ask all of them to risk their jobs. Maybe their lives. And while she was accustomed to risking her own on a regular basis, she didn't like to drag others along for the ride. She reminded herself that they were here as much for Alex as they were for her. It was her job at stake, but his life.

"Marie," she said, "where's 7 from here?"

"I'll get a map," she said, and exited.

Jaguar turned to Rachel again. "The stone?" she asked.

"Funny you should mention that," Rachel said. "I checked the inventory of Karena's personal items post mortem, and sure enough, she had a grey stone in her pocket. She didn't have one coming in. But she wasn't the only one."

"Fiore, or Terez?" Jaguar asked.

"Neither. The woman Alex is accused of murdering. Found clutched in her hand."

Jaguar whistled, long and low. "Can you get it?" she asked.

"Not even close. All the evidence went to one of the governor's. Miriam Whitehall."

Jaguar closed her eyes and smiled blissfully.

"What do I owe you?" she asked.

"Your life. So don't go throwing it away."

"No plans in that direction," she said. She turned to Marie, who had come over with the map. Jaguar opened it as the others drew in close around her.

"There," she said, pointing at Normal house Seven. She smiled over at Marie. "Perfect."

Marie made a dismissive sound. "You have the devil's luck, Jaguar."

"Sometimes I suppose I do," she murmured. "Wish it was a little more consistent."

"What?" Gerry asked. "What're you talking about?"

"Just something Marie and I cooked up earlier as a preliminary plan. We didn't know if it'd work, but now it looks good."

Rachel picked up a piece of bread and began tearing strips off it.

Pinkie shifted in her seat, and then reached across, grabbed the bread from Rachel. "Look," she said. "If you're hungry, eat it. If not, leave it alone."

Rachel scowled at her, and folded her hands hard.

"What's the plan?" Pinkie asked.

Jaguar moved her finger from Normal House seven, in a direct line to the breeding complex, which was separated from it by a few hundred yards of wood. Her finger landed on the jaguar cages.

"Somebody's gonna let the cats out of the bag," she crooned.

"Fuckin' jam," Pinkie said. "I'm not going near those things."

Jaguar jerked her head up. "You don't have to. You and Gerry are in costume. Animal control, patrolling the Normal house area to make sure they don't get in there. Bring an extra suit, for our guest."

Gerry nodded.

"Rachel, you stay in the truck. Can you hook your computer into security?"

"I—for what purpose?"

"Shut down the Normal house security system."

Rachel's hands twisted as if they were tearing bread. Pinkie rolled her eyes, and sent the loaf sliding across the table to her.

"Thanks," she said. "I think."

"Can you do it?" Jaguar asked.

"Well, of course I can do it."

"Good. Blow the implant circuit when they get her. Once she's in the truck we'll take it out. I don't know what kind they have in her."

"It should be in the files."

"Okay," She looked at Rachel hard. "I'll need a shuttle pass for us, too. Can you arrange that?"

Rachel thought hard, then nodded quickly. "Where you going?"

"Home Planet. Bird sanctuary just outside her town. It's got a few hundred unpopulated acres."

Jaguar had struggled about where to bring Fiore. Part of her wanted to stay on the Planetoid just because that was the last place Alex was seen. She kept expecting him to turn up in the same vicinity, in the way you expect a lost item to be in a particular place, sure that you put it there, sure it couldn't have just walked away.

But Alex had just walked away, and he had shuttle tickets, but there was no record of him boarding, though Jaguar knew he had ways get on unrecorded if he wanted to. Finally, she decided that she had to bring Fiore to the home planet in hopes of getting a location for the processing plant. Any information she could find on that would ultimately do them only good.

"Are you sure this is a good idea?" Rachel asked, her hand finding the bread and tearing at it.

"No," she said. "You got any better?"

" I guess not. Anything else you need?"

"Just try and stay clean. I don't want anyone else losing their jobs. And I may need someone who can be inside. Offices, computers, that sort of thing."

Jaguar turned to Gerry. "Anything from your friend the sniffer?"

"I sent it out."

Jaguar sighed. "We can't wait for him. We go tomorrow. If he shows up, tell him what the assignment is. He's to track Alex and bring him back safe."

Gerry shook his head slowly from side to side. "If he shows up, it won't be here."

"What?"

"It'll be wherever you are."

"How'll he know where I am?"

"He's a sniffer, Jaguar."

"Well, what's he look like, so I'll recognize him."

Gerry pinched his nose with his fingers, rolled his eyes toward the ceiling, and then gestured toward it. "He's big. He's got a lot of hair. Light colored."

"Gerry, that could be Santa Claus."

Gerry shook his head. "No beard. And his nose's probably broken in more places. I guess you could say he looks sort of like a mountain, with a boulder on top. That'd be his head."

Jaguar sighed. "Okay. I'll keep an eye out for a walking mountain."

"With lots of gold hair. Golden retriever, remember? Oh, and he has a black and gold ring. Wears it on his little finger."

"Okay. I'll know him if I see him. Pinkie? You set on your part?"

She held her hand up with her thumb and her silver pinkie extended.

Then, Jaguar thought, we are ready to roll.

On the Home Planet, Pasquale sat at a café drinking a cup of espresso, his white dress shirt and pants spotless and creased, his great mane of gold-blonde hair tied back in a neat ponytail. He was considering a small and ancient Etruscan coin that sat on the table in front of him. He liked

Etruscan artifacts. They reminded him of where his blood flowed from. He was glad this one had come home to him. Now he had to determine what it asked of him.

He sipped from his cup. Put the cup down. Picked the coin up and smoothed it with his fingers, which made it look dwarfed, as if it was the coin of a midget people. He put the coin down. Picked up his cup and sipped. Put the cup down. Narrowed his eyes and raised his massive head, sniffing the air around him. Picked the coin up and smoothed it some more.

He held it between his thumb and index finger, held it up to the background of the very blue sky. Brought it to his face and took a long breath through his nose. Closed his eyes and leaned back, palming the coin and continuing to smooth it.

Scenes unfolded for him. People moved in their disorderly courses, and places became visible. The interaction between people and place created sense, and understanding. There was hunting, and the scent of the moon. There were women, and there was the sweetly acrid aroma of money. Lots of money. There was sex, or the possibility of it. And something else. A plan he'd nurtured for a long time, that had the possibility of reaching fruition through the confluence of events he'd found himself involved in.

He so enjoyed it when synchronicity ruled. It had always been his best friend.

It would still be tricky, though. He'd have to work it just right, and he'd need to balance every aspect perfectly for it to work.

He frowned, muttered, the small muscles around his mouth and nose twitching. Without opening his eyes, he lifted the coin and pressed it against his lips. Flicked out his tongue and licked at the old metal quickly once. Twice.

Then he chuckled.

A waiter walked over and stood at the side of his table. Cleared his throat.

Pasquale opened an eye and grinned at him. "It's a good day," he said to the waiter.

The waiter peered around him. "The sun is shining," he agreed. "A good day. Can I get you anything else?"

"Just my bill," he said, smiling. "I'm afraid I have to leave."

CHAPTER TWELVE

Alex could no longer determine if he was in adept space, empathic space, or simply going mad. He woke from dreams that hadn't occurred to face waking that felt like a dream. The only way he could tell the difference between the two was that Jaguar often visited his dreams, and he knew she wasn't with him because he longed for her so completely when he was awake.

He saw he was seated on a tree stump, peering at a sun that set red and orange beyond the horizon. On the ground at his feet was a small, round stone. He had the sense that it had fallen from his hand, which was cupped as if it had been holding something. He pushed at it with his toe, not wanting to pick it up. Touching it seemed to make the worst problems. When Brendan had one, the world turned strange, but actually holding it was worse. He pushed it away with his food, and looked around.

They had moved to the western edge of the rainforest, where the canopy thinned and the sound of animal chatter, bird talk, was muffled and distant. That meant they'd walked a good ten miles that he had no memory of walking. If they kept walking, they'd eventually make their way to one of the outlying towns where Teachers often took their rest leave. It was land not made available for prison work. He hoped they didn't end up there.

Or maybe he would end up there alone, because he didn't see Brendan anywhere.

Part of him thought that it would be as good a time as any to leave. He could walk back to the city zone. Find Jaguar. Tell Paul what happened. Get some help.

Another part of him didn't want to leave Brendan alone. He had to know what the plan was. There wasn't anyone else to know. Somebody had to stay and figure this out, and if the stone wasn't pushing him into a land of insanity, if he could avoid touching them, he still could do this. If he could find Brendan.

"Brendan?" he asked.

"Right behind you, idiot," Brendan said.

Alex jerked around and saw that Brendan stood at his back.

"Why are we here?" Alex asked.

Brendan chuckled. "Is that a metaphysical question?"

"No. Purely practical." He squinted past the glare that the sun cast on Brendan's glasses. "I want to know what we're going to do next."

Brendan nodded. "I told you. We're here to work for The Mother."

"But what does she want you to do?"

"Save her," he said.

"How?" Alex asked pointedly.

Brendan gazed down at the ground, bent over and picked up the stone Alex had pushed away. He held it in one hand, and put his other hand in his pocket and lifted out a plastic container about the size of a water bottle filled with clear liquid. Alex thought he was going to open it and drink from it, but instead he lifted it high, so that the golden rays of the sun filtered through it and cast rainbows on the earth at his feet.

"She said give them this."

"What is it?" he asked.

Brendan lowered the bottle. "The Mother is coming back to live here before she makes her way back home."

Alex took a moment and let the words sink in. "The Mother is coming to the Planetoid first?" he asked.

"Yes. I have to get it ready for her." He regarded Alex quizzically. "I told you that before, didn't I?"

"I forgot. Is that why you haven't killed yourself yet?"

He nodded. He rolled the bottle around in his hands and sighed as if he was very tired. "I'm to distribute this to the people."

"How?"

"I don't know yet. The Mother will tell me."

"When?" Alex asked.

"When I'm told."

"How does she tell you things?" Alex asked.

Brendan tapped his finger against his skull. "She speaks to me. Here."

Alex struggled with a thought, then formed words around it. "What are the stones for?"

The motion of Brendan's hands stopped. He held the stone in front of Alex's face. Alex jerked back but Brendan moved forward, pressing the stone against his face.

"They're her body. Can't you feel her in them?"

Alex tried to respond and found he couldn't because his head was filled with words that flowed on and on inside him.

She's the only one after all, the only one who knows what's right, not sex or love not babies or food or compassion or healing or love or love. This one is asking for death.

Alex closed his eyes. Words filled his brain, some of them his own.

Death? She wants death?

A high-pitched hum filled the inside of his head, somewhere between bone and the thin membrane that protected his brain from invasion.

Death. Like the woman on the bridge. And you know how, you know who you know who you should kill first. You will kill her.

Kill her? Kill who?

Jaguar. Kill Jaguar. You will kill her, for the Mother. For yourself. To save her. To save her.

Sound reverberated inside the cavity of his skull and he felt it as a weight, substantial as stone. Brendan tossed the bottle of poison high into the air and Alex felt his hand shoot up, felt it land solid in his hand like water-weighted stone and as it hit he fell into Brendan's left eye, himself a stone weighted with water, unable to swim, unable to see, unable to care about either anymore.

The Sanctuary Animal Patrol received word that the jaguars were loose at just the wrong time. Mid-afternoon, on a Saturday, when the most people were out viewing the animals. With their children.

"Shit," Allen Dolpern said. "Suit up. We're going. Got a truck?"

"Getting it," Susan replied, and moved toward the garage, grabbing her suit on the way.

In the garage, a truck was waiting, but Susan was surprised to see someone standing next to it, already suited up. Under the protective head-gear, she could see a fluff of what looked like blue hair. She wondered vaguely who it was.

"Hey," she said. "How'd you get ready so fast?"

"I'm a boy scout," a voice replied. "Always prepared."

Susan shrugged, turned and opened the van door. She barely felt the prick of a needle engaging with the muscles of her backsides. All she knew was that suddenly she felt quite light. Light enough to float away. And even if she was falling, that was fine, because she would simply drift up to a place of quiet, and float there for as long as she wanted to.

"Night night," Pinkie said, catching her as she fell. She pulled her head-gear off, stuck her fingers in her mouth and whistled. Gerry and Jaguar, suited, walked over.

"In," Jaguar said to Pinkie. "I'll take care of the supervisors."

Gerry and Pinkie gunned the motor, and Jaguar stuck her head in the door.

"Hey," she said to the supervisor. "We're rolling. I'll call in when we get there."

"Oh—sure. I didn't know you had the others."

"I'm fast," Jaguar said. "Fast and easy. You heard that about me, didn't you?"

They moved the van out, and made it to the sanctuary in good and easy time.

A woman screamed.

A child screamed.

A man swore.

A black jaguar, panthera onca, flung itself against the fencing between breeding complex and Zoo, claws catching in the metal edge as he pulled himself up and over. People scattered like coins tossed on the street as the white van pulled up, and three animal control workers got out, suited for action.

Panthera onca ignored them, and ran his paces into the heart of the Sanctuary.

"Get 'em out of here," Jaguar said to the security guard. "We'll take it."

Jaguar nodded at Gerry and Pinkie, and they followed the big cat, who led them directly to the fencing that backed onto the normal house area.

Jaguar pointed to the van, and they returned for it, drove it through the walkways.

"Hey," the security guard said. "You can't bring that back there. That's secure."

"Tell it to the cat," Pinkie said, sticking her head out the window.

The security guard scratched his head and moved his hand toward his belt sensor, but was interrupted by the sound of a low growl behind him.

Jaguar stifled a chuckle. She turned to Rachel, who sat in the back of the van, head bent over her computer. She was dismantling the security system.

"Got it?" Jaguar asked.

Rachel shook her head. Held up a finger. Jaguar waited.

"Now," she said. "Got it." She raised her head. "So go. We've only got five minutes before it reverts.

Jaguar got out of the van and held a hand up to the security guard, whose face was quite pale. "Try not to pass out," she said. "Remember, they're opportunistic hunters."

His legs began to shake visibly. Jaguar moved forward two steps. Waved a hand at the van. "Go," she said. "Find the other one."

The security guard, who imagined he could feel hot breath at his ankles, didn't argue.

A few dozen feet away, another security guard held back a group of spectators.

"Cool," someone said.

"Jam tight," someone else agreed.

Jaguar approached Chaos. "Here, kitty kitty," she cooed. The guard stood and shook.

"Move one step to the side," Jaguar advised him. "Very small step. Very slow movement."

The guard did so.

She walked to his right, and the guard would later say he swore she started singing. Using words he didn't know. A tune he'd never heard. But dammit, she was singing, and that damn cat turned right away from him and toward her.

It prowled, he said, just like a housecat. Real low to the ground. Ready to leap but she just stood there singing.

Not an eye moved off the scene, as the van pulled around behind the fencing. Inside the van, Rachel spoke. "Seven," she said, pointing ahead. "Move. You've got four minutes."

Outside, Chaos leaped and Jaguar let herself fall under him, shouting at the guard, "Don't shoot. Don't raise a weapon. He'll go for you."

And she continued to sing while the crowd gasped and the van rolled up to normal house 7. Two people in animal control suits knocked on the door, and Peter, the Teacher who now had Fiore's assignment, opened it.

"Come on," Rachel muttered at Pinkie and Gerry's back. "No time for small talk."

The teacher was talking to them, friendly, easy, asking about the escaped cat. Gerry was talking back, friendly, easy. Then Pinkie made a small, quick movement and the teacher slumped onto Gerry's chest.

The two dragged him inside.

But nobody noticed because all eyes were glued to Chaos, who had both his paws on Jaguar's shoulders. He held her down and growled, breath hot in her face, mouth large enough to engulf her face as she lay still, singing.

And inside normal house 7 Fiore crouched in a corner in the kitchen. Gerry picked her up, slung her over his shoulder where she began to beat on his back and scream.

"Christ," he groaned. "You got another one of those needles, Pinkie?"

She did, and she used it. Fiore was loaded in the van, covered with blankets, and they drove out of the normal house area. Rachel lifted a tense face to Pinkie. "Half a minute to spare on the five," she said.

And they rolled back to the sanctuary area as Chaos lowered his open mouth over Jaguar's face, brought his tongue out, and licked her.

The crowd was still, trying to interpret this gesture.

He licked her again, and she reached up, scratched the front of his head, pulling a panther-sized purr from the base of his throat.

"Aw," someone said. "That's so *cute*."

Jaguar pulled herself out from under him and stood, singing as she led him, like the Pied Piper, through the Sanctuary, back to the breeding complex.

"When the van arrives, can you tell them where I've gone?" she requested as she passed the guard who watched the crowd.

"Um—yeah. No problem."

The crowd watched her leave, waited until the breeding complex gates were shut, then cheered mightily. They were still cheering and clapping when the white van pulled in.

"The other one's still in the cage," Gerry said, out the window.

"Yeah. Great. Your friend took care of the big guy." He pointed. "Breeding complex."

"Thanks," Gerry said. And they rolled away.

Fiore regained consciousness before they reached the shuttle station. When they got out of the van, Jaguar held her eyes hard for a minute.

She didn't fight. Didn't want to.

"You're coming with me," Jaguar said. She nodded.

Then, she turned to Rachel. "I'm all set for the shuttle?"

"I recoded the retinal scan to pass for you and Fiore. Passes here," She handed over two cards. Jaguar pocketed them.

"Thanks. Look," she said, "I don't know what'll happen, or if I'll be able to contact you for awhile."

"I know. Just—be careful." Stupid to say that, she knew, but someone had to.

Jaguar nodded.

"Okay," Rachel said. "Jaguar—you know you'll be *persona non gratis* after this. If you show your face, you'll be taken in."

"Paul's gonna have diarrhea of the cerebral cortex over it, I'm sure."

"Should I call him or something? Try to explain?"

Jaguar considered this. She supposed it would be courteous. But hadn't he said he didn't want to know what she was doing? Had he ever wanted to know what she was doing?

"No," she said. "Either he gets it, or he doesn't. If he gets it, he'll figure his own way of dealing. If he doesn't—well, the less he knows, the better."

She reached over and squeezed Rachel's shoulder. "Gotta go," she said. "Be good."

She took Fiore's arm and led her out of the van, toward the shuttle that would take them on the next leg of their long journey.

CHAPTER THIRTEEN

Pasquale looked perfectly at home in Larry Barone's penthouse living room. His massive shoulders and head were not out of place among the portraits of men, ancestors of Barone, that hung on the wall. And his large hands held the fine china as carefully as if they were tying ribbons in a little girl's hair.

He'd been here before, quite a few times, and always found the business as good as the food he was offered. Today, he thought, would be even better.

"I told you," Pasquale said to Larry, "I don't do take out. And I can't recommend anyone who does. You're on your own."

Larry, who looked as if he hadn't been sleeping well lately, stopped stirring his tea. "How do you know that's what I want?" he asked.

"I can smell it on you," Pasquale said. He lifted his head half an inch and breathed in through his nostrils. "Smells like fear."

Larry felt a muscle in his arm jerk, as if he was about to defend himself. Pasquale always knew too much, and said too much about it. "You don't make any exceptions?"

"No," Pasquale said. He sipped at his tea and leaned back in his chair. "This is nice," he said. "What kind is it?"

"Green tea mixed with jasmine. My own blend."

"Nice," Pasquale repeated.

"What if," Larry said, speaking carefully, choosing his words, "what if you had compelling reasons of your own?"

"To off someone? I never found any yet."

"Self-defense?" Larry suggested.

"That's not killing. That's—self-defense."

"But you have had reason to use it, haven't you?"

"Once or twice."

"Self protection?"

"Same thing, isn't it?"

"What about protecting your client?"

Pasquale put his tea cup on the table. "Say what you mean."

"Miriam has plans to kill me," Larry said grimly.

Pasquale chuckled. "You sure? Maybe it's just a little communication trouble."

Larry grimaced. "I know her. She wants it all, and that's her plan."

"Yeah. But I'll bet she wants to marry you first."

"So?"

"So, don't marry her. Then she won't kill you."

"It's not that simple," Larry said, his jaw tight and his teeth clenched. "For all I know, she plans to kill me as soon as the Hague repeal comes through and I've got my—"

Larry shut his mouth. He hadn't meant to say any of that to Pasquale, who should know as little as possible. Though from the way Pasquale's silent eyes looked at him, Larry imagined he already knew it.

"Skip it," Pasquale said, and his eyes expressed disgust for Larry, who couldn't even come up with a good story to buy a hit. He leaned across the coffee table and tapped a broad finger against Larry's knee. "I tell you what. It's your woman. Why don't you kill her?—in self defense, of course."

Larry retreated from Pasquale's gesture. "I'll give you five times to your usual rates," he said.

Pasquale picked up his tea cup and stirred it, a meaningless motion, meant only to buy him time for thought. He sipped at it, stared at the ceiling, then put the cup back down.

"I'll have to go the Planetoid," he said. "Take care of it there."

"I can arrange—"

"I make my own arrangements," Pasquale cut in. "But I want you there. If I'm protecting my client, client's gotta be there, right?"

Larry shifted in his seat. He had no plans to visit the Planetoid until after their plans were complete, which should be within the week. Certainly he didn't want to be there when it happened, though Miriam said she would be. It would look better, she said, and she knew how to protect herself.

Of course, if he was there, perhaps to meet with governors like Shafritz who still supported the idea of a processing plant, and the timing was right, then it could seem like Miriam died in the general chaos, which would be good. And he'd be on hand to survey the damage, take a hand immediately in what happened next.

But the timing was crucial. She had to instruct Brendan to complete his task before she died, and she shouldn't be around too much after that. He could get enough support from Shafritz and Malor for the plant, and he didn't want her taking over at such an early stage.

"Tricky timing," Pasquale echoed his thoughts, keeping his observant gaze on Larry. "And the other players involved—they're not so easy to get around."

"Other players?" Larry asked. "I don't know what you mean."

"Sure you do. Dzarny and Addams. What about them? I hear she's especially tricky, though he's no slouch either. Just not as flashy."

"Miriam's taking care of Dzarny, and Addams is out of the way for now."

"And you're counting on that?"

"Are you offering to take care of them, too?" Larry shot back. He was tired of being interrogated as if he was a novice at hard ball.

"Only," Pasquale said, "if it's in self-defense. Or in defense of my client, of course."

Larry paused. That might be good. A back-up plan. Yes. But Pasquale was talking again.

"Of course, that sort of thing can be arranged, but it ain't easy. And sniffing through all that shit Miriam's got ain't easy. You're screwing yourself with that moondust, you know that?"

Larry found himself once again irritated with Pasquale's arrogance. "What we do to screw ourselves pays you, Pasquale. I wouldn't complain if I was you."

"I'm not complaining. Just telling you. It means extra work for me. Take more thought and involve more risk."

So that was it. Pasquale could squeeze hell out of a job, always accepting the usual rates, then adding expenses from here to the poor house. "Then maybe a bonus would compensate you for your trouble," he suggested. "Ten percent?"

Pasquale rubbed thoughtfully at his rock-like jaw, and the muscles of his thick face manipulated the possibilities. "I think that five times the normal rate should be ten times. And I think I should get half up front, half right before the job's done."

Larry swallowed hard. "That's a little steep, isn't it?"

"What's the return you expect? Maybe you'll walk away with a Plane-toid?"

At that, Larry felt himself smiling. When he was focused on completing a job, or a sale, he didn't allow himself the luxury of fantasizing about the rewards of success. But to hear it said like that felt better than anything he'd ever known. He was out to own a Planetoid. A whole world to do with what he wanted. It was like being God.

"Ten times," Larry said, "Half up front, and half after completion. Expenses in between."

"Good enough," Pasquale said. He pressed his broad hands onto his knees and pushed himself to standing.

"When do you want me on the Planetoid?" Larry asked.

"I'll let you know. Soon, though, so be ready. And tonight, I want you to call your old lady."

"What for?" Larry asked.

"Tell her you're worried about her. Women like it when you worry about them. Tell her you're so worried, you hired her a bodyguard." Pasquale grinned. "That would be me."

"She won't go for it. She doesn't like to be interfered with."

"She'll do it if you put it right," Pasquale said, and then made a sound of derision. "Don't you know anything about women? You soft soap her. Talk up the danger. Tell her I won't be in the way. In fact, she'll hardly see me except once so I can introduce myself. But you'll feel better just knowing I'm there. That's the truth, ain't it?"

"Okay," Larry said. "The timing—"

"Leave that to me. Like I said, I make my own arrangements."

He shook down his pant legs, jiggled his keys in his pocket, and gave Larry one last grin. "It's always a pleasure," he said, "doing business with you."

When he'd left and the door closed behind him, Larry said, "I wish I could say the same."

They were having a philosophical discussion. Alex recognized his own voice, saying words he didn't know if he believed, but saying them with conviction. His hand was stretched out in front of him, and in it was the bottle of what Brendan called poison. He stopped speaking, midsentence.

"What?" Brendan asked.

"Nothing," Alex said lamely. "Never mind." He looked around. It was dark out. The stars pierced their holes of light in a black sky. The moon hadn't risen yet, and they cast the only light he could find, either outside or inside. As he sat and thought about it, he realized he felt horrible. His skin itched, he'd give a lot of money for a toothbrush, all his muscles ached, and his belly felt weighted with sorrow, heavy and complete.

"No," Brendan said. "You were saying something important. You were talking about the Killing Times. That it was a matter of population control, and with ten million people dead, the planet had a chance to renew herself a little. Please keep going."

They were still at the edge of the rainforest, he saw. In fact, he didn't seem to have moved from the stump he'd been sitting on, so not that much time had passed since the world appeared to him last. But he had no memory of what he'd been saying, or why he'd been saying it. The Killing Times as population control? Certainly he'd heard that theory expounded, but he didn't subscribe to it. There were better ways to create zero population growth than that.

He searched the rounded out corners of his skull to see if any possible reason why he might have been talking about that appeared, but nothing did. In this moment of clarity, his one thought was that he'd better find a way to get Brendan moving forward into healing, or he'd end up a worse case than his prisoner.

He turned the bottle over in his hand. Had he agreed to help with this? He had a feeling he had. Not a surprise. It was a good strategy to use with a prisoner like Brendan. But did he mean it? And if he said it, would he actually go through with it in one of those strange dream states he kept falling into? He couldn't remember when he and Jaguar speculated about the effects of Artemis on men. A few days ago? A month? A week? They thought it would increase aggressiveness, and he supposed in a way it did. Maxxed it out. But mixed it so with passivity that it didn't look or feel like aggressiveness. It was just the inexorable surge of death. Thanatos and Eros, at odds.

Jaguar had once told him that she had a theory about men and death. She said that women face death regularly, bleeding every month, having babies at the edge of possible disaster. Facing death was built into the normalcy of their lives. But it wasn't for men, and so they chased it, looking for ways to face it down by acting badly, bravely, or foolishly. At the time, he told her she shouldn't generalize. Now, he thought maybe she hadn't. Maybe she was accurate in her assessment.

To conquer death and tell the story was maybe what all the wars were about after all. But for Brendan, the appeal was different. He wouldn't be a conqueror. He would perhaps be rescued by the mother if he was a good boy and did as he was told. Or he would merge with her in death, relinquishing all self into the void she promised him.

Alex didn't feel that, though. His urge was not for Thanatos, not for merging with the Mother. It was to save or kill or some combination of the two. Brendan was the martyr, but he was the hero. Only, he could no longer tell who was the enemy, and who was the ally. Not in any consistent way.

Brendan walked a little bit away from him and dug his toe in the dirt. "What's this place made of, anyway?"

"Dirt," Alex said. "Like earth. It's a reconfigured asteroid."

Brendan continued to dig at the dirt. He bent down and picked up a handful, put it to his tongue and then spat it out. "It doesn't taste right," he said.

Alex twisted around to look at the trees growing in back of him. "They like it," he said.

He stood and walked to Brendan, his legs a little wobbly from sitting for so long, but still holding him up. If he was going to play the hero, he should clear a few things up. For instance, whether Brendan had a communication device for the mother, or if it was empathic contact. He regarded Brendan's profile for a moment, then put a hand on his shoulder and turned him around. Brendan blinked at him, but seemed to feel no threat in the gesture. He smiled softly, sadly, as if at someone who refuses to understand. Alex reached a hand tentatively toward him, ran it over the space around him. If there was a transmitter, he should be able to feel it pulsing just below the surface of skin.

He let the air flow between his hand and the surface of Brendan's skin, feeling for the different blip that indicated technology. Nothing in his neck or head. Nothing in his arm. Nothing along his back or in his groin or his legs. Nothing, finally in his feet.

Nothing.

Which meant it was empathic communication. Or madness, because there was still the possibility that Brendan was communicating only with the inside of his own head.

Brendan stood very still, but seemed to somehow approve of what Alex did. When Alex put a hand to his forehead and their eyes locked in the beginnings of empathic contact, Brendan smiled. "You're like her, aren't you?"

"What?" Alex asked.

"The Mother. You asked how she talked to me. I think you talk the same way. I wish I could, too."

Alex took a chance and went subvocal.

How does The Mother talk to you?

"Like that," Brendan said. He smiled, pleased. "Just like that."

Alex felt a thrill run through him. Either they were dealing with an empath, or something about Artemis increased receptivity to empathic contact. Brendan wasn't one. Was The Mother?

"I want to do something," Alex said softly. "I want to talk to The Mother inside you. Will you let me do that?"

Brendan nodded. "I think she'd like you, anyway. You're here to help."

He closed his eyes, as if waiting for a kiss. Alex pressed his fingers against Brendan's face and allowed the empathic space to open between men more fully. Somewhere he heard Jaguar growling at him, telling him to back off, take care. But that wasn't how heroes were made, was it?

He would go in as far as he could, and come back out with as much information as was currently available.

As Jaguar and Fiore boarded the shuttle, she knew nothing about the shit hitting the fan with Paul Dinardo, but if she had she would have been pleased both at his distress, and his response.

Alex's replacement supervisor, Rod Galentas, called him first when the news broke that one of the Death Sisters was missing, either escaped or taken hostage when a couple of big cats broke loose at the sanctuary. Reports coming in said that a tall woman with green eyes and dark hair subdued the jaguar. Rod knew who that was.

So did Paul. And whether it was knee jerk response, or he was trying to do the right thing would never be clearly ascertained, but when Rod grimly filled him in on the news, he only smiled.

"It's part of her program, Rod," Paul said without breaking stride.

"Her what? I thought she was suspended."

"Not Addams," Paul said. "The prisoner. Another Teacher took her. It's part of her program. Weren't you informed?"

Rod deflated. He'd apparently been looking forward to a ruckus.

"No, I was not," he said sternly. He was the type of supervisor who didn't like any breach in protocol, which was probably why he hadn't fared too well on Planetoid Three, where most programs involved some breach of protocol. Paul knew he'd applied for transfer to Planetoid One, which was more conservative in its approach to Prisoner programs, and he was just waiting out his time to leave.

Paul sighed. "Well, you should have been. And so should Peter. I put the paperwork through on it."

"This is highly irregular, sir," Galentas said disapprovingly.

So will I be, before this is all over with, Paul thought. "Maybe," he suggested, "that's because of your status."

"What?"

"You're awaiting transfer into zone 12, right?"

Galentas nodded. "But what's that—"

"The situation is highly classified. I guess you and Peter would automatically be booted from the information loop on it. He doesn't have the right code classification, and you're not really part of the system if you're not officially transferred in. Not as far as the computer's concerned."

"Classified?" Rod asked, his back stiffening. He did believe in this kind of protocol. "I wasn't informed—"

"Yeah, well I'm informing you now. That prisoner has classified information, and the feds need her. And you're to keep this quiet, Galentas. Understood?"

"Of course, sir," Rod said. "Of course. As long as you're sure it's all right."

"Yeah," Paul lied. "I'm sure."

CHAPTER FOURTEEN

Rachel had arranged for a car to be ready for Jaguar and Fiore at the home planet shuttle station. Fiore remained silent in the shuttle, in the car, all through the drive that took them to the bird sanctuary where they'd be doing their first round of work.

She didn't seem afraid. Didn't seem anything. Perhaps patient. She sat, treelike, and looked ahead. Sometimes, she twisted her neck to peer out to window, up at the night sky.

Jaguar set up rough camp about a mile into the woods, and waited until the moon rose. Then she led Fiore deeper into the woods they occupied. When they were well out of sight of the others, she stopped and gave her a throwing knife.

"See," she said, demonstrating how it could be balanced on the edge of a finger. Then, with a flick of her wrist, she sent it flying into the bark of a tree. She retrieved it, and handed it to Fiore.

Fiore held the knife as if it was precious, balancing it as Jaguar had done, caressing the edge of it. She lifted it to the moon, watching the light play against the metal, then brought it to her lips. Jaguar saw the tip of her tongue flick out to taste it. Then, sighing with profound pleasure, she brought her arm back and tried a throw.

The knife turned end over end and landed true, with its point piercing a tree.

"Good," Jaguar said, watching as a broad grin formed on Fiore's face. "Now catch me supper."

Fiore walked over to the tree, pulled out the knife, and then dropped to her knees. Jaguar observed the way she sniffed at the loamy earth, her fingers moving just behind her face to touch what she had just smelled. She trailed after her, staying within her shadow as she made her way sniffing into the forest.

When she stopped, Jaguar stopped and watched as her hand folded in a satisfied way over something on the ground. She squinted at it, brought it close to her nose and inhaled, then smoothed it over her cheek, leaving a dark smear from the edge of her eye to her jawline.

"Deer?" Jaguar whispered.

Fiore dropped the spoor, grunted in the affirmative, and stood. She began running, low to the ground, her movements silent and sure. Jaguar followed, and in a sheltered spot beneath a grouping of trees, they saw the deer, nested down for the night. As they moved closer, a buck lifted his head and gave warning to the others. They clamored into wakefulness, scattering through the trees, and Fiore pinpointed the slowest.

She pulled her arm back and let the knife fly, her aim as sure as her steps had been. It pierced the neck of the deer, who stumbled, stood, took a step forward, stumbled again, and finally fell as blood poured out of its artery.

The women waited as the deer's legs jerked spasmodically, kicking at the ground. When all movement ceased Fiore walked over and pulled the knife out, brought it to her lips and licked at the blood which covered it.

Jaguar pushed Fiore's face into the deer's. "Breathe," she said. "Breathe and say thank you."

She heard Fiore's breath moving with the last breaths of the deer, and then she said, "Now take the heart. It's yours."

There was a moment of hesitation, but only a moment, before Fiore cut through to that organ, pulled it from the chest cavity and held it up, steaming, and still pulsing weakly, moonlight and blood pouring down her wrists and arm.

"Go ahead," Jaguar whispered. "It's yours. And you're hungry for it, aren't you?"

Fiore brought the heart to her lips, and held it there, suspended. Then she bit into it, teeth working hard against muscle, the red splashing her face and running over her breasts.

Jaguar rocked back on her haunches and sang a wordless melody, watching the movements of death around her. She heard Fiore's feast, gruntings and slurpings and small laughter in the darkness. Then, it all stopped. Silence, and an absence of motion surrounded them.

Jaguar stopped singing. Fiore was staring at her hands, catching the rich scent of blood and shit. Now she saw what she wanted. Now she saw herself.

Jaguar scrambled to her side and wrapped her hands over Fiore's face, finding her way in.

See who you are. Be what you see.

And Fiore relaxed into her hand, not resisting the sensation of Jaguar moving through her memories, her experiences, her fears and hopes.

Jaguar started with surface material. Recent memories of daily events. But all she found here was what she already knew. The pleasure Fiore took in the sweat lodge, in the fiery stones. Jaguar pushed further, going back in time to when Fiore was trying to get pregnant, the time of frustrated desire. She saw Fiore's face, hot with rage and grief and the tears that expressed them. Fiore, slamming a hand down on the doctor's desk, screeching at him to do something for her do something dammit. The doctor looking at her hesitantly, telling her there is one thing. Experimental. But he knew someone who might be able to help.

Fiore, walking, head bent low, toward a lab that had the sign La Femme on the door. The research labs of La Femme. Fiore being told the vitamin she was receiving wasn't a fertility drug. Just a way of increasing her health so that she might get pregnant. And Karena at the lab, taking different vitamins for different reasons.

Fiore, not telling her husband or anyone about this, but taking her vitamins. Fiore, asking questions and being told the vitamins formula couldn't be disclosed. Fiore discovering her pregnancy. Fiore one day looking into the mind of the researcher who took data from her, and Fiore, one day tracking a truck from La Femme to the place it got the vitamins, her curiosity and capacity for tracking leading her to—to a crystallization plant. Fiore, standing and looking at the plant. Clutching her rounding belly under a rounding moon.

Realization dawned on Jaguar. Fiore knew what she was taking, and she continued to take it. More importantly, she knew where the plant was. Probably knew who ran it.

Where is it? Show me.

Fiore struggled under her hand, and her clear response came back to Jaguar.

No. I will not.

There. Jaguar was not surprised. Fiore was an empath. A real one, not

Artemis-induced. An empath and pyrokinetic and a hunter. And she didn't want to be any of those things.

Why didn't you stop taking the compound once you knew?

I wanted—a baby.

And Karena? Did she want a baby?

She wanted money. We were paid well for our time. Terez didn't know. Her husband gave it to her to make her want sex more. He worked at the plant.

Stupid. They bought the lie. Fearing themselves, they thought they could make themselves over in the right image, if only they had the right chemicals. She spoke harshly into Fiore, telling her the truth.

Fiore, you're an empath. A hunter and pyrokinetic with it. You'll never be anything else without twisting yourself into little bits. Artemis won't change that. Won't make you a normal woman with a baby and a husband and a house.

Jaguar placed an image in Fiore's mind, of the moon sailing weightlessly over curtains of clouds.

Look at her. She's powerful, but she'll only tell you the truth. The only power you get from the moon is the power you already own, and that's what terrifies you most, isn't it? Your own power. That's why you were so willing to give it away to a little pill.

Fiore scuttled back on her haunches, trying to escape these words, but Jaguar wouldn't let her. She lunged, pressed Fiore hard into the ground, feeling the fire that lingered behind her eyes.

Fiore struggled, then ceased struggling, a hiss of air escaping her lips as her eyes became heated stones, eyes of the earth.

And under this well-hidden fire, she was earthy, her hair the screaming grass of a forest where animals foraged and slept and fucked and were born and died and were eaten, so that the bones would dissolve and feed the trees and grasses that were her hair.

Fiore's voice whispered to Jaguar in this place.

It will kill me.

Jaguar laughed. She thought of Kali dancing while thousands died. A woman breathing while thousands were born. Fiore was ancient. Her wisdom was the raw knowledge of life and death. She contained fire, which contained both, and she'd have to learn how to own that. Direct it. Stop fearing who she was. Slowly she let the knowledge take hold, let it seep like moonlight into the deepest places. Then she dropped her hand.

She waited until Fiore opened her eyes and sat up. Her breathing was ragged and the corner of her mouth twitched. She dug in the earth with her hand, brought earth to her mouth and ate.

"Hecate," Jaguar said sharply, and prepared to slap her on the back, but Fiore grasped her wrist and stopped her. Jaguar looked at the hand that held her, felt the heat of it, and the intense strength. She relaxed, and Fiore released her hold.

"Okay," she said. "It's all yours."

Fiore stood, pointed her body east, and ran. Jaguar pulled in breath and ran behind her, working to keep up. The moon poured light down, and they ran through it, under it, until woods gave way to road. And Fiore kept running.

Jaguar wasn't sure how long they kept this up. She was in good shape, and a fairly good runner, but her limit was an hour. When she began to feel defeated by her legs, she figured they'd passed her limit. Fiore kept running, and Jaguar followed. She tried not to think about how much ground they were covering, for fear the thought would stop her from continuing to cover it. She just ran, let her feet pound earth, let her heart and lungs do their job, kept Fiore in her sights.

The road turned toward a gravel path, and here, at last, Fiore stopped. Jaguar, her legs weak and her breath short, stopped behind her and waited. Fiore looked left, and right, then walked forward on the path. Jaguar followed.

After what Jaguar thought might be another mile, Fiore stopped, raised her face and sniffed the air, then made a sound like growling. Jaguar followed her gaze toward a long low building a few hundred yards away.

There were lights on behind the windows, vehicles in the lot. Fiore walked forward.

"Wait," Jaguar said, catching up to her, grabbing her arm. "Wait. Is this the plant?"

Fiore nodded.

"I'll call it in," Jaguar said. "This is all we need. Proof. Evidence."

Fiore stared at her. The spirits of the night blazed at the back of her eyes.

"Fiore," Jaguar said sharply. "No."

Fiore held up a fiery hand, and Jaguar clutched it at the wrist.

No. Not this. Not here. Not now.

But heat surrounded them, and fire bit at her face, her hair. Fiore shoved hard and pushed Jaguar to the ground and ran toward the building.

No time to think. Jaguar rose and ran after Fiore, knowing she had no weapon, no defense except to kill Fiore, and she wasn't willing to do that. She'd mistakenly killed one prisoner already.

Fiore was standing at the plant door, hand raised, and Jaguar could see the outline of fire in her thoughts. Jaguar's only thought was to tackle her, but before she could move a man appeared from the side of the building and moved toward her.

"Hell," Jaguar said. "Hell no."

Jaguar dove for his knees. He lost his balance and went down over Fiore and she, undeterred, scrambled out from under him, ran to the door and pressed her fiery hand against it.

"Uh-oh," Jaguar said. She turned and rolled into the bushes as the sound of fire engulfed her, as fire in a great rolling sphere engulfed the building, and thunder boomed out across the sky.

When Jaguar rose from the bushes, it was to see the man dragging Fiore by the left arm across the parking lot, illuminated by the wall of fire the building had become. She didn't wait for him to get to her, but strode out to meet him, landing a punch hard on his jaw as soon as she was close enough.

His head snapped back, and he rubbed at his chin while he regarded her. "What the hell was that for?"

"You attacked her. You attacked my prisoner."

"I was trying to stop her."

"Well, who the hell told you to do that?" Jaguar demanded.

Pasquale held a hand out, palm up. "Could we maybe discuss this somewhere else? We're not gonna be alone very long."

Jaguar knelt down to Fiore. "She's not dead, is she?"

"Don't think so. Burned bad, though. It's a shame. She's good."

Jaguar looked up at him. "How do you know?"

"I been watching the two of you. In the woods. She could be trained for tracking."

Jaguar pushed herself to standing. "She doesn't need training. She needs a doctor. We have to get her to a hospital."

"She's going nowhere."

"She's coming with us."

"No."

Jaguar looked up at him, about to ask him who the hell he was, and then she saw.

A boulder on top of a mountain, and a great head of golden hair. A small black and gold ring on his pinkie finger.

"Shit," she said. "Golden Retriever."

"That's right," he agreed, " And I understand you want my services in a big way. Which means you do what I say."

Jaguar fought with herself for a moment. She needed him. She hated needing people. It left you with so few options.

"Anyway, you're not thinking straight," Pasquale continued. "She'll get to an ambulance quicker if we leave her here."

The sound of sirens in the distance told Jaguar he was right. Dammit, she thought. She'd found out nothing useful, and all evidence would be destroyed in the fire. If she brought Fiore, she might be able to get her to talk. But she might not survive rough and fast travel, and she probably needed a doctor faster than Jaguar could get her to one.

Pasquale was right.

"Let's get out of here," she said.

Pasquale gave her a small bow. "My wings are just around the bend."

Jaguar made herself as relaxed as possible for two of her least favorite activities—flying, and flying when someone else was in charge. They kept low and not too fast so Pasquale could scan the road for an open bar. Jaguar wanted a drink, and she wanted to talk while not in motion. She needed to concentrate with this man, she thought.

They entered and Jaguar looked around. Noted that the only other people present had very few teeth and wore flannel. That felt safe. When Pasquale went to the bar and then returned to the table with her two shots of tequila and a pack of cigarettes, she felt even safer.

He plunked them both in front of her, with lime and a shaker of salt, and sat down across from her to watch the proceedings. Jaguar stared at the sticky table top, picked up the salt and cupped the lime between thumb and index finger.

The first shot felt good.

The second one felt better.

Pasquale shook his head. "You out to do some damage?"

She shook her head hard as the burning coursed its way down her throat, and rasped back at him, "I already did some damage. I'm out to stop feeling it."

She wiped the back of her hand against her mouth, shook her head again, and opened the pack of cigarettes, and lit one. This wasn't the kind of place where anyone would call the cops for illegal smoking.

Pasquale lifted his glass of beer and took a sip. He lounged back in his chair, leisurely, relaxed. "That's bad for you. Smoking."

"My life is bad for me," she said.

Pasquale shook his head. "You hurt?"

Jaguar took a deep pull on the cigarette, felt the nicotine course through her, making her dizzy. She didn't smoke often enough, she decided. "My left leg is killing me," she noted, "and there's something going on in my ribs I'd rather not think about. How do I look?"

Pasquale chuckled. "You know how you look. You look like a really good meal."

"Yeah," she said, "well, don't get too hungry."

"Not me," he said. "My grandmother taught me better than that."

She narrowed her eyes at him. "What?"

He turned his glass around and around, lifted a hand philosophically and let it drop again. "My grandmother made homemade pasta," he said. "From the time I was a little boy, I ate good homemade pasta. It was great, except that now, I can't eat the crap that comes in boxes."

Jaguar felt hot anger rise from the back of her neck. "What's that mean?" she hissed.

He grinned. "I won't try food that'll spoil me for what's available on a regular basis. I hear that's you."

"Oh," she said, anger receding. She supposed it was a compliment. "Well, at any rate, this is business. That's all. Remember that."

"From what I here, that only encourages you."

She startled, flicked ash onto the floor. "What do you know about it?"

Pasquale shrugged his mountain shoulders. "When I take on a job, I find out everything. So I know everything about you."

"Then," she said, "you know what the job is, don't you?"

"Yeah," he said. "I know. You're looking for Alex Dzarny. And I owe a friend of yours, so if it all checks out, I'll find him for you."

"What's to check out?"

"How come you're doing this."

"I thought you were a mercenary. What do you care why I'm doing this?"

"On this job, I'm not a mercenary. I'm paying a debt. That means I get to ask. So why are you doing this?"

"If you know everything else, then you should know that," she said.

Pasquale shook his head. "I know he's gone with a man named Brendan Farley. I know about the moon mining and that you want to stop it. I know about that plant you blew up tonight. I wanna know why *you* would do this for *him*," he said, punctuating the words with his finger.

"Because I need him to stop the moon mining," she said.

"Bullshit."

Jaguar lifted her glass, saw it was empty, and licked the bottom of it. Then she put it down on the table, hard. She didn't take offense at what he said. He was right, and she didn't blame him for calling her on it.

"Because," she said, "he'd do it for me."

"You think?"

"I know."

Pasquale considered her, and nodded as if concluding a conversation in his own head. "You're not telling me all of it, but that's enough. How do you know he's still alive?" he asked next.

"If he was dead, I'd know it."

"How?"

"How do you know things?"

Pasquale chuckled lightly and considered her some more, turning his glass around and around. He lifted his head and sniffed the air around her. "You smell like mint," he said.

"I know," she said.

"Mint, and—" he lifted his mouth in a grin. "You know what you smell like, don't you?" he asked.

"Look," she said, "I'm not the one you're supposed to sniff. Can you find him?"

"Does he want to be found?"

"No," she said honestly. "In fact, I think he's hiding."

"From what?"

"Me."

"Why?"

"So he won't kill me."

Pasquale looked at her keenly. "He's good at hiding?" he asked.

Jaguar nodded. "Among the best."

"Then I'll need something from him."

"What?"

"Something important to him. Something he holds in his mind that he can't hide from. Something that stays with him, regardless."

Jaguar dropped her cigarette on the floor, ground it out with her foot. "I don't have anything like that here."

"That's okay. He ain't here anyway."

"Not on the home planet? You know that?"

"I know that. I checked it out."

Jaguar leaned back in her chair. "How much?" she asked.

"What?"

"How much do you want from me? What'll you try to soak me for? What's your game?"

"What the hell are you talking about?"

"I'm talking about your game, you arrogant son of a bitch. Just like that, you checked out the whole goddamn world and you know he's not here, but you need something to find him. You sell snake oil on the side?"

Pasquale smoothed his lower lip with his tongue, lifted his glass and drained the contents down his throat. He carefully placed it away from him on the table, and swiftly, easily for a man his size, reached across the table and pressed the blade of a knife against her throat.

She hadn't seen it coming. She sat very still, staring at his hand, with the small, unlikely ring on his pinkie. It was intricately carved, she noted, with a circle of leaves and the face of an animal with two pieces of ebony for eyes.

"I don't like insults," he said, smiling. Anyone watching would think he was caressing her, from the way his hand moved, the knife cupped hidden within it. She knew this move. She'd done it herself more than once.

"I don't like assaults," she replied, flicking her knife out from her wrist, letting her hand stay still on the table, lifting her eyes from his knife and ring to his face and holding him in a steady stare.

"Don't try that on me," he said, still smiling. "I know about empaths, and I know what to do about them, too."

She felt the blade against her flesh and figured her odds. She'd beaten worse, she thought. "Maybe," she said.

He ran the edge of the blade against her skin, and with his other hand smoothed her hair back from her face. He chuckled again. "Now who's being arrogant?" He asked, and retreated into his seat, the knife disappearing. "If I was looking for money, I wouldn't be trying to get it from a Planetoid Teacher. I know what they pay you. Ever think of that?"

She shrugged, and stayed silent.

"Ever think it's a little easier to find where someone *isn't* than to find where they *are*, especially if they don't want to be found?"

She shrugged again.

"You're not gonna trust me, are you?"

"Not even a little bit," she replied crisply.

"Tell you what, then," he said. "Let's say you go ahead and not trust me, and I'll go ahead and do my job—which I'm doing because I owe someone a debt of honor. That's important in my family. That work for you?"

Jaguar relaxed. She pressed the button that retracted her own knife. "It'll do. You got a shuttle pass?" she asked.

"A few."

"Ever been to the Planetoids?"

"Once or twice. Never as a prisoner. And I plan on keeping it that way."

"Suits me," she said. "Just fine."

CHAPTER FIFTEEN

Barone heard about the fire in the plant in Connecticut over the news, which called the building an abandoned government facility. It was completely destroyed. The charred remains of three people were found inside. They were believed to be homeless people who had found shelter there. He listened to the complete report, and then put a call in to Miriam, who appeared on her end of the telecom looking calm and collected.

"You heard?" he asked.

"Yes," she said. "Interesting, isn't it, the way our enemies can work for us when they're trying their best to do us in."

"What does that mean?" Larry asked.

"I was just wondering what to do with the old place," she said, "and how to make sure the workers weren't indiscreet."

He felt a twitch in his groin, reminding him of why he'd started working with her on this in the first place. Millions of dollars in loss, not to mention all the information stored on the computers which they'd have to slowly retrace from whatever they could salvage, and she bypassed all that to move directly into the advantages the situation presented.

"Good save, Miriam," he said, "Unless—is it possible you arranged the whole thing yourself?"

She laughed lightly. "You do know how to compliment a girl, Larry. Was that your only concern?"

He leaned back in his chair and thought a minute. "How are the plans moving along?"

"All in the pocket, sweetness. And ready to go."

He shook his head slowly back and forth. "What about Dzarny?"

"Him, too."

"Are you sure?"

"Very. And Addams."

For once, he believed her. She spoke with a great deal of conviction, for one thing. For another, he knew what had happened with both Addams and Dzarny in the last few days. He certainly didn't rely only on her for information.

Now he turned a serious and concerned aspect her way. "Miriam, I'm worried—not for our plans. For your safety. Listen," he said, leaning in more closely, more intimately, "I did something today. For you."

Her face softened and she lifted a fluttery hand to her collar, adjusting it. "You did? What, dearest?"

"I hired a bodyguard."

The softness turned to consternation, and looked like moving over into petulance, but Larry kept going. "He's the best, and I don't care how much he costs, you're worth it. He'll be up there in the next few days."

"Larry, I don't really want anyone hanging around—"

"Oh, he's very discreet. You won't even know he's there. He only wants one meeting with you, just to make sure you know what he looks like and so he can find out more about you. Honestly, darling. I think it's the only way for me to feel secure about you."

"If you insist," Miriam said, trying not to sound cold. She had obviously expected diamonds, or a house or maybe a yacht. Or, knowing Miriam, a small country. But she wasn't fighting it either, and that was good. Larry smiled.

"I do," he said. "I really really do."

She leaned away from the screen, and he felt as if he could breathe again, realized he hadn't been breathing throughout. This was tricky business. "I'll be on the Planetoid tomorrow, and I know we can't meet, but if you can sneak away, I'll be at the Governor's Inn on Yonge and Vine."

"You're coming to the Planetoid? Is that a good idea?"

"Shafritz requested a meeting. Everyone knows I'm vying for a processing plant there, so it would seem strange if I refused."

Miriam shook her head. "Just be careful," she said. "We're almost there. And Dzarny is secure, so don't mess with the program."

"I wouldn't dream of it," Larry said. "Not at all."

On the inside of his mind, and within all his vital emotional space, Brendan was two years old and alone. He stared out of the low window near the kitchen table, and waited for something to happen.

Nothing did. Almost wordless, almost without thought, he turned away from the window and went to the refrigerator and tried to open it, but he wasn't strong enough, so he sat down hard on the kitchen floor.

Alone was what he felt, and to him, and to Alex who felt it with him inside the cocoon of empathic space, alone felt like death. It was blank and void and without meaning. It was big and empty and too much to cry about. But he cried anyway. Usually when he cried his mommy came and helped him. He knew that without words, without reason, without thought. So he cried very loudly.

Nothing happened. The feeling of that was too big for him to handle, and too big for Alex to endure with him. Alone. Alone. Alone.

She's dead, Alex whispered into him. *She's dead and she won't come back. It's not your fault. You'll have to find someone else to be your mommy.*

Whispers moved through him, and Alex moved with them, prepared to go anywhere except here. He didn't think he could take much more of here. But they went nowhere except into the living room, where nobody lived anymore, where curtains moved in and out of open windows as if someone had lived here once. Brendan toddled over to a small table and picked up a grey crayon. A green crayon. He clutched it in his hand and went to the wall, began making swirls of grey on the wall.

Grey swirls, circles, curves, spirals. Grey filling in the white of the walls. Grey growing on the wall like blood on a rug. It pulsed and spread of its own accord, wrapping Brendan in it, wrapping Alex in it. Wrapping them both in it.

No, Alex said into him. *Don't stop here. Move on. Move on.*

This was what he'd wrapped himself in from the start. This piece of his life, static and unchanged at his core. The beginning of Thanatos. The beginning of despair, hidden deep inside him, waiting for a space and time to flower.

Brendan, it's over. Move on. Move on.

But he couldn't because the grey was a tombstone he'd laid over life too long ago to even have words to talk about it. It was a tombstone lodged inside his psyche so deep it would take the whole world dying to satisfy its prerogatives. The whole world.

But not Alex. He wasn't prepared to move that way yet.

Brendan, he suggested. *Show me The Mother. Let me hear her.*

With the same abrupt stillness of a child who stops running, the grey stopped whirling around them and was still.

Alex saw scenes shift and melt, saw time occur in events following one another swiftly and smoothly. An orphanage. A school. A college. No girls, he noticed. Never any girls.

Then an office. Quickly like smoke in mirrors, another office. Then, a white room.

Very white. Windows open. Curtains blowing in and out softly, silently. A woman in the room. He couldn't see her, but he caught the scent of her and it was familiar. Brendan stood at a white desk in the white room and opened a drawer, took out stones. Grey, smooth stones. He pocketed three, continued to hold one, and when the woman stepped close to him, he accused her with it. Held it up to her and shook it at her. She grabbed his arm and held it tight. Pulled him close and held him. Just held him.

There there, she said. *There, there. It's all right. Mother is here now. Mother is here.*

Deep peace pursued him and led him to a white couch, where he sat with her and let her hold him, rock him, hold him more. With Brendan's breath he breathed her in. And with Brendan's eyes he saw her face.

Miriam Whitehall.

Alex was so shocked he let go of Brendan, snapping the empathic contact with painful sharpness. Brendan reeled back from his hands and clutched at his head, stumbled left and right and left again.

"Jesus, I'm sorry," Alex said. He put his arms out to keep Brendan from walking into a tree and instead Brendan walked into him, leaned on his shoulder and sobbed.

Alex closed his arms around Brendan's thin back and held him. "There there," he said. "There there. It'll be okay."

CHAPTER SIXTEEN

They took public transportation to the Toronto Zoo and Animal Sanctuary, on Pasquale's advice. He said it was the last place anyone would think to look for her. Nobody would believe she'd ride an airvan back there after the prisoner disappeared. She figured he was right. She walked him through the Sanctuary, down the long path to the breeding complex, where Marie was waiting to let them in.

Marie took a look at her—a little scraped up on the face and arm, dog-tired and depressed—and shook her head. "When's the last time you ate food?" she asked, leading them inside.

Jaguar shrugged. "It's been awhile. Anything new here?"

"Nothing."

"Anything from Rachel?"

"Nothing new. She'll be here later."

"Everyone come out clean?"

"Rachel's okay. Pinkie's hiding. The Animal control people spotted her hair."

"I told her," Jaguar said. " What about Gerry?"

"They're watching him, but haven't pulled him yet."

Jaguar sighed. Not too much damage then. And, if they survived this—if they could bring it to something like a conclusion—nothing they couldn't repair.

When they entered the house, walking through the hall and into the kitchen, Pasquale looked around appreciatively.

"Nice place," Pasquale said, looking around. "Good kitchen."

"Marie likes good food," Jaguar noted. "Too bad we don't have time to enjoy it."

"We don't?"

"We don't. We've got work to do, remember? Find Alex. Now."

Pasquale shook his head. "For a woman who's not paying me anything, you sure ask for a lot. I told you I need something to track him with," he said.

Jaguar turned from him, tapped a finger thoughtfully against her lip. "Marie," she said, "can Rachel get into my place, or Alex's?"

"Gerry says they're both being watched."

"Then Alex's office. Could she get into that?"

"Sure," Marie said. "But I don't know if Galentas' cleared out Alex's stuff."

"They put Galentas in his place? I'm glad I'm suspended then. But even if he cleared stuff out, he'd have it all stored nice. Anal retentive types have their uses. Call Rachel. Tell her to bring something from his office."

"What?" Marie asked.

"Something—personal?" she turned her question to Pasquale.

"Personal," he agreed. "But not like underwear. It should mean something to him. The more he thinks about it the better."

"Okay," she said. "Okay. Tell her to look for a little clay figurine of a panther. It's painted black, and—" she paused. Naming the objects in his office did something to the inside of her chest. The thought of Galentas occupying it didn't help, either. "Tell her if she can't find the panther, look for a clay bowl with a red feather in it. She'll know. And in case anyone's listening in, come up with a reason for it, okay?"

Marie made her way to the telecom in the living room, and Pasquale seated himself contentedly at the kitchen table, where two loaves of fresh bread and a jar of homemade jam kept him busy. Marie brought out juice and slices of meat and cheese to go with them, and Pasquale and Marie talked about ways of preparing game meats like venison, ways of preparing fresh fish, the secrets of good sauce for pasta. Jaguar sat at the table and ate nothing. While they talked, she waited.

"You should eat something," Marie said to her.

"Yeah," Pasquale agreed. "This is very good food."

"Not hungry," she replied.

He leaned over and tapped her arm. She gave him her attention. "You wait too hard," he told her. "Time's gonna pass whether you're watching it or not."

He tore off a chunk of bread and handed it to her. She took it and chewed on the end, then tossed it away.

When Rachel arrived, she was still waiting hard. Pasquale was making himself a cup of coffee, showing Marie the proportions of water to caffeine that he preferred.

"Hey," Rachel said, going over to Jaguar. "You okay?"

She waved a hand noncommittally. Rachel shook her head, then looked over toward Marie and Pasquale, at the stove. "Who's he?" she asked, jerking her head toward him.

"Old friend of Gerry's. Here to help. What'd you bring from Alex?"

Rachel handed over the small panther, and Jaguar took it from her, stroked it lightly. She'd given it to him, and it sat on his desk. She smiled at it, like seeing an old friend, and then felt sorrow stab somewhere in the middle of her chest.

She was aware of Pasquale's eye on her, and thought, *I will not let him see me upset. I will not let him see me cry.*

"Don't touch it too much," he said quietly. "Here. Let me take it."

She handed it to him. "Will it work?"

Pasquale shrugged. "I'll give it a shot."

He put it down on the table, and turned back to the coffee.

Jaguar felt sorrow turn to rage. "Hey," she snapped at him.

He turned and stared at her.

"What're you doing?"

"I'll go after I have my coffee," he said.

"How about now?" she asked, being particular to fully articulate each syllable.

"After I have my coffee," he repeated, with the same articulation. Then he shrugged. "Look, I just got off a shuttle after a somewhat difficult time, and I've eaten a good deal of food. If I jump up and go now, my belly'll be working harder than any other part of me."

Jaguar receded grudgingly into her chair. Rachel took a seat across from Jaguar, reached over the table, grabbed her hand, squeezed it and released it. Rachel was one of the few people who could get away with such a gesture, especially when Jaguar's mood was up to feral on the scale between wild and tame.

"We'll find him," Rachel said. "It'll be okay."

While Pasquale and Marie chatted and drank coffee, Jaguar brooded as plainly as she could, until Pasquale thumped her on the back and said "Okay."

"Okay what?" she asked.

"You got your wish. I'm heading out.".

She pushed her chair from the table and stood. "Ready when you are."

He grinned. "Not a chance, little sister. I'm like you. I work alone."

She put a hand on her hip and stared at him hard. "I'm going with you."

"No," he said.

"What if you find him in a situation you can't deal with? You know very little of what's going on here."

He raised his massive hand and patted her three times on the cheek. "I know everything about what's going on here."

She counted to ten silently, closed her eyes and opened them again. "If you ever pat me like that again," she said softly, "I'll bite your nuts off."

His face worked on this for awhile, the massive jaw muscles twisting, the droopy eyes going narrow and then wide. Finally his mouth opened in a wide grin. "Okay," he said. "It's a deal."

Jaguar let her back settle. "When will you be back?"

"Depends. I'll know pretty quick if I can't pick up a trail. If I can, I'll keep going until I can bring him back."

She receded into her thoughts. Pasquale gave a neat bow to Marie and Rachel, and exited by the back door.

And they waited.

He's going to kill me, Alex thought, looking at Brendan.

It was a new thought, so he wondered if Brendan had just decided to do it, maybe because the empathic contact brought up too much for him. Or it was possible that Brendan meant to kill him all along, and Alex just couldn't see it.

Either way, it was true now. He'd sobbed on Alex's shoulder for a long time, let himself be held and rocked as if he was a baby, and then, he'd pushed himself away from Alex, walked a few feet away, shuddered once or twice and was silent for a long time.

When he turned around to look at Alex again, he was smiling, and Alex knew what his intent was. Brendan meant to kill him.

As they prepared for sleep, Alex could read it clearly. He was going to kill him, and—No. That wasn't it. Have Alex confirm the water supply source, first, then pour his stuff into it. Then Alex was to do something else. Kill her. Yes. That was it. Kill her. Then, die.

"Tired?" Brendan asked him, smiling sweetly.

"Yes," Alex said. "You?"

He nodded. "We have some busy days ahead."

"Yes," he agreed. "The Mother told you when, didn't she?"

He was almost beatific, with the moon pouring light onto his face. "She'll make it easy for you, at the end," he promised. "You won't feel a thing. Won't even see it coming."

"Thank you," Alex said, as he lay down, hands behind his back, and considered the stars.

"But—you're not going to sleep, are you?"

"No," Alex said, "I'm just—thinking."

"Yes. You know what to do? You remember?"

Did he remember? Something he was supposed to do?

Brendan sat up and leaned on one elbow, looking down at Alex. In his hand, he rubbed a stone. *Remember? You have to kill her. You have to kill her.*

Kill her?

Yes. He had to kill her. Kill her and then return. Let Brendan know she was dead. Then it could begin. The work of the Mother. All the work of the mother must be done. The world was very green here, and the color was all that mattered to him, because he could smell it, and it would tell him where to go, what to do, how to do it.

Brendan pressed the stone into his hand.

Take this. It will lead you there, and back.

Alex felt the pleasure of something smooth and cool in the palm of his hand. He stood up. The world turned many colors around him, and he found himself walking forward. Listening to the palm of his hand, knowing what to do.

Kill her. Kill Jaguar, with her green eyes, her silky hair, her body like that of any animal, unaware of its own grace, immersed in unselfconscious beauty. Kill her kill women like her are the cause of all the trouble, wanting life, seeking life, working for life which always ends in death so kill her now.

He breathed in deeply, absorbing the truth of all this, his thoughts turning toward her as he walked and walked. Brendan was right. She had a hold on him. He wanted her. He remembered the feel of her lips against his. He remembered her hand clasping the back of his neck, pulling him close, her body pressed against his.

His legs felt weak with the memory of desire and he stopped walking. His hand began to shake, and the stone dropped from it onto the ground.

He gasped, as the world came back into his vision, dark and full of night sounds, none of which spoke in human tongue.

"Jesus," he said, looking around.

He was standing just outside the ecosite, looking at the barren zone between it and the nearest road.

He looked at the stone on the ground at his feet and waited for his mind to start working again. What was he doing? Going to see Jaguar. He wanted to see her. To kill her for the Mother? He shuddered. No. Desire moved in him too strongly for Thanatos to take over completely. He wanted to see her. He wanted to leave this place, go back to himself.

He wished his brain would work more coherently. He pushed his hands through his hair, moved his feet up and down on the ground, trying to feel connected to something real again. He had to think.

Brendan was sending him to kill Jaguar, and the stone would tell him, somehow, what to do after that. Go back and bring Brendan to the water supply, he supposed. Then, Brendan or someone would kill him, make it look like suicide, as if Alex had gone mad and done this thing and his body would be found after the devastation had occurred. Jaguar would already be dead at his hands, so she couldn't tell the story. And if Brendan's plan for the water supply went through, there'd be nobody else worth listening to on the Planetoid.

But how much did Jaguar know anyway? He wondered, for the first time in days, what was going on with her. He'd been isolated here with this madman, going mad himself. But what was Jaguar doing? Did she think he was dead? Gone mad? Disappeared? Did she think he'd broken his word about staying in touch? Was she alive and well? Did she know as much as he did, or maybe more?

He'd find out soon enough, he supposed. But there was one more thing he had to do. He was wearing a t-shirt under his jacket. He took it off, and tossed it on top of the stone. Then he bent down over the stone and picked it up, wrapping the t-shirt around it in as many layers as he could, making it tight and small, with a sort of handle that he could hang onto.

He would have liked a better container for it. He didn't know if he had to be holding it for it to work its tricks on him, because he wasn't sure how it worked. But he had to get it to Jaguar, so that Jaguar could get it to someone who would analyze it and say it was Artemis. It was their only evidence of moon mining. He had to get it to her, and then leave her, before he did any harm because one thing he did know was that he could not trust himself.

Jaguar continued to sit at Marie's kitchen table, waiting. Rachel had gone back to work, and Marie was in the yard nursing a sick Meerkat back to health. Jaguar waited.

The door opened, and she picked her head up. Pasquale stood framed in the doorway. She looked at him and waited some more.

He shook his head. "There's interference," he said. "I can't get a trail going."

"Can't get a trail going?" Jaguar repeated, voice dangerously low and soft.

"Yeah. In fact, every time I tried, it pointed me back to you."

"But—why?"

He lifted his shoulders and let them fall. "Maybe you touched the piece too much. There's too much of you in it and not enough of him. From what I hear, that'd be about right."

She wondered briefly if he knew he was insulting her and wanted to get her angry enough to put her off balance, or if he was just an asshole. "What kind of shitty editorial comment is that?" she demanded.

"You got more ego than anybody I ever met, and it don't leave much room for anyone else. But you already know that, and seems like you're kinda proud of it, so I'm not telling you news." He shrugged and turned up a large, elegant hand. "If you thought about him as much as he thinks about you, I might get some luck. As it is, I can't do a thing."

She pushed her chair back and stood. "You can't?" she asked, voice still soft and low.

Pasquale glanced at her suspiciously. "That's what I said."

She shoved her chair out of the way and walked to where he stood. She spoke clearly, and still softly. "If you can't find him from something I made for him that sits on his desk and has his thoughts that often, either your reputation is bullshit, or you're giving me bullshit."

Before he could respond, she flicked her blade out from her wrist and held it up to his face. "Now which is it?" she asked. "Are you incompetent, or a liar?"

She took a step forward. He took a step back. She took another step forward. He took another one back. She took one more step, but he could go no further, because he was against the wall.

"What's your game, asshole?" she hissed, and brought her blade up to his throat.

The door creaked open, and Jaguar heard Marie gasp. "Mary and Joseph," she said.

Jaguar ignored her, kept her eyes hard on Pasquale. He stayed very still, like a mountain with a boulder on top.

"What's your *game*, asshole?"

Marie took two steps back and stood very still.

"I can't find him," Pasquale said calmly. "There's no game. I just can't get a trail on him."

"It's your job to find him," Jaguar asked, pressing the edge of the knife closer to his throat. "You just tell me what you need to do it."

"Why don't you bring me his heart on a platter? That seems like your style."

Rage flashed in her eyes, moved through her body and into her legs. She brought her knee up to his crotch and slammed it in hard enough that his eyes bulged. She took a step back and he lunged forward, wrapping his meaty hand around her wrist and holding her there. She didn't struggle against him because she knew that would be useless. She just let him hold on, keeping her eye on his pinkie ring as his hand moved with increasing and lessening tension.

She was aware that Marie had left the room, and figured she had gone for her shotgun. She could easily stand here like this until Marie returned, staring at the black glittering eyes in his pretty little ring.

Then, she blinked. Looked again. Cursed softly under her breath and raised her gaze to his.

He was focused, alert to whatever move she might make next. Jaguar's eyes glittered, and a smile formed itself on her face. "Hello," she said. "So nice to meet you."

Pasquale's heavy brows folded down hard. "What?" he asked.

"Let her go," Marie's voice said behind them, and Jaguar turned to find herself staring at the muzzle of a shotgun.

"Christ," Pasquale said, "You're all whacked around here." He released her arm, and she rubbed at it.

"It's okay, Marie," she said. "Just a discussion we had to conclude."

"Did you? Conclude it, I mean," Marie asked.

"Oh yeah," Jaguar said. "I think we understand each other perfectly now. Or, at least, I think I understand him."

She turned back to Pasquale. "I'll find something else for you to track him with. Something he can't possibly hide from."

She headed for the front door, kicking a lamp over just for fun on her way out.

CHAPTER SEVENTEEN

The Townpark offices were locked up tight with nobody around when Alex stumbled in to the village. He made his way to the airvan office and found that also closed for the night. He'd forgotten that some people actually kept regular hours, went home after work and slept. He made his way to the back, and found the airvans parked and empty, with two empty hovercabs nearby.

"Not even a cabbie," he muttered. "Shit."

He went to them and found them locked. Fatigue coursed through him, and the weight of the stone in his pocket didn't help. He leaned against the side of the cab and felt himself falling into darkness.

No, he told himself. Don't fall. Stop it, now.

With great effort, he lifted his head up and looked at the lock. He thought of Jaguar, who knew how to manage a lock and had taught him a trick or two. It wouldn't be the first time she'd saved his life, he thought, and he focused his attention on the door to the hovercab. If he could get it open, he knew how to get it started, which was something Jaguar never got the knack of since it involved overriding the computer in the ignition complex. She was great with locks, but hell on computers.

When a small click told him he'd done it, he almost sobbed with relief. The door opened, and the ignition kicked in easy, and he was off. As he flew, he put the stone in the glove compartment. Whether psychological or physical, his relief was immediate.

Then he realized he wasn't sure where to go. To his apartment? To Jaguars? He tried her place first, but moved on quickly when he saw the surveillance vehicle parked in front of her building. He swooped low and away, to his own apartment, only to see another surveillance vehicle on his street. He moved on. He turned the corner and put a few blocks between them, then brought it down onto the street. Now what?

He wanted a closer look to see if he could spot the team in the vehicle. They might be just as inclined to give him information as to arrest him, if that's what they were after. Or it was possible they were looking at someone else's place, nothing to do with him except coincidence. Possible, but not likely. He retrieved the stone from the glove compartment, feeling again the burden of heaviness that seemed to sink into his bones with it. Then he got out of the hovercab, and walked, whistling softly as he went.

After a block he stopped at a shop window to give himself time to look around. In his peripheral vision he caught sight of a familiar face. He looked into the window, and as the person passed, saw their reflection in the window. At first he thought it was just one more hallucination, and waited for it to sprout wings and fly away, or dissolve into colors that poured strange energy through him. When it didn't, he turned and called to it.

"Rachel," he said. "How's it going?"

She stopped, turned, gaped. "God almighty," she said.

"Not yet," Alex said, "though I may have come close a few times." He walked to where she stood and took her arm. " I think we should walk, don't you?"

"Jesus—I mean, Alex—it *is* you. I thought it was, and then I thought I was crazy for thinking that. Where've you been? And what's that beard about? Are you okay?" she asked.

He took her questions methodically, in order. "Camping out with lunatics, where there's no shaving apparatus, and I'm sometimes okay. I think. My turn. Why is there a guard at my door?"

"Because," Rachel said, "there's a warrant out for your arrest. We're waiting for one on Jaguar, too. She borrowed a prisoner. And lost her."

Alex stopped walking, and pressed a hand to his forehead. Not much had changed in his absence. Chaos ruled, and Jaguar helped.

"You better start from the top," Alex said. "What am I charged with?"

"Murder," Rachel said.

Alex frowned, looked up and down the street. The woman on the bridge. They were putting that on him. "Maybe," he said, "we better keep walking."

As they walked, Rachel filled in the remainder of the gaps for him, from the hearing that left Jaguar suspended, to current events, which included Jaguar's return from the home planet without Fiore, and with Pasquale. About Pasquale's failure to find him, which she'd just heard about, and Pinkie's state of hiding. As Rachel spoke, Alex began to realize that they were in just as much trouble as he'd anticipated at the start of this. Rachel told him everything she knew, up to the story Marie had told her about Jaguar's fight with Pasquale.

At that point, Alex stopped walking. "Where is she now?" he asked.

"At Marie's. She's staying there, in the attic room. She's been half out of her mind trying to find you."

He felt the pull to see her, inevitable, undeniable. *You want her. She makes you want her.* He took in a deep breath and released it. He would not allow himself to sink into surrealism. The feeling passed, and was replaced by a hopefulness he hadn't felt in days. He wondered if it acted as an amplifier of the emotions in the people around you. With Brendan, he felt despair. With Rachel, he felt hope.

"Alex?" Rachel asked. "Are you okay? What's that bundle you're carrying?"

"It's a long story. Listen, Rachel. Do me a favor. If I sort of space out, slap me or something. I've been taking hits off of Brendan's Artemis, and it's making me strange. Where's your car?"

"A few blocks down. I've been parking and walking at night, to see if they're still watching your place and Jaguar's. Why?"

"Go get it, then come get me. No. Wait. There's a little store a block east. A drugstore. They have mints that come in tin boxes. Get some."

"A craving?"

"I want the box. And get some tissues, too."

She frowned, shrugged, then went. She'd done stranger things lately.

He waited, staring at a window which he supposed was a shop window. Saw that he was staring at a display of women's cosmetics. Thought of Brendan. Thought of Jaguar, thinking of him. All thoughts, leading back to that home. Desire, a winged creature taking flight inside him.

Rachel pulled up to the curb, and he got inside her car. She handed him the tin and he carefully but quickly unrolled the stone, slipped it into a bunch of tissues, and from there into the tin box, which he closed tightly and wrapped in the plastic bag it came in.

He let it rest on the dashboard and again, felt immediate relief. An immediate lightening.

"You got your notebook with you?" he asked.

She reached into her back seat and pulled her computer up, handed it to him. He opened it up and stared at it.

"Password?" he asked.

"Depends," she said. "Whose file you want?"

He grinned, and shook his head. "You know, Rachel, I remember a time when you were reluctant to play hacking games. I don't know that Planetoid work has been good for your morals."

"It's been very good for them," she said. "taught me right from wrong, and when to use which one. Whose file?"

"Miriam Whitehall," he said. "Her private files."

Rachel glanced at him.

"That's E 5 Sam Sam control 18," she said, punching it up, "but we've already been through it a few times. There's nothing on it we can use. Nothing to prove anything against her."

"You know about her?" he asked.

"We know she's up to something. Jaguar's known since she got suspended. She just can't figure out exactly what, or prove anything, and it's making her crazy. You know how she is."

He nodded. He knew. She'd be even more crazy when she found out what Miriam's plans were. Sabotage, to be seen as the work of a crazed supervisor and his prisoner. But he had the moonstone now. That might provide the proof they needed. He put the computer away.

"Okay. Then let's go."

Rachel didn't ask where. She pulled out into traffic, and pointed the car toward Marie's. "I can get you through the checkpoints with my pass, and then I have to pick up Gerry. I'll bring him back to Marie's in case you need us," she said. She glanced his way, looked him up and down. "You can grab a shower there, too."

"You trying to tell me something?" Alex muttered.

"Well," Rachel said, "I don't think I have to, really."

"No," he said, "You don't."

Alex put his head back, closed his eyes. They'd be there in ten minutes. He'd find something better to contain the stone in, and take a quick shower, wash the moon off his skin before he exposed it to anyone else. He'd wait for Rachel to come back with Gerry, and they could all go talk to Jaguar together. That would be safest.

If he wasn't alone with her, then he couldn't kill her.

"I'll need you," he said. "Somebody has to keep an eye on me, apparently."

Rachel unlocked the door for him, and left him to shower and shave, which seemed to clear away the cobwebs he'd been living in for the past however many days he'd been with Brendan. Then he wrapped himself in a robe, put the box in the robe pocket, and sat at the kitchen table to wait for Rachel's return.

The house was quiet. Outside, there were no sounds of the city. Only peepers making their small sounds in the dark, calling for a mate, a mate, a mate. Rachel had said Jaguar was in the attic. She was very close. He closed his eyes and searched for her thoughts, wanting the jungle of her dreams if he couldn't have her presence.

He had a clear sense of her, breathing softly, body relaxed, mind wandering through scattered images of a large man who wore a strange ring. Then his own face appeared in her thoughts. His own face next to hers, mouth on her hair, her breath against his neck.

Jaguar. I want you.

Her breathing the only reply. His face the only image in her mind.

Do not stand up, he told himself. *If you stand up, it's all over.*

He rose and made his way to the attic.

The door to her room was closed and he opened it carefully, silently, then stood inside and looked at her. He put the stone down on a bureau and watched for a moment. He took a step closer to the bed, and then another. She was asleep, and he was reluctant to wake her too swiftly, both as a matter of courtesy and as a matter of safety. He knew what her reflexes were, and he could see her knife, gleaming at her wrist, under the nightshirt she was wearing. She'd kicked herself loose from the covers, and her legs were naked. He resisted the urge to touch them. Even from where he sat, he could smell the moon around her and feel how it pulled him to her. Different than Brendan, though. Lively and full of fire. Alive and prepared to kick. It seemed like a long time since he'd seen her.

Stay where you are, he told himself. *Don't go any closer. It isn't safe.*

He walked silently to the foot of the bed and stood there, watching her sleep.

Jaguar. I want you.

He saw himself reaching for her, his hand moving against his volition and his direct command to stay still. He reached for her, leaning over the bed.

Before his hand touched her skin, she shot upright, grabbed his wrist, twisted and pulled. He rolled with the twist and was on the bed with her, making a grab for her arm as her blade shot out from the sleeve of her nightshirt. He rolled onto his back and she was over him, straddling him, her arm raised high, blade gleaming, but he had her wrist locked in a firm grasp, pushing it away.

Jaguar, it's me. It's Alex.

She looked at him hard, and gasped, eyes growing large in the dark, her mouth forming the syllables of his name.

He let go of her arm. She retracted her knife and swayed over him for a moment. Then she reached down to his face, pressed her palm against his cheek and held it there. Sweet. It felt sweet.

"Alex?" she asked. "You're here?"

"Yes," he confirmed. "Here. I'm here. But not for long. I have to go back. I can't stay. I came to tell you—"

"No," she said. "No. You can't go."

"Jaguar, listen to me—"

"You're not going back," she insisted, lowering herself closer to his face, the weight and smoothness of her skin against his thighs.

She was the color of sand on the floor of the desert. Her eyes caught moonlight and held it. Somewhere far away he was telling her that there was no time and it wasn't safe. Not safe for him to be here and he didn't know what would happen. He thought he spoke, but maybe he didn't. The skin of her legs was pressed into his and there was no barrier left between them. There was fire in her skin, the moon in her eyes. She was close enough for him to breathe into her lungs, and the moon was in her, washing through her and into him and he could no longer instruct his hands not to pull her down to his mouth.

Hush, he said to her, to himself. *Hush, Jaguar.*

He told himself clearly and firmly that he shouldn't. Not yet. Not here. Not this way, with the moon in her eyes and fire in her skin. But it felt so good and he would rather drown in her eyes, be burned by her skin than fade into Brendan's despair, a shadow of a shadow of fear. Her eyes could swallow him right here. Her eyes and her hand, and he would be content.

Then his mouth was against hers and hers was warm as light and she was pressing herself into him, kissing him, her desire an animal with wings that carried them both over the edge of the abyss they'd skirted for so long.

She struggled with his robe, pulling at the belt, tugging at him her eyes hungry and her body warm and sweet and naked under the thin nightshirt.

"Wait," he whispered hoarsely, "Wait. Jaguar."

"No," she said. "I won't wait. No more."

He laughed softly. "Until I get this thing off, I meant."

It seemed to him as if they fell off the dark side of the moon into a space empty of everything except the two of them. All his fear was gone. He wasn't here to harm her. He knew what he was doing, and meant to do it, meant to find his way to her in this unexpected night.

He fell into her as if she was the bottom and center of everything he'd ever wanted, his hands recognizing her shape from the memory of many nights he'd gone to sleep dreaming of it, his mouth knowing the taste of her from long desire.

Her hands soothed all questions, left none remaining except one—how much pleasure he could offer her, in exchange for the bliss she was giving to him.

Gerry was walking from his apartment toward Alex's to relieve Rachel, when he thought he saw someone he knew. He passed the window of the diner. Stopped. Backed up. Looked hard.

"Hey," he said to himself. "It's Pasquale."

He was going to go in, but just then a woman seated herself at Pasquale's booth. She was older than Pasquale, which surprised Gerry. He didn't think Pasquale liked older women. But she was nice looking, and she had a nice smile as she held out her hand and let Pasquale take it and kiss the back of it.

What a guy, Gerry thought. Always the romancer. Gerry thought he knew the woman's face, but he couldn't put a name to it, and he wasn't sure where he knew it from. He stood and stared into the window, mouth slightly open, asking himself what was the right thing to do here. He didn't want to interrupt anything, but it would be good to say hello. On the other hand, if it was business, he really didn't want to interrupt. He knew how Pasquale was about business.

Finally, he decided to move on. Maybe he'd head over to Marie's. If Pasquale was here, that meant Jaguar was back, too. He'd probably find out more when he got to Rachel's, who was supposed to drive him back to his own place and fill him in on anything he might need to do.

He walked at a leisurely pace to her building, which was just a few blocks away, and would have rung her bell but she was just coming out her door.

"Hi," she said. "You're late. I almost left without you."

"Left? For where?"

"Marie's. I'm staying there tonight. You want to, or will you head home."

Gerry looked around, lifted his wrist and looked at it, scratched his belly and looked down at his hand. When the answer was in none of those places, he shrugged and followed Rachel to her car. He opened her car door and got in. Settled himself.

She yawned big, saying words through the yawn he couldn't understand.

"What?" he asked.

"I said, you missed all the fun. I found him."

"Who?"

"Alex. Or he found me. I dropped him off at Marie's."

"Cool," Gerry said. "And Jaguar's back, with Pasquale, right?"

"How'd you know?"

"I saw him," Gerry said.

"You stopped at Maries?"

"No. I saw him on the way over. At the diner. With this pretty woman."

Rachel swerved to avoid a dog running across the road. "Again?" she asked.

"No. Not that I know of. At least, it's the only time I saw."

She ground her teeth. "No. Say that again."

"Oh." Gerry repeated what he'd said.

Rachel frowned. "But—that doesn't sound right. What'd she look like?"

"Older. Nice looking. Brown hair that's all soft around her face. Soft face. I think I know her, but I'm not sure from where."

Rachel tried to place the description. Thought it sounded familiar. Like someone she knew.

"Y'know," Gerry said. "She looked an awful lot like Governor Whitehall. Miriam, right? I didn't now Pasquale knew any governors."

Rachel chewed on her lower lip. Miriam? Meeting with Pasquale? Could it really be, or was Gerry off on one of his own little journeys? She felt inclined to tell Jaguar about it right now. But—if Alex was with her, maybe they had things to talk about. Or not talk about, if she was reading the wind right.

She'd go to Marie's and see if Pasquale was there, see if Jaguar was available. If not, first thing in the morning, she'd have to let her know.

Alex trailed a finger down the road of Jaguar's spine. He let his hand come to rest on the back of her thigh, which he considered as a thing of beauty.

She had filled him in on most of the details of her last few days, and he'd told him what he could remember about what happened with Brendan. She knew about the stones, because her prisoner had one. And she knew Miriam was involved. But she didn't know the extent of their plans, or how Brendan fit in until he told her. And even so, he could only tell her that he believed it to be true, with the disclaimer that right now his belief system might be a little off.

And none of that was half as interesting to him right now as finding the exact middle of her spine.

"Jaguar," he said, "I have to go soon."

She lifted her head from her pillow and looked back over her shoulder at him. "Are you well enough to leave?" she asked.

Fair enough question, he thought. Too bad he didn't have an answer for it. "I got here," he said. "It seems that right now, it's handy being an adept. I think it's pulling me through the strange bits even when I can't do that consciously."

"That doesn't mean it's safe for you to go back to Brendan. "

"I have to bring him in."

"We could tell Paul. Let him send someone else."

"By the time they get done arresting me and trying me, it might be too late."

"Then I could go."

"No," he said. "Absolutely not. I know him. I'll bring him in."

"That's fine, if that's all you plan to do," Jaguar said, "But it isn't."

He was silent. Of course he wasn't just going to bring Brendan in. Now that he'd had a chance to rest and review the situation, he planned on trying to get The Mother close enough to reel in as well. Jaguar would tumble to that quick enough.

"I'm doing my job, Jaguar," he said.

"Which is?" she asked.

He traced the line of her jaw with his finger, and she caught it at her chin and held on. "Okay," he said, "I know. But this is our only chance to connect Miriam to this mess."

"Then I'll come with you. You need back-up."

"Not likely. I want you off the Planetoid as of this morning's shuttle."

She released his finger and raised herself on one elbow. "And miss all the fun? With governor's screaming and so on? I don't think so," she said.

"I do," he replied. "Someone has to get the Artemis stones to a scientist I know in Jersey. We'll need an official analysis for the Hague."

She shook her head. "I hate Jersey. Send Rachel. I'll go with you. You shouldn't be alone with him."

"You shouldn't be alone with me. You're the last person. " He stopped and considered her spine some more. "He wants me to kill you, Jaguar. There've been times when I thought." He stopped again. Too much to feel tonight. Not enough reason to balance it. "Jaguar," he said, "I don't know what I'll do if he gets the Artemis near me. I might kill you."

"You won't," Jaguar said.

"How do you know?" How could she know how close he'd felt to what Brendan believed, how that invaded him, and touched the part of his own fears that were most likely to rear up and attack. Attack her.

She sat up and stretched. "Because I'll kill you first, okay?" she said. Then added more reasonably, "Look, we can bring Gerry if you want. I'll bet he's immune to Artemis. Way too crazy."

He considered the situation. She was right. He shouldn't go back alone. And he was right. She was the last person who should back him up on this, though as far as he could tell there was no one else for the job. He could keep arguing with her about it, but he'd have to knock her out cold to keep her away, and for all he knew that was how she'd end up being killed. If they brought Gerry along, though, it might work. It might keep them both safe.

"Okay," he said. "But I think," he added, surveying her, "you should get dressed first."

"You too," she said. "Where's the address of the Jersey guy? I'll give it to Rachel, and dig up Gerry."

"It's taped to the box," Alex said. He sat up on the bed, felt a momentary dizziness come and go, and stood. So far so good. He reassembled the robe from the heap on the floor it had become and wrapped it around himself. "My clothes are downstairs. I'll meet you in the kitchen when you're ready."

She stood and reached for a pile of clothes on the chair next to the bed. He found his feet reluctant to take him out of the door. He moved back toward her and touched her cheek, kissed it lightly.

"You understand," he said, "that right now I'm thinking I'm one of the luckiest men alive."

She regarded him coolly. "Then stay alive," she said.

"Those were my plans, Jaguar. "

She nodded, her sea-eyes gone dark in the darkness, wide as the night sky and twice as deep.

He stroked her hair one more time, to have the feel of it in his hand after he left the room.

CHAPTER EIGHTEEN

He dressed in the darkness, moving quickly. It would take Jaguar time to rouse Rachel and tell her about the stone, the plans. Time to dig up Gerry.

But as he dressed, he felt space opening up around him. Felt himself fall into it. Felt himself dying, cells sucked dry of life.

Am I having a heart attack? he asked himself. Am I dying? No, he said. This can't be. Not now. Not now. Artemis, maybe. Residual affects. Something in his clothes. If he could stick it out, he'd come back. He'd learned that, hadn't he?

He leaned against the wall, feeling its gritty texture under his hand, relying on this physical sensation to keep him where he was while he waited to see what would happen. No voices told him to kill. No despair filled him, or hopelessness, or desire.

What happened next was that he saw Jaguar standing in front of him, saw his hand going to her throat, reaching for it, saw Brendan standing behind her smiling and Miriam standing behind him, her face triumphant.

The space closed itself, spit him back out into Marie's kitchen, where he leaned against the wall and felt it with his hand. He listened to the house a minute, and heard its silences. So, he thought. He was right. It was that way, and this was no Artemis affect or heart attack. It was the adept space, giving him fair warning. He'd take it.

He found the keys to Rachel's car on the kitchen table, as if they'd been left there just for his use. He let himself out the back door, and left.

Jaguar made her way to Rachel's room with the material from Brendan. Rachel was sleeping, but she woke when Jaguar whispered her name and put a hand on her.

"What?" she asked, sitting up fast and blinking at Jaguar. "Is it for me?"

Jaguar laughed and sat down on the bed next to her. "Sort of, " she said. "You awake?"

Rachel blinked some more and rubbed at her face. "Not sure. What time is it?"

"Nighttime. But I have to go."

Rachel looked at her hard. "You look—different."

She peered down at her green work shirt. "Good color for me?" she asked.

Rachel shook her head. "Something else. Did Alex find you?"

"He did," she said. "We're on our way to get Brendan, and we need you to do something."

"We?" Rachel asked.

"Alex, and me. Or Alex and I depending on how fussy you are. Are you awake, Rachel?"

She shook herself. "I'm awake. I just don't often hear you use that word. We."

"We're going to get Brendan," she repeated patiently, "and we need you to do something."

She handed her the material, and the name and address of the scientist Alex knew. "Get this to that person. As soon as you can. Call in sick and take a shuttle out today. Don't open the box. It'll hurt you. You got it?"

Rachel nodded, then looked at Jaguar questioningly.

"No time for answers," she said. "When we get back, okay?"

"Okay," Rachel said. "No wait. There's something you have to know. It's important."

"Okay. Be fast."

"It's Pasquale," Rachel said. "Gerry saw Pasquale, at a diner with Miriam."

Jaguar's lips went thin. She closed her eyes and pressed two fingers against them while Rachel reported what Gerry had seen. Jaguar's mouth twitched, and then she opened her eyes and smiled. "Is he here?" she asked. "Did he come back here?"

"Yes," Rachel said. "At least, someone's in his room snoring."

"Okay. Then don't tell him where I am. If he asks, say I'm off sulking somewhere. Tell Marie to try and keep him here, one way or another. I can't take care of it until we get back."

"Okay. Jaguar—be careful, right?"

"Always," Jaguar said. She stood up and left the room before Rachel could offer further comment. She wanted to get moving, and she kept feeling twinges of anxiety, as if she was waiting for what would go wrong next. Which, she realized, she was.

Downstairs, the kitchen was quiet and dim in the night that had turned the corner toward dawn. She recognized the voices of morning birds outside.

"Alex?" she whispered. Nobody answered.

She went to the laundry room, but he wasn't there. Went to the living room, but that was empty. Made her way down into the basement and in the damp, cool dark asked again, "Alex?" No answer. Her heart began to beat abnormally fast for the amount of energy she was expending. Maybe he was upstairs waiting for her, looking for her. She took the steps two at a time and opened the door to her attic room.

It was empty. Her heart skipped a few beats before it got back on its track. She pressed her hand to her chest, asking herself why she was so afraid.

And then, she went to the attic window and saw why.

There was only one car in the lot. Rachel's car wasn't there. She slammed a fist into the wall.

"No," she said. "No, goddammit."

She clattered down the attic stairs and threw open the back door, ran to the parking lot, where she saw the tracks of a car just gone.

"No," she gasped. "No."

She turned back toward the house, thinking she'd get the keys to Marie's car and follow him. She wouldn't be that far behind him, could catch up with him. And then, at the door of the house, she stopped dead in her tracks.

She didn't know where he was going.

He never told her where Brendan was, and she didn't ask because she thought she'd be going with him.

He was gone. Alone, and without weapons because he never carried a weapon casually, said he wouldn't since the Killing Times. Damn him. He was gone.

If she didn't have the evidence of her skin still tingling to his touch, she would have thought the whole episode with him a dream because she couldn't have found and lost him again so quickly, and she could no more get to him now than she could before he dropped into her bed, into her. But he had been there, and her skin still tingled with his touch. She still smelled of him.

His scent was on her, in her. She raised her hands to her face and smelled his soap on her.

"Pasquale," she murmured.

He was all she had now. Pasquale, who met with Miriam, and claimed he didn't have a strong enough scent to track Alex. Pasquale, who was snoring in his room.

"Okay," she murmured. "So he's available."

And if she was walking into a trap, at least she was doing it with her eyes open.

She went back into the house, walked down the hall to Pasquale's room, entered it and closed the door behind her. He was lying under the covers, hands behind his head, eyes open. She wondered if he'd been waiting for her. She supposed that would at least save time.

She unbuttoned her shirt and let it drop to the floor, let her pants slide down after them. When he sat up and gaped at her she knew he hadn't expected this, no matter what he knew.

Pasquale shook his head. "Put it away. I told you I'm not here to—"

"You're here to find Alex for me. And you need something to track him with. Something with his scent."

She could see thought chasing thought behind his eyes He rubbed at his chin. He paused and chewed on this, then shook his head at her. "He was here? With you? Then, you know where he is, right?"

"He left before I got his forwarding address."

He ran his gaze down and back up the length of her body, then held her eyes with his for a long moment. "He left you behind."

She nodded.

"He's in trouble," Pasquale said matter of factly.

She nodded again. "But the one thing he can't hide from is standing naked in front of you right now." She lifted her arms wide. "His desire."

Pasquale knit his thick brow, unknit it. He grabbed a robe from the chair on the side of the bed and put it on, and went to stand facing her. He touched her hair with the tips of his fingers. A gesture of intimacy and admiration. She closed her eyes.

He walked a circle around her, stopping to breathe deeply at the back of her neck, stopping again to press a hand against her thigh, at the place where Alex's hand had pressed so recently. He stood still, breathing in and out, deeply.

"Nice," he murmured softly. "Very nice."

She opened her eyes. "Then it'll do?" she asked.

"Just fine," he said. "It'll do fine. Lemme get dressed, and I'll meet you downstairs."

He waited until he could no longer hear her steps going down the hall, and then pulled out his cellcom and made a call.

"You ready for action?" he asked when he heard Larry Barone on the other side.

"What?" Larry asked.

"Today's the day," Pasquale said.

There was a pause, then Larry spoke. "Today? But we haven't—"

"You have to. Today. Tell Miriam Dzarny and Addams are clued in and it has to be today. Get her and bring her along."

There was a longer pause, then Larry's voice came back. "Are you sure?" he asked.

"Now," Pasquale said, " Or never. You pick."

Larry's voice again. "Where?"

"Rainforest site. The far side, where it goes into the wetlands, in a clearing between the two. You'll see them."

"Okay," Larry said. "Okay."

"And bring my money," Pasquale said. "All of it."

When he hung up, Pasquale smiled at his cell com. He'd delay here for a while longer, and Jaguar would be suspicious, but she'd made a choice to take the risk anyway, so that didn't matter. He looked at his watch. Half an hour. He'd time it so they left in half an hour. By then Alex would be almost there, and Larry would have Miriam. He'd delay a little more on the ride there, and the timing should end up just right.

Everything was going just the way he liked it to go. Exactly designed to match his needs.

When Alex arrived at the ecosite, Brendan was still sleeping peacefully, face angelic and serene. He liked to sleep, he told Alex. It reminded him of death. In his presence, Alex immediately felt heavier, as if he'd swallowed lead. He wondered if Brendan had more stones on him, or if it was just him. Just his despairing presence.

Alex nudged at him with his foot, and he opened his eyes, blinking in the light.

He grinned broadly at Alex. "I was having a dream."

"Good one?" Alex asked.

"Very good. There was a man in it. He—he seemed to be my father. I was very young, and he took my hand, said we could go for a walk."

Alex waited for more, but it didn't come.

"It was very pleasant," Brendan said. He sat up and stretched, rubbed at his eyes, then reached in his pocket for his glasses. When he pulled them out, a stone fell with them.

Alex took a step back.

Brendan picked it up, and held it up to the light. Through a world that was beginning to pulse like a drum around him, Alex saw Brendan's face grinning.

"Did you do it?" he asked.

"Yes," Alex answered truthfully. "We did."

Brendan nodded. "Then we can go on. Will you be my father?" he asked.

Or at least Alex thought he asked that. Maybe he didn't.

"Will you?"

Yes, Alex wanted to say. Of course I will. He understood that Brendan needed that more than anything else. A father. Not a mother. Male energy, good and strong. But he didn't feel very strong right now, or at least not strong enough to shift Brendan's energy around.

He saw Brendan looking at him, his eyes glittering and grey like the stone he held.

If I can block his energy, Alex thought, I can do this for him. He slowly raised a hand, watched it lift as if a crane was pulling it up. He lifted it, then let it fall on Brendan's shoulder. Time seemed delayed, but that didn't matter. It was still moving.

"Yes," he said, "Of course I will."

For a moment, Alex saw a shift in Brendan's eyes, as if a veil of grey was lifted to reveal a clearer blue beneath. He was aware that Brendan caught at his lower lip with his teeth, and shook himself as if he was seeing something clearly for the first time in a long time. Good, Alex thought. Good.

But now was a delicate moment. Prisoners, when they first cleared, were at their most vulnerable. They had to be held in a careful stillness while they adjusted to what they learned about themselves because otherwise they might back into a grief so deep at what they'd done, who they were, that they'd get suicidal, go mad, choose to go back to what they were. It was when they were clear that they understood the waste of their own lives, and their grief could be bottomless.

Alex stood for what might have been minutes, or hours, without moving, waiting to see what Brendan would do next. He was about to go subvocal and see what he could see, offer what comfort and reassurance he could, but he never got the chance.

Brendan gasped, and scrambled away from Alex, standing quickly and turning away. He walked a few feet away, then stopped with his back to Alex and pressed a hand to his temple. With his other hand he clutched at his stone.

Alex felt the return of normal space and cursed under his breath. Close. He'd been damn close. Well, that was a good sign, he thought, and at least he felt clear right now. Maybe he was learning to deal with this stuff. He looked at the sky and saw that the sun had crept a little higher, but not too much. It was still early morning. He hoped it was the same day he remembered waking up to.

"Brendan?" he asked tentatively. "You okay?"

"We have company," Brendan said, not turning around.

"Company?"

"Mother's coming," he said.

"She is?" Alex asked. "When?"

Brendan turned around to face Alex. "Now," he said, looking over Alex's shoulder.

Alex twisted around. Saw Miriam Whitehall and a man whose face he knew from televised interviews—Lawrence Barone. She was holding his arm with one hand, and in her other hand was a laser-fire gun.

"Hello, Alex," she said. "Nice day for a major tragedy, isn't it?"

Alex thought of the night he'd just spent. No regrets there, at least.

"A good day to die," he agreed.

CHAPTER NINETEEN

They took Marie's car out of town, Pasquale driving. Jaguar, an uncomfortable passenger at the best of times, alternated between tapping her foot nervously and twirling the music program for something to listen to.

"Relax," Pasquale said. "I'll get you there in one piece."

She did not ask him and then what. She continued to play with the music program, tap her foot.

Pasquale pulled the car to a stop at the border of the rainforest ecosite nearest the swamps. He got out, and invited her to do the same.

"We walk from here," he said.

"How far in?"

"Half mile or so."

She followed to where the trees just began to crowd, and then he stopped her with a hand held up. He walked ahead until she just couldn't see him, then came back and whispered to her.

"In that clearing. I'll go with you. No trouble, right?"

She looked at him, said nothing.

They walked through a final row of trees and emerged in a clearing where the grass was soft and full, and tree stumps told the story of cutting having been done recently. As they entered, Jaguar felt cold metal at the back of her neck. She stopped walking.

"Don't try the knife," Pasquale said. "I'll get my shots in first."

Jaguar surveyed the faces of the people there. Miriam and Larry, Brendan and Alex. She let her gaze stop at Alex.

"Hello, Alex," Jaguar said. "Thought you'd get away from me that easy?"

Miriam didn't turn her attention from Alex, who stood with his hands up at the end of her weapon while Barone patted him down for weapons of his own.

"No, Jaguar," he said. "I thought maybe for once you'd be smart enough to stay away."

She narrowed her eyes at him and made subvocal contact. *Then you've forgotten everything you know about me.*

A ping of laser fire landed near Jaguar's left foot and she narrowly avoided jumping in response. When she looked away from Alex, she saw Miriam glaring at her.

"None of that here," she hissed. "Do you understand?"

Jaguar shrugged. Apparently Miriam could pick up on empathic contact. "You always were an eavesdropper, Miriam," she said.

Miriam said "hmmph," then, to Brendan, "I thought you said he did it."

Brendan ogled her and said nothing.

"We did," Alex said, looking to Jaguar for confirmation.

Jaguar nodded. She smiled at Miriam. "And it was great. I just dropped by to let him know that the evidence was safe and en route."

Lawrence Barone stepped forward, his face hard and grim. "What evidence?"

She flashed a smile. "An Artemis stone."

"Miriam," Larry started to say, but she cut him off with a wave of her hand.

"So what?" she said. "The only other person who'll have them are him," she pointed to Alex. "And once the toxin's in the water, everyone will be far too busy counting bodies to care."

She held her hand out to Brendan, who handed her a small bottle. She held it up to the light. "At least, until the home planet intervenes and the place is cleaned up. Then, of course, decisions will have to be made about what happens next to Planetoid Three."

"We'll track it to you, Miriam," Alex said. "Neurotoxins carry chemical tags. You know—"

"—But nobody has ever tagged this kind," Miriam cut in. "In fact, it doesn't even exist as far as the chemists are concerned. It'll read like water with a little extra potassium in it." She grinned and lowered the bottle, put it in her own jacket pocket. "It's an Artemis compound. Designed to bring out the real you. For most people, that's not a good thing."

Jaguar understood. Some people would die instantly, but many more would just go mad and start killing—themselves or others. Those who didn't go mad or die might be killed by those who did. In any event, the Planetoid would be discredited as a prison system. Officials would say it made people mad.

"Cute," Jaguar said. "And what about us? You shoot us?"

"No, no," Miriam said, "Something much more beautiful than that." Miriam turned glittering eyes to Brendan, who jerked his head up and glued his beatific gaze to her face.

Jaguar watched, fascinated in spite of herself as Brendan held out his hand. Miriam placed a stone in his palm. Silence passed between them, but it was a silence rich with energy. He nodded, walked to Alex, and held up the stone.

"You see," Miriam said, "Larry's insurance company doesn't have to pay full claim if a Planetoid workers are involved."

"Jesus," Jaguar whispered. "We're an insurance break?"

Miriam gestured sharply at Brendan, who grabbed Alex's hand.

"No," Alex said sharply, making a fist, but Larry knocked it down and Brendan grabbed it, pressed the stone into it. Alex made a fist with his other hand and brought it up, then stopped.

Jaguar heard him groan in pain, in despair.

"Don't," Jaguar said. "Don't. Alex—" She took a step forward and a large hand fell on her shoulder, jerking her back. Pasquale put his weapon to her temple and his mouth to her ear. "Stay put," he whispered.

She turned her head to the left, causing the barrel of his weapon to push into her flesh. He shoved it in just a little further. She could not establish contact, but she could open herself to it, and she did so, feeling the thick fog of despair that moved from Brendan to Alex, feeling how it closed in on him, shut him down, Thanatos smothering Eros.

"Jaguar," Alex gasped, "They want me to. I can't . . . Don't let me."

Kill her. You have to. You know you promised and you're a man of your word. Kill her and you won't be tormented by your desire. She is too attached to life and if you kill her it will be gone. No more desire. No more pain.

Jaguar felt pain, very deep. Alex's or Brendan's? She couldn't tell because what was Brendan's seeped into Alex and stayed there, seeking a place to attach itself, a place where it might fit and grow and become part of Alex for good. Pasquale's hand on her arm tightened and she heard Brendan, soft and seductive as death.

whose hands do you want to kill her mine or yours because she will die like all

humans she'll die soon and I could take her or you could do it kill her because she's
beautiful. She's beautiful.

She's too beautiful.

Kill her.

"Alex," Jaguar cried aloud, "Don't listen. Don't."

But he couldn't not listen. Brendan stood with a hand on his shoulder, another hand pressing the stone into his. Alex's face was beaded with sweat and his arms were shaking. Words were torn out of him, pushing past what was happening inside him.

Jaguar. Kill me first. You said you would.

"No," she said, not sure what she was saying no to. "No."

Miriam laughed.

Kill her. Go. Now.

Jaguar twisted to see her, and Pasquale pulled her back, but she'd seen enough in one swift look. Miriam knew. If Alex tried to kill her, she would kill him first. But that didn't matter to her. One or the other of them would be blamed. He would kill her, or she would kill him. Would she? Would she? If she didn't, he would kill her. There was no way out. No way to win. She would have to and she couldn't.

Pasquale whispered in her ear, "He's gonna go for your throat."

Alex lunged toward her, eyes not seeing. Pasquale took a step back and moved his aim to the back of her head. Jaguar thought of the knife at her wrist. How much time would she have to use it? And who would she use it on? Every muscle in her body tensed.

Alex. Alex, no. Don't.

Then, she relaxed. Stopped everything in herself of fear, or tension, or preparation for death, his or her own.

Her fear, her sorrow, her despair, was what they wanted. The stone would amplify it, send it to Alex, and they'd be killed by their own fear for each other's safety. The minute she bought their program, it became real. Reality be damned, she thought. Let it go. She focused on what she knew to be true. Who he was, and what she was to him.

Alex's hands stretched around her neck, and Pasquale's gun pressed at the back of her head.

She looked at Alex's face and saw it as she saw it last night in the dark, his eyes alive and searching her face as if it was the most precious thing he'd ever seen. She thought of him caressing her in the dark, his mouth on her skin and her hair.

Alex, she whispered into him, and desire, that animal with wings, spread itself through her and into him. Desire, that presence, alive and joyful. Abundant. Eros, spreading soft wings over Thanatos, and leaving it obscure.

It didn't matter that they had guns all around them. It didn't matter that despair filled the air. It didn't matter that all the people in their immediate vicinity wished death on them. They were here. Alive. His hand on her skin. His eyes searing her. His hand moved against her throat, caressing her skin.

"Beautiful," he murmured. "So beautiful." He leaned forward, and put his lips to the crescent at the base of her neck.

"What the hell—" Miriam said, and took a step forward. "What the hell?"

"Can't beat that with a stick," Pasquale commented.

"Do your job, Pasquale," Larry barked. Miriam whirled to look at him.

Pasquale raised his weapon and fired at her once. Her eyes grew wide with terror. She pressed her hands to her stomach, looked down at it, and then she dropped.

Brendan's scream would have been piercing, but Pasquale turned his weapon toward him and cut it off with another shot. The sound jolted Alex back to himself, and he dropped the stone, stepped back from Jaguar, a hand still on her arm.

"How's that?" Pasquale asked Larry.

"Good," he said looking down at the bodies. " Very good. Now those two. Make it look like one's a suicide."

Alex jerked Jaguar back from Pasquale and prepared to whirl on him, but Jaguar stepped out in front. "Ladies first?" she asked.

He surveyed her, considering. "If you insist," He turned his weapon toward Jaguar. "Don't take it personal, okay?"

"I won't," she said.

Alex, still confused from the effects of Artemis, even more shocked that she didn't make a move, put a hand out. "Wait," he said. "Wait. Don't."

Pasquale tilted his head to one side and grinned, "Yeah? Gimme one good reason why not."

Alex hadn't expected that. Nor did he understand Jaguar's unwillingness to attack. Something was going on here that he wasn't getting.

"Stop fucking around," Larry said. "Do it."

"I'll do it my way," Pasquale shot back. Then, to Alex, "So, go ahead. Talk me out of it."

"You need a reason?" Alex said, "Jesus. Just look at her. Then, look at him." He indicated Larry. He waited while Pasquale did so. "Isn't that reason enough?"

Pasquale considered. "Y'know, I think you got something there." He turned to Larry. "I think he's right, don't you?"

"This is ridiculous," Larry hissed. "Stop it. I paid you to do a job here."

"Yeah. You got the money, but I got the gun. Why don't you tell me why he's wrong?"

"I—what?"

"Can't do it, can you? I'm not surprised. Apple don't fall far from the tree, and your father was a slimy son of a bitch who stole money he didn't deserve from dead women. I think he taught you to prefer your women dead. And I think your money is rightfully mine no matter what I do, because that woman your father stole money from was my family. You got a clue what I'm talking about?"

Larry licked his lips. "I don't—I don't have any idea."

"Yeah," Pasquale said, "You do. You remember Anna Burhasa. You just don't like to think about it. Lemme help you with that unconscious thing."

Pasquale aimed his weapon at Larry's chest, grinned broadly, and fired.

Larry continued to stare at Pasquale as he fell. There was hardly any blood, Alex noticed from where he stood. But he fell anyway.

Pasquale lowered his arm and walked over to Larry's body. Jaguar came around Alex and kept going toward Pasquale. Alex grabbed at her arm and missed. She kept walking.

Pasquale had reached into Larry's pocket and pulled out an envelope, which contained a thick wad of bank notes. He was counting them carefully when Jaguar reached his side, bent down and touched the side of Larry's neck. She twisted around and looked up at Pasquale.

"All there?" she asked.

"Looks like it," he said.

"What'd you hit 'em with?"

"Rezonine."

"Jesus," she said. "I hope you got the dosage right. You could've killed them."

Alex felt as if he was beginning to wake from one dream, into another. Somehow, though, it was starting to make sense. He went to Miriam and checked her pulse. Slow but steady, and no wound in her belly, where she should have a bloody hole. Son of a bitch, he thought. Pasquale used a tranquilizer gun.

"I know what I'm doing," he said, and put the bank notes away. "One thing, they won't be up for a while. You got plenty of time to get some back up."

Alex straightened up and approached Pasquale and Jaguar. Pasquale smiled and stuck out his hand, which Alex took. "I'm Pasquale. Pleased to meet you."

"Alex," he said. "Equally pleased."

"Yeah," Pasquale said. "We been looking for you."

"You found me. You wouldn't happen to have a cellcom, would you? I need to call this in."

"Oh sure," Pasquale said, and reached into his pocket, pulled one out and handed it to Alex.

"Great," Alex said. "If you'll excuse me, then." He walked a few yards away, leaving Jaguar and Pasquale alone. Pasquale jerked a thumb toward Alex.

"He's a nice guy," he said.

"He is," she agreed.

"Don't make him too crazy, okay?"

She rolled her eyes. Pasquale laughed. "You thought I was doing a double-cross, didn't you?"

She shook her head. "Just not sure of the script. But I figured any odds you want against a double cross."

He stopped counting. "Against?"

"Against. I knew who your grandmother was. Anna Burhasa."

Pasquale looked her up and down admiringly. "How'd you get that one?"

She tapped his hand. "Pinkie ring. Family crest."

Pasquale looked down at his hand, the little ring with the leopard face and engraved grape vines. "Not too many people know about that."

"I do."

"She was a good woman," Pasquale said, stretching his hand out and musing on the ring. "Made great pasta. She would've hated what Barone was doing."

"So why didn't you kill him?" Jaguar asked.

Pasquale dropped his hand to his side. "I don't do take out. Grandma told me not to. Besides, I figure he'll end up on the Planetoid."

"Yeah?"

"Yeah. And there's this Teacher there who owes me. She'll make sure he gets the right treatment."

Jaguar put her hand out and he took it, shook it and held on. "My pleasure, Pasquale. My pleasure."

He let her hand go. "Well, I better head out. Don't wanna be here when the party starts." He handed her his tranquilizer gun and patted her hand. "I'd appreciate it if you didn't mention me."

"Of course," she said. "Where you heading?"

"Back to the Home Planet," he said. "I wanna track this woman I know who'd make a good hunter. See if she's interested."

Jaguar nodded. "Say hello for me."

Pasquale gave her a bow, turned and walked away. Alex came over to where she stood and watched his receding back.

"Backup's on the way," he said.

EPILOGUE

"Hi there," Jaguar said, as she took a seat across from Alex at the small table where he sat nursing a tall beer. She looked around. The bar was still sparsely populated at this hour. Gerry's band didn't start for another three hours, but he'd be here any minute with Rachel and Pinkie, all of them cleared by the review committee they'd just met with. They'd gone to Marie's to drag her along with them to celebrate.

Alex and Jaguar had already had their review meetings, but they'd done it in the presence of the Hague last week. They were sequestered away from each other for the duration, and had dutifully refrained from empathic contact so as not to taint the hearing. When their testimony corroborated not only with each other's but also with the findings of a certain scientist from New Jersey, they'd been cleared in the same procedure that determined to maintain the moratorium on Lunar mining. The only difficulty they had was in explaining the tranquilizer gun, but Jaguar had solved that by asking Rachel to make sure to sign one out in her name, from some time ago.

Alex picked up his beer and took a sip. "It's been awhile, Dr. Addams. How are you?"

"Not too bad, now that the dust is settling," she replied. She reached over and wrapped her hand around his beer, pulled it toward her and took a sip. "How about you?"

He retrieved his beer. "Better now."

They were silent. Uncomfortably so. Looking at each other as if they'd suddenly become different people. As if they were strangers. After all this

188

time, it happened a little too fast and not the way he expected it would—with some sense of intent on both their parts instead of this falling off the edge of the moon into each other. Jaguar was right when she said it would change everything. It already had.

"Alex—" she started to say.

"Jaguar—" he said at the same time.

They both stopped.

"You go," he said.

"No," she said. "You."

He turned his beer glass around and around in his hand. "Why'd you sleep with me, Jaguar?" he asked.

She startled, then covered it with a quick smile. "That's a funny question," she said. "What're the usual reasons?"

"You're not the usual sort of person," he noted. "And the circumstances weren't usual, either."

"You want to blame it on the moon?" she asked.

Yes, he thought. That's what they both wondered. If Artemis pushed them into doing something they shouldn't have, wouldn't have otherwise.

"Do you?" he asked.

"Maybe it was Artemis," she mused, "That's one possibility."

"You have another?"

She shrugged. "Maybe I wanted to see if you kept your eyes open, or closed."

He leaned forward. "And?" he asked.

"I couldn't tell," she whispered, leaning across the table to him. "It was too dark."

He leaned back away from her, turned his beer around and around in his hand. She shifted in her seat, gave him her profile.

"So what now?" he asked.

She pulled his beer to her again and took a longer sip. Her eyes peered at him over the glass, cat-like, discerning all the unspoken subtleties passing between them. It seemed they had a whole new language to learn with each other. If they wanted to.

She put the beer down a little too hard. "It doesn't have to be a big deal," she said."I mean, you enjoyed yourself, didn't you?" she paused. "Didn't you?"

Words wouldn't begin to cover it, so he inclined his head forward. Yes. He enjoyed himself. Very much.

"So we're adults, and if we want, we can try it again, see if we continue to like it. That's easy enough, isn't it?"

Easy. She was making this easy for him. He could reap the benefits of her bed with no strings attached, and if he turned his attention elsewhere she wouldn't give him a hard time about it. Like an old song, she'd just turn her pretty head and walk away. And he would do the same for her. The perfect arrangement. And in the past, with other women, it was pretty much what he insisted on.

But not with her. Real desire was too powerful a force, and he would no more touch it lightly than he'd try and harness the moon. He heard her voice recurring in his thoughts. *Do not fuck with this stuff, Alex. It'll eat you alive.*

"I'm not sure that would work," he said.

She tilted her head to one side, pulled back a little. "Okay, then. We don't have to repeat ourselves," she said, voice a little tense. "We can go back to the way it was. Blame it on the moon."

Back out gracefully, with no hard feelings, and take no more chances. Again, she was making it easy for him. Too easy. Like a story where you're offered the small loaf of bread and the large, and the large seems by far the better, but as it turns out, that's exactly the wrong choice. No. He supposed if he wanted easy, he wouldn't be chasing the edges of her life.

"That's not what I want," he said definitively. "What about you?"

She ducked her face down and stared hard at her hands, which were folded on the table, tight and still.

He reached across and put a hand on hers, called her eyes to his. She lifted them, sparking gold inside the green. He had a sense of *deja vu*. They'd done this before, in exactly this place. It wasn't that long ago that they sat in these chairs and she allowed him entry into the wilderness of her soul, where he found an integrity more certain than any Planetoid code book would ever allow for or recognize. Clean as the scent of mint after lightning. Purely Jaguar. He put a hand to her face, found entry, and sought it again, moving past the places she showed the world to where she lived when she was telling herself the truth.

What do you want, Jaguar?

No words. He could discern no words here. But there was motion. The movement of fire, quick and hungry. The movement of earth, patient, slow, and relentless. What she wanted had no words. What she would offer him could not be spoken. It could only be lived, and either they would dare that, or they wouldn't.

He released her, leaned back in his chair, drank his beer. They were where they'd always been, circling each other, circling their own emotions, waiting for guarantees that would never come.

"Why don't we play it by ear," Jaguar said quietly, "and I'll let you know if it's working out okay for me?"

He lifted his eyes to her face and went subvocal with one more question.

Trust me, Jaguar?

She let her eyes rest quiet in his for a moment, touched her hand lightly to her neck.

With my life.

Behind her, the door to the bar opened and voices and laughter floated toward them. She turned away and waved a hand at Rachel, who had her hand in Pinkie's, with Gerry hovering behind them.

"Here's the others," she said. "A helluva team."